MW00711584

The

Prodigal Daughters

ANGELA D. SHEARRY

From Heaven to Earth Publications

The Prodigal Daughters

by

ANGELA D. SHEARRY

Published by:

From Heaven to Earth Publications
Post Office Box 166138
Irving, Texas 75016-6138
http://www.fromheaven2earthbooks.com

Copyright © 2000 by Angela D. Shearry

All rights reserved. No part of this book may be reproduced or transmitted in any form or by any means, electronic or mechanical, including photocopying, recording or by any information storage and retrieval system without the written permission from the author, except for the inclusion of brief quotations in a review.

This book is a work of fiction. Names, characters, places, and incidents are either products of the author's imagination or are used fictitiously. Any resemblance to actual events or persons, living or dead, is entirely coincidental.

Scripture quotations are from the King James Version of the Holy Bible. Copyright © 1972, Thomas Nelson, Inc., Publishers.

The song "Were You There?" is from The New National Baptist Hymnal. Copyright © 1977, Triad Publications, Publishers.

The poem "I Choose" and the song "In Your Presence" were written by the author, Angela D. Shearry. Copyright © 2000.

Printed and bound in Canada

Cover Illustration: Derrick Glass and Angela D. Shearry
Cover Design: Wendy Gonzales
Interior Design: Defae Weaver

First Printing, June 2000

Shearry, Angela D.
The Prodigal Daughters/ Angela D. Shearry
ISBN 0-9673477-3-4
Library of Congress Card Catalog Number 00-090199

For book signings and direction on booking Angela D. Shearry:
E-mail: ashearry@ureach.com

Dedication

To my mother, Eva L. Glass

Thank you for every time you took me to church. Thank you for every prayer you prayed for and with me. Thank you for fervently speaking life and purpose into me. Thank you for sharing with me so much of the wisdom that is imparted to you by the Holy Ghost. Thank you for supporting me emotionally, spiritually, and financially during this project. Thank you for always — ALWAYS — believing in me! I love you SO much!

Your creed of life is now mine: Get busy living or get busy dying! Like you, I choose to live!!

Acknowledgements

I thank **God** and His Son, **Jesus Christ**, for the many tests and trials I've endured in my lifetime . . . and for the ones I failed. For both have made me the person I am today — a person who knows that it is *only* the grace of God that completes and sustains me and that it is my destiny to fulfill His will in my life.

I thank my sister, **Toknoka Glass-Lott**, who is a dynamic, praying, devil-chasing woman of God in her own right. Your financial support of my endeavor is typical of your ever-present love and kindness. Your talents and achievements are poignant testimonies of your spirit of excellence. And your forthcoming doctorate degree will be the icing on the cake! To be the baby of the family, you didn't turn out half bad ☺.

I thank my brother, **Derrick Glass**, who, I am highly persuaded, has the comic ability to bring a smile to a dead man's face. Thank you for all the times you unmercifully tickled our funny bones and for bringing joy and laughter to our family. And thank you for lending me your artistic abilities during this project — who else could have drawn such magnificent clouds? No one!

I thank my nieces **Alexis, Crystal, and La'Nicea** for being a special part of our lives. The mere fact that you were born is a clear indication that God has chosen you to do a special work for Him. Even in your youth, you *must* seek to know and do His will. Never forget that greatness and power are in your genes — not because of your earthly lineage, but because you're children of the King! And never forget that Auntie Angie loves you very much.

I thank the man I love and adore, **Derek Sneed,** for entering my life one blessed day. Because of you, I learned through painstaking and glorious revelation that God is *truly* a God of second chances. Thank you for the love and strength you've brought to my life. Thank you for striving to be the man God has called you to be. And thank you for the monetary sacrifices you made to financially support this dream of mine. I love you!

Thank you: **Ann Fields,** for enthusiastically welcoming me to the book-writing profession and for pointing me in the right direction so many times; **LaRee Bryant,** for your editorial insight; my cousin, **Glenda Sterling,** for being the first to read the beginning chapters so long ago and — amazingly enough — liking them even then; **Patrice Lowe,** for reading my work from start to finish and for the tearful and glowing praise you gave it; and **Bishop T. D. Jakes,** for so profoundly revealing to me mind-blowing things about my God that I didn't even know and for teaching me how to "maximize the moment."

Special Acknowledgements

My heart is expanded with gratitude for each of these people. Throughout this endeavor, many others did lend me a helping hand in the way of providing informational support and hearty encouragement, but the helping hands that these people extended toward me had money in it! I could not have accomplished this feat without them and my heartfelt prayer is that God will reward them bountifully for being such a great blessing to me:

Van Banks-Simpson – My instant friend. Never before have I met anyone with whom I so quickly developed a genuine bond of friendship, nor so strongly. Your godliness, thoughtfulness, and realness convinced me that God *meant* for us to be friends.

Kelly A. King Causey – One would only have to meet you to understand why I often refer to you as "such a sweet spirit." Your bright eyes and ready smile *always* cheer me. And the fact that you eagerly volunteered to support me after knowing me for only a few weeks brought tears to my eyes.

Evangelist James E. Flowers – *Thank you so much* for so graciously supporting me in this endeavor. Thank you also for praying God's blessing on this book, and I pray that the seed you planted in my ministry be the source of the overflowing abundance in your own ministry.

LaShonda N. Harris – My sweet cousin. Did I ever tell you that you were the first to send me a check?! I leaped and cried with joy! I wish God's best for you.

Tammy Hudson – It was when I met you that I started thanking God for placing *real* people in my life: people who are willing to admit that living for the Lord can sometimes be a struggle and yet know that having the presence of the Lord in your life is worth *every* struggle. I love you *dearly* for being one of those people and for being such a true friend to me. I'll never forget the look of excitement on your face the day you placed a check in my hand. You were more excited to give it than I was to receive it. How can that be? ☺

Vincent E. Pewitt – Thank you for supporting me so willingly. Even if I knew every police officer in the state of Texas, I'd still say you were the best of the whole bunch!

Timothy W. Williams – I've always known that we were friends, but when you — the king of investments — chose to invest in me, well, my heart just swelled with pride! Thank you for believing in me.

"I will arise and go to my father,
and will say unto him, Father, I have sinned against heaven,
and before thee . . . the father said to his servants,
Bring forth the best robe . . . And bring hither the
fatted calf, and kill it; and let us eat, and be merry . . .
And they began to be merry."
Luke 15:18-24 KJV

The

Prodigal Daughters

Chapter 1

*S*he moaned softly, then shifted her upper body to a more pleasing position. Her slow, hushed breaths gradually quickened to deep, heavy panting, as if she were experiencing the intense sensation of falling from the aerial peak of Mount Everest. And just as if she'd fallen to rock-solid ground, her body went rigid and her breathing stopped. Seconds passed . . . before a deep moan escaped her loosely parted lips and her body trembled as it slowly relaxed. Then, with the speed and force of lightning, blissful serenity, intent on ravishing her with its languid potency, spread throughout every inch of her body. She smiled softly. This is exactly what she'd needed, even hoped for. Shifting again, she pressed the front of her mellowed frame into the feathery-soft cushions of her leather sofa, unconsciously begging the penetrating sensation to possess her forever.

Sleep had seduced Sasha as sweetly as any man could, and just when its touch had become caressingly deep, the phone began to barrage the room with loud, piercing rings.

Sasha's body jerked at the intrusion, then stirred reluctantly. In the deep recesses of her mind, she begged the ringing to stop, stop, stop. Sleep hadn't stroked her this well in a long time, and she wasn't quite ready to leave its warm, soothing arms.

Still, the phone kept blaring, demanding to be answered.

Sasha's eyes fluttered as if to open, but fell closed once again, too heavy with sleep. Groaning softly, she blindly reached over her head to the small chrome and white end table and lifted the phone's cordless receiver. "Hello," she purred, still under the effects of sleep. Turning, she snuggled her face and body once again into the cushioned back of the sofa.

"Sasha?" the caller asked, as if uncertain she'd dialed the right number.

"Mm-Hmm," Sasha mumbled affirmatively.

"What are you doing?" the caller asked with a questioning laugh. When Sasha didn't respond, the caller continued. "Sasha? What are you doing?" Still no answer. "Do you have company? . . . Did I interrupt something? . . . Look, if you're over there gettin' busy," the caller said, chuckling lightly, "I can call you back later."

At first, Sasha felt dopey, like she'd been hit hard in the head. *I need more sleep,* she thought, trying to find a more comfortable position on the sofa. As she slowly turned to lie flat on her back, a feeling of tingling warmth began to course through her body. It felt good. No, it felt better than good — it was invigorating. She could hear the persistent questions being fired at her over the phone, but she ignored them. Wanting to savor the moment, she grinned happily as every limb of her body began to stretch in luxurious and stimulating harmony, doing countless wonders for her body. How could she feel so good after having slept for only . . . How long *had* she been asleep? It felt like glorious days.

"What time is it, Zandy?" she quietly asked the caller.

"I was just about to hang up this phone, girl. Didn't you hear me talking to you?"

"Mm-Hmm. What time is it?"

"It's *time* for you to tell me who you have over there making you purr like that, especially at this time of the day. I *knew* something was up with you," Zandy said with thrilled conviction. "I *knew* you were keeping something — or should I say *somebody* — away from me. The cat is out of the bag now, girl, so you might as well c'mon and tell girlfriend the whole story. Who is he, Sasha?" she asked like a child anxiously waiting to be told a secret.

Sasha slowly sat up on the sofa. Feeling a yawn about to overtake her, she covered the mouthpiece with her hand and opened her mouth wide to let the yawn pass through. For the first time since she'd awakened, she opened her eyes fully. The sun's brilliance poured through the glass of her patio door and ricocheted off the opened vertical blinds and into her eyes. Squinting, she looked at the clock on the wall. It was just minutes after four o'clock, which meant she had slept for . . .

"So you're not going to tell me?" Zandy pressed, intruding on Sasha's thoughts. "I can't believe you!" she cried in mock rage. "But that's okay. It's quite alright. I guess I *am* getting a little bit ahead of myself. I shouldn't expect you to tell me *all* of your business when we've only been friends for a little over a month. You can go ahead and keep your secrets from me," she pouted. "I don't care."

Sasha smiled. "I have no idea what you're talking about, Zandy. I was sleeping when you called, and I was resting quite well until you woke me up. *Thank you very much,*" she added, laughter rippling her belly.

"Yeah, yeah, yeah. Tell me any old thang," Zandy continued to jest. "I've called you before when you were asleep and you didn't sound *nothing* like you did a few minutes ago. And why didn't your answering machine pick up?" she asked rhetorically. "I know why — because *you turned it off* so you and *what's his name* wouldn't be disturbed. Over there gettin' your groove on. That's what you're doing."

Sasha glanced at the answering machine near the base of her phone and mentally kicked herself for forgetting to buy a new tape. "The reason my machine is off is because I took the tape out of it. It got tangled up in the machine."

Zandy sucked her teeth as if she wasn't buying Sasha's explanation.

"Really, Zandy, this is my father's old answering machine. I guess it's just time for a new one."

"A new man or a new answering machine?"

"Zandy!" Sasha cried, blushing with embarrassment. "You know what I mean."

Zandy laughed out. "Alright, alright, alright. I'll let you off the hook this time. Go and buy yourself a *digital* answering machine — one that doesn't require a tape — so you'll have to come up with a better excuse next time. For now, we'll go ahead and play like you *really were* sleeping when I called."

"I *was* sleeping," Sasha said, another yawn escaping her. "I can't believe I fell out like I did. I even slept through class."

"That's exactly why I called you. I didn't see you in English/Lit, and I was wondering what happened to you. You did know you were supposed to turn in your paper today, didn't you?"

"Oh, my goodness!" Sasha jumped quickly to her feet, almost tripping in her long skirt. "I completely forgot! What did Dr. Avery say?" she asked anxiously. "Oh, never mind. I know how she is about late papers." Groaning, she fell back onto the sofa.

"Now you know that Dr. *Sasha-Can-Do-No-Wrong* Avery ain't worried about *your* paper. Dr. Avery worships the ground you walk on. Oh, Sasha, dear," Zandy said, imitating the professor's extremely syllabic and brisk way of speaking. "I do understand that your pinky toe was hurting you to distraction, so much until it affected your fingers and you were helplessly unable to write. Do you think you can have the paper in by . . . let's see . . . the end of the semester? Yes, that should do it. That will give you another two whole months to complete it." Zandy finished with a perfect mimic of Dr. Avery's well-known hoot of a laugh.

"Zandy, you should stop it!" Sasha yelped, her body shaking with laughter at her friend's remarkable imitation. She had Dr. Avery's voice down pat. "Dr. Avery would never be that easy on me, or anyone else."

"Anyway, "Zandy stated blandly, all humor aside, "I told her that you *had* completed the paper and that you probably went home for the day." She paused before saying pointedly, "I told her that you haven't been feeling too well lately."

Sasha, still smiling at Zandy's foolishness, slowly became aware of the change in her voice. Sasha's smile faded. "Why . . . why did you tell her I wasn't feeling well?" she asked timidly. Not waiting for a response, she continued with forced cheerfulness. "I . . . uh . . . I feel fine. I had planned to be in class today, but I came home at one because my Computer Org class was cancelled, and, somehow, I fell asleep on the sofa.

Sasha rubbed her eyes as if to wipe away the last traces of sleep. "I don't know how I did that when I knew I had Dr. Avery's class at two." She exaggerated a chuckle. "How was class anyway? Did I miss anything besides turning in the paper?" When there was no response from Zandy, Sasha wondered if she was still on the line. She couldn't even hear her breathing. "Well, I guess I'd better get over there and turn my paper in." Still no response. Apprehension crept into Sasha's voice. "Zandy, you're not saying anything. What's wrong?"

"I was about to ask you the same thing, Sasha," Zandy finally said. "Look," she continued in a voice that was concerned, but matter-of-fact, "I know that we haven't been friends long and maybe I'm not even the one to be talking to you about this, but I can see that something is going on with you, okay? You haven't been your relaxed and cheerful self these past couple of weeks. I mean, you seem so . . . so distracted now, like you've got something pretty heavy on your mind. At first, I thought it was me, that maybe you weren't down with us being friends. I thought that maybe you were trying to give me the brush-off or something. But the other day I saw you sitting in the campus Snack Bar and you looked like you were way off in another world. That's when I realized that something else had you buggin', and the only reason I didn't come over and talk to you then was because I didn't want to intrude. That was more than a week ago and," she added somberly, "you haven't gotten any better. For some reason, you're stressed out, and it shows.

Zandy sighed into the phone. "Listen, I'm gonna stop right here, because I don't wanna push the issue. I just want you to

know that I'm here and if you want to talk, I'm a good listener."
She chuckled. "I know what you're thinking, and you're right —
Zandy is *not* the one to be listening to other people complain
about their problems. You know that much about me, if nothing else. But I want you to know that there *are* exceptions to
that, Sasha. When it comes to people I really care about — my
family and my very few friends — there's not much I wouldn't
do for them. Any one of them will tell you that. Well, except my
father," she snorted, "but that Negro doesn't count. But," she
continued kindly, "*you* count, Sasha. I think of you as a friend,
and I never use that term lightly, either. So-o-o," she said, slowly
inhaling and exhaling a deep breath, "with all of that said, I guess
I'd better let you go so you can get your paper over to Dr. Avery."

Sasha found herself at a loss for words. Zandy was known
to be straightforward, mischievous, facetious even, but rarely was
she so serious. Had she offended her? "Zandy," she said slowly,
searching desperately for the right words, "I'm really sorry. I
know that I've been kind of out of it lately, but the last thing I
want to do is offend you, to make you think I don't want you as
a friend. I truly apologize for allowing you to think that I have a
problem with you, because I don't. In fact, I'm really glad we
met. And you're right - I do have a lot on my mind, but I'm not
sure I'm ready to talk about it yet. I've thought about talking to
you a hundred times, but I don't seem to be able to get it out.
Maybe it's because I've never been one to really talk about my
personal problems. Anyway, I wouldn't even know where to start.
There's just so much going on in my head right now. I'm sorry.
I really am."

Zandy laughed. "Sasha, there's really no reason for you to be
sorry about anything. I brought all of this up because I wanted
you to know that I care, should you ever want to talk, and that's
it. Anyway," she continued in an urgent tone, "you'd better get
your paper on over to Dr. Avery. Girl, she told me to tell you
that if you were going to miss class, you should've turned your
paper in early." Her voice took on a low, menacing tone. "*And*

she said that she'd better have that paper in her hands by five o'clock *today*. She's not concerned with how you get it to her, either. She said you can have it delivered by the neighborhood *cat* if you want. But if you *don't* have it to her by five, she said that she's going to give you so many 'F's for the remainder of this semester that you're gonna cry for the *rest* of your life every time you *see* the letter F, big *or* small!"

Sasha sat straight up on the edge of the sofa, temporarily forgetting how pleased she was to know of Zandy's concern for her and just how much she really did need to talk to someone. "Zandy! I thought she said I could turn the paper in later!"

Zandy, expecting this reaction from Sasha, burst into laughter. "Did *I* say that?" she asked, feigning total ignorance. "I don't remember saying that."

Sasha fell clumsily to her knees and threw her hand beneath the chrome and white coffee table, searching frantically for her shoes. "Well, what was that *Dr. Sasha-Can-Do-No-Wrong Avery* business all about!" Hearing Zandy still laughing on the phone, Sasha began to get tickled, too. "Did she *really* say that about giving me 'F's?" She found her brown, leather flats and hastily slipped them on her stocking-clad feet.

"No, but I heard that she said all of that stuff to this guy named Daslin last year when he claimed that he missed two weeks of class because he was sick. Sasha, you gotta forgive me for joking with you so much. I know how important your grades are to you, but I just couldn't resist the temptation to tease you. I never can. Still, I really didn't mean to string you on for so long. I meant to tell you earlier that you needed to turn the paper in today, before Dr. Avery left her office, but, as you know, the conversation took an unexpected turn. I'm so sorry, but I would've given anything to see the look on your face, girl!"

"I bet you would have. My heart felt like it wanted to jump out of my chest. Don't scare me like that anymore, Zandy."

"But really, though," Zandy said, "you and I both know that Dr. Avery thinks you're the cream of the crop. She thinks you're the perfect student, and the only reason she set a short deadline for you to get that paper in, is because she only gave me a few extra hours to turn one in last semester when I took one of her writing classes. I bet she thought I would have a fit if she gave you until Monday to turn it in. It wouldn't have bothered me one bit. My paper was late because I didn't start on it until the day before it was due. And I *still* got an 'A' on it," Zandy said triumphantly. "But don't you dare tell Dr. Avery that. She'd go back and change my grade."

Sasha envisioned Dr. Avery's tall, slim figure strutting over to the Registrar's Office in one of her many chic, eye-catching out-fits and a pair of her exquisite, high-heeled pumps and demand-ing that Zandy's grade be changed from an 'A' to an 'F'. The vision made her smile. "Dr. Avery is too nice to do something like that."

"Yeah, well, I still wouldn't put it past her to do it to me, because I'm not her *girl*. You are, and you know it, too. Teacher's pet," Zandy teased.

Sasha was perched on the edge of the sofa, listening intently to Zandy and smiling broadly. Dr. Avery and Sasha *had* devel-oped a close, almost maternal relationship, but still Sasha didn't think she was the object of classroom favoritism. "No, I'm not the teacher's pet, and you will soon know that, too, if I don't get over there and turn my paper in. And you're the one to talk. You and Dr. Avery go at each other like two loving sisters – squabbling with each other one minute and laughing with each other the next. Dr. Avery loves every minute of it. And you do, too. So, *now*, who's the teacher's pet?"

"I still say that you are, but I guess that's an argument I could never win with you. I do like the woman. She's just so . . . wholesome, *without* a man. I love that. And she's a literary ge-nius in the classroom, too. I swear, she can make *The Canterbury Tales* as interesting as *The Young and The Restless*."

"And don't forget that she dresses very well," Sasha piped in. "I know you like that."

"She's da bomb!" Zandy quickly agreed. "Ol' girl definitely has style. It's in everything she has and in everything she does."

"You're right about that. So I'd better get over there right now before she gives me an '*F*' in style." Sasha paused, then said, "I really want to thank you for the call, Zandy. You know it would've been another headache for me to deal with if I didn't get this paper in . . . even if Dr. Avery does think I'm the *cream of the crop*." She laughed softly. "I always enjoy talking to you, Zandy. I can't think of anyone who makes me laugh as much as you do. So, thanks. A lot. And thanks for the concern, too. I really do appreciate it."

"No problem," Zandy told her. "Call me when you get back. I'm still on campus right now, but I should be at home by the time you make it back in. Maybe we can find something to do tonight. That is, if you don't have any other plans," she said, hinting again that Sasha was hiding a guy from her. "Okay?"

Sasha missed the hint. "Okay. I'll talk to you later. Bye-bye."

"*Au revoir!*" Zandy said, speaking French. Before Sasha could hang up, she added, "Tell Dr. Avery I said, *'Bonjour'*!"

"That means hello, right?" Sasha guessed.

"*C'est correct* — that's right," Zandy praised. "And make sure you say 'Aleczandria' because you know she can't stand my nickname. She says it sounds like the name of a cartoon character. She likes the sound of *Aleck-zahn-dria* better," Zandy uttered with Shakespearean luster. "I told her, 'I can't help it if your mother named you Theola.' Hmph! Hatin' on *my* name."

"*Theola*?! That's not her name. Her name is Kinsari."

"Theola Kinsari Avery. Her first name is a combination of her parent's names — Theodore and Ceola. Uggh! Her mom's youngest sister named her Kinsari. Dr. Avery said that her aunt hated her first name and begged to give her a middle name. I told Dr. Avery she should *still* be thanking her aunt, because that first name of hers is whacked!"

"It really is," Sasha agreed, shaking her head in disbelief.

"And you know how she says her name, too. Like she stood right beside God when He made the world. Hello class," Zandy mimicked, "my name is Dr. *Kin-sahhh-ri* Avery." Zandy's voice crackled with laughter. "I told her if she keeps picking on me about my name, I'm gonna tell everybody on campus that her name is *Theee-owe-la* Avery. So tell *Theola* that *Aleczandria* said, 'Hello'."

Sasha laughed. "I will *not* call her that, but I will tell her that you said, 'hello'. Bye-bye."

"*A tout àl'heure!* — see you later!"

Sasha looked thoughtful as she hung up the phone. She was starting to like Zandy more and more. And she really did appreciate the call, because the last thing she wanted was to miss turning in her Lit paper, or any paper for that matter. Her watch showed it to be 4:23. It usually took her all of ten minutes to drive to the campus, but traffic at this time of the day would slow her down. And she would be in big trouble if she missed Dr. Avery.

Whistling winds drew Sasha to the patio's glass door. The October sky was sunny bright, but the brisk winds hinted that winter was just around the corner. At home, in Milwaukee, Sasha had hated the harsh, snowy winter months, but Mississippi winters weren't nearly as bad, especially here in Jackson. They were mild in comparison — a little cold weather, but no snow. She'd always liked that. Mild winters made her think of two lovers taking long, romantic strolls in the cool of dark, moonlit nights, hand in hand. Sasha wrapped her arms around her midriff and smiled knowingly. This winter she hoped to be one of them, walking hand in hand with her very own . . . lover. The thought was absolutely incredible, and she shook herself out of the fantasy. Reaching out, she pulled the dangling string on the vertical blinds to close out the glare of the sun.

Flipping on a light switch, she looked down at her matching silk skirt and blouse and saw that they were both very wrinkled from her long nap on the sofa. With quick movements, she ran her hands down the front of the blouse in unsuccessful attempts to smooth out the wrinkles. She tucked the blouse tightly into the small waistline of her skirt and then shook the loose skirt lightly. She frowned. The skirt's wrinkles were locked in, too. They needed the aid of a warm iron, but she didn't have time for that.

She dashed out of the living room, into the master bathroom and right up to the mirror over the sink. Seeing that her velvet black, shoulder-length hair hung limp in disarray, with little sign of the loose curls she'd put in it that morning, she picked up her hairbrush from the counter and hastily ran it through her hair, brushing it all to the back to put in a ponytail. Holding her hair up with one hand, with the other she threw the brush on the counter, yanked open one of the drawers, and picked up the first ponytail holder she saw — a black and yellow one, which clashed noticeably with her attractive, although wrinkled, brown and beige outfit. She wrapped the ponytail holder carelessly around her hair. She then jutted her face close to the mirror and searched the corners of her brown, almond-shaped eyes for any of the repulsive tiny bits of crinkling crust. She saw none. But she did notice that one of her smooth, cocoa-colored cheeks was lined with dried up dribble. *Disgusting*, she thought. She wet and soaped a wash cloth from the nearby rack and scrubbed her entire face.

She needed to do something about her mouth. It was desert dry. Pushing her face up to the mirror once again, she tightened her lips then drew them back, revealing a perfect set of sparkling, white-white teeth. *Braces can do wonders*, she thought. Reaching for her bottle of mouthwash, she remembered that she'd used the last of it that morning. Toothpaste would have to do. She picked up the tube from its cup, plopped open its cap, squeezed the white substance onto the tip of her index finger, cast the tube onto the counter, and proceeded to swish the pasted finger up and down and around her teeth and gums. Quickly turning on the cold faucet, she let a liberal amount of water gush into a small cup, and practically throwing the water into her mouth, she swished it rather comically over her teeth and gums before spurting it into the sink. *That feels better if nothing else,* she thought, wiping her mouth of excess water. With her teeth feeling cleaner and her mouth refreshed, she smiled into the mirror that killer, dimpled smile that was so much like her father's. At the same time, Sasha realized that her mother would have been horrified had she been there to see her daughter using her finger in such a ridiculous manner rather than a toothbrush. Her smile grew larger and she said softly, "Forgive me, this once, Mom."

The sound of the gushing tap water snapped Sasha back to attention. Snatching a bar of soap from its dish, she washed her hands vigorously in the cold water and then, dropping the soap back in the dish, she hastily rinsed her hands and then dried them on a fluffy white towel hanging on the rack. After turning the faucet off, she allowed herself one last look at her wrinkled clothing and then her reflection in the mirror. With a brief hunch of her shoulders, she said under her breath, "I guess I don't look *too* bad" and then she turned and fled from the bathroom.

In the bedroom, she swiped a light jacket from the walk-in closet. Throwing one arm into it and then the other, she rushed back into the living room and grabbed her book bag from the coffee table. Spotting her keys on the table, she snatched them up and bolted out of the front door, quickly locking it behind her.

Off she flew down the stairs from her apartment, the high winds lifting the jacket behind her. At the bottom of the stairs, she stopped long enough to enjoy one more spine-tingling thought of she and her lover strolling in the cool of the dark night, before she was off and running again.

Chapter 2

Sasha's insides churned incessantly with butterflies. Spilling her troubles to Zandy had seemed like a good idea earlier, but now, just thinking about it made her uncommonly nervous. In an effort to calm her nerves, she anxiously paced back and forth through her apartment under the pretense of last minute straightening and cleaning. The luxury two-bedroom apartment was already immaculate and its contemporary style and decor made it look more befitted for the pages of a home designer's magazine than the abode of a sophomore college student. Still, she aimlessly dusted ultra-clean furniture, wiped crystal clear mirrors, adjusted perfectly aligned frames, swept spotless floors, fluffed fluffy pillows and picked invisible lint, and all the while her eyes darted constantly to the clock on the wall. It was 6:47 p.m. and Zandy would be there at 7:00. She still had more than ten minutes to wait.

I'll be out of my mind by then, she thought.

Her eyes cut to the phone. "Maybe I should try and catch Zandy before she leaves home," she said aloud. "I can tell her that I was a tad bit impulsive when I invited her over here to talk about my stupid problems." Sasha took the pillow she'd been holding unconsciously tight in her arms and laid it on the leather loveseat along with the other decorative pillows. Moving toward the phone she stopped suddenly, threw her hands up in frustration and fell back onto the sofa. "Ugh-gh-gh! Zandy has already

13

left home by now," she said, scowling at the clock on the wall. *Why didn't I think to call Zandy earlier and tell her not to come? Why did I even call her in the first place?*

"Oh well," she said. "What's done is done. And who says I can't tell her when she gets here that I changed my mind?" Closing her eyes, she tried once again to will the jitters away.

She wasn't sure she even wanted to change her mind. Although a part of her was very reluctant to opening up and pouring out everything to Zandy, another part of her felt that she *really* needed to do this, regardless of how difficult it was to let someone else in on her personal thoughts and feelings. She could use a good ear and some advice, too. The conversation she'd had earlier with Zandy was all she could think about during her drive over to the campus to see Dr. Avery. She thought about it during her drive back home, too. Thinking that talking to Zandy might help to relieve some of the frustration and confusion she'd been feeling lately, she'd rushed into the apartment and called Zandy on the phone. Without any preliminary remarks, she'd boldly told Zandy that she was ready to talk, if she was still willing to listen. After Zandy queried her as to whether she was absolutely sure, Sasha assured her that she was and then invited her over for the evening. Sasha had warned Zandy that she had a lot to talk about. She told her to come prepared to spend the night.

But now Sasha questioned her decision. She didn't know Zandy all that well. She'd met her at the beginning of the semester when they'd teamed up for a co-writing assignment in Dr. Avery's English/Literature class. After the assignment was completed and turned in, they'd remained friends, hanging out on campus sometimes during the day and phoning each other sometimes in the evenings. Since she'd known her, Zandy had been nothing but friendly, easy-going, and a huge barrel of laughs. But still, she had a bit of a no-nonsense edge to her and that made Sasha a little uneasy.

What if she thinks I'm being silly and immature? What if she just wants to be nosey?

But, then again, she did express concern for me today, and she seemed genuine enough.

Maybe I can talk to her. God knows I need to talk to someone. I know I haven't known her long, but she just doesn't come off as the type who wants to know your business just for the sake of knowing it or to blab it to the world. There's a down-to-earth honesty about her, and I like her.

Sasha made the final decision to bare her soul and tell all.

A quick, triple-knock on the door caused Sasha, lost in thought, to jerk with surprise. 6:53. That must be Zandy. Early. With a brief look around the living room, Sasha stood, released a deep breath, then walked quickly to the door and opened it.

Zandy stood in the doorway frozen in an en-vogue model pose, both hands pointing elegantly toward her head. She was grinning from ear to ear.

Sasha's hand flew to her mouth. "What did you do to your hair?" she asked in a surprised whisper.

"You like?" Zandy asked. Still standing in pose, she turned her head slowly to give Sasha a side-to-side view of her new precision cut.

"It's really cute, but how could you get it cut so . . . short?" Sasha eyes perused Zandy's layered cut with a look akin to amazement. She mentally recalled how Zandy's natural, sandy-brown hair had swished and swirled around her shoulders like it had a life of its own.

Zandy sashayed into the apartment and threw her overnight bag on the floor near the sofa. "Girl, I got tired of combing that stuff. And it's not that short. I still have quite enough to curl if I want to. Or I can lay it down and keep on going. Why do you keep looking at me like that? You don't like it?"

"Yes, I like it. I told you, I think it's cute, especially the long layers at your temples. I'm just surprised, that's all. Have a seat." Sasha closed the door then turned back to Zandy, who had flounced down on the sofa. "When did you get it done?" she asked Zandy.

"Yesterday afternoon. I went in to get a touch-up and ended up telling Rob to cut it, too. He cut it some, but you know what I said?"

"What?"

"I said, '*Plus court, s'il vous plaît.*' — make it shorter, please. Rob was surprised that I wanted to get it cut, too." Zandy looked at Sasha's hair, still pulled back in the ponytail. "You should let him hook you up. The girl is bad when it comes to hair."

Sasha drew her chin in, confused. "Is Rob male or female?"

"Didn't I tell you about him?" Zandy didn't wait for an answer. "Rob is gay with a capital 'G'. Even if he never does your hair, you have *got* to meet him. He's very sweet and will keep you laughing, although he does get on my nerve sometimes. He wants to be treated as if he's, quote-unquote, one of the girls and not a guy. We have to call him Robin, else he may not respond. I've called him 'girl' so much in the salon, I'm starting to do it outside the place, too."

"So you don't care that he's gay?" Sasha asked, surprised at Zandy's nonchalance.

"As long as I don't have to participate, I really don't care what gay people do. I try to stay out of other people's business. As long as Rob continues to wash his hands before doing my do, he will always make money off this here head. Nobody in Jackson can do hair like Rob. He's good. *Real* good. So when can I make you an appointment?"

"Why? So I can get my hair cut, too? No, thank you. I'm ready for a change, but not *that* kind of a change. You don't like the way I wear my hair?" Sasha asked, smiling.

"Your hairstyles are simple. Cute, but simple. What I'm saying is, if you want something more sophisticated and stylish, Robin, I mean Rob, can hook it up! And he don't need nobody's scissors to do it, either." Zandy laughed, then peered at Sasha, her head cocked to one side. "What do you mean, you're ready for a change?"

Sasha began to fidget with the gold band on her pinky finger. "Oh," she stammered, "nothing much. You want something to drink?"

Zandy could see that the question made Sasha uncomfortable, so she let it slide. "Something to drink? I want something to eat! I'm hungry as I don't know what. I thought we were going to order a pizza."

"Oh! I forgot. I should've called while you were on your way over. I'll get the phone book and call now." Sasha retrieved the directory from a cabinet on her wall-sized entertainment center and headed toward the kitchen counter with the cordless phone in tow. "Well, make yourself comfortable while I order the pizza."

Zandy stood to her feet and removed her windbreaker. She looked around the living room. "I know I told you the last time I was here, but I just *love* this apartment. It's so nice and spacious. And you have it decorated so well. I love these colors," she said, admiring the white leather furniture and the yellow, rose, and sky-blue hues that softened the room. "And I don't know how you keep this white carpet so clean. Wait 'til you see my apartment. Almost everything in it came from garage sales."

"You can get some nice things from garage sales," Sasha said, holding the phone to her ear. "My mom and I used to go all the time."

"I know this stuff didn't come from no garage sale."

"No, my father bought it. He—" Sasha signaled that someone had answered the line. "Yes, I'd like to order a pizza, please." As soon as Sasha had stated her request, the perky voice that answered the line put her on hold.

Unaware that Sasha had been put on hold, Zandy browsed Sasha's book and tape collection, displayed on the entertainment center.

Sasha watched Zandy as she casually flipped through a book from the shelf. *Zandy's hairstyle really is pretty, and now,* Sasha thought, *she looks even more like someone you'd expect to see modeling in the pages of a fashion magazine.* The short, layered hairstyle only emphasized her doe-like eyes, high cheekbones and flaw-less, copper-toned skin, her most prominent features. Like Sasha's, Zandy's cheeks were imprinted with dimples, too. But Zandy's were more long than deep. And while Sasha had a few com-plaints about her own slightly medium frame — like her rear end and hips seeming too wide at times — Zandy evidently had none. In fact, many — guys and girls alike — would say that Zandy's rear-end and hips were just perfect. To see her head on, no one would guess that she was lugging such a full, nicely rounded bottom behind her. Standing approximately five feet, five inches tall, her frame was more slender than skinny and at-tractively toned without being muscular. Though most girls usu-ally disliked their breasts, their thighs, their hips, their rear-ends, their something, Zandy was evidently pleased with all of her body parts. Her pleasure showed in the way she dressed. All of her clothing fit as if they were perfectly tailored to every inch of her body. Like the jeans she had on now — she looked like she'd been poured into them. The fitted, short-sleeved T-shirt cropped just above her navel, too. Never had Sasha seen Zandy in any-thing loose or baggy. Looking down at the big jumper dress she'd thrown on for comfort, Sasha knew that Zandy wouldn't be caught dead in it.

All in all, Zandy was gorgeous by anyone's standard. *And the great thing about it all,* Sasha thought, *she doesn't seem to have a conceited bone in her body. Confident, but not conceited. It's funny how someone with her stunning, cover girl looks can get just down-right silly. The crazy way she acts sometimes, you'd think she looked more like Bozo the Clown than the JET beauty of the week.*

The perky voice returned to the phone, and Sasha completed her order. After hanging up the phone, she walked over to Zandy, who sat cross-legged on the floor reading a book. "What book is that?" she asked her.

Zandy looked up, surprised to see Sasha standing near her. "What'd you say?" she asked, distracted. "Oh," she said, Sasha's question dawning on her, *Woman Thou Art Loosed.* She held the front cover up toward Sasha as if she hadn't seen it before. "You read it?" Zandy asked, standing to her feet.

"Yes. It's pretty good, but I enjoy *listening* to him much better. When he speaks you can *hear* the power and the anointing of God in his voice."

Zandy read the author's name out loud. "Bishop T. D. Jakes."

"He is *awesome*," Sasha said. "I used to have one of his tapes, but I loaned it to one of my cousins back home. I don't think she ever gave it back to me."

Sasha reached over and pulled a handful of tapes from the shelf. After looking at the titles on the tapes, she quickly browsed through the remaining tapes on the shelf. "No, it's not here. She still has it. Anyway, if you ever want to hear him, he comes on BET Sunday mornings at six o'clock. He comes on TBN, too. I just don't know when."

"Alright," Zandy said, "I don't watch a lot of TV, but maybe I'll get a chance to watch him sometime." She pointed to the tapes in Sasha's hand. "What's on those tapes?" she asked.

Sasha looked down at the tapes. "Oh," she said, then added somewhat reluctantly, "there's preaching on these tapes, too."

"Who?" Zandy asked.

"*Who?*" Sasha repeated.

"Who's preaching on those tapes?"

Sasha looked straight into Zandy's eyes. "My father." She placed one of the tapes in Zandy's hand.

Zandy read the name on the tape. "Elder Pearson Lindsey. Your father is a . . . preacher?"

Sasha laughed at the serious look on Zandy's face. "Yes, he's a preacher. You don't like preachers?"

"No, that's not it," Zandy said, shaking her head. "I just didn't know." She began to chuckle softly.

"What's funny?"

"Nothing, really. I guess I feel like I should've known."

Sasha smiled. "Now what's *that* supposed to mean?"

"It's not meant to be a put down or anything. I guess what I'm saying is that there are so many things about you that I should've picked up on. You're different." When Zandy saw the questioning look on Sasha's face, she continued. "No, you really are. You're quiet and calm. You're always so proper and very well mannered. You don't party and stuff. You don't curse. I never see you hanging out with any guys, so you can't be gettin' your groove on."

"But you thought I had a guy here making me *purr* earlier today."

"Hey, you did sound pretty . . . um . . . you know what I mean. Besides, I didn't know you were a preacher's daughter then. And I guess I should have. Even the way you dress is different."

"Excuse me?"

"Don't look at me like that. You know what I mean. You know I don't mean you dress whacked or anything. We both know that your clothes are *tight*."

Sasha frowned. "I don't wear tight clothes, Zandy."

"No, no," Zandy laughed out. "Tight means good. Like, you know, you got some sharp clothes and you look really nice in them." When Sasha's face registered understanding, Zandy continued. "Let's just say this, you don't dress like *me*. The average guy probably wouldn't even think you *had* a shape under some of the clothes you wear. But no one would ever accuse *me* of being a preacher's daughter. Now that I think about it," she added, smiling, "they say that preacher's kids are the worse kids. Evidently, they didn't mean you."

"No, but sometimes I wish they did."

"Why?"

Sasha looked intently at Zandy. "Listen, that's kind of what I want to talk to you about. But let's eat first. After that, I'll spill it all out. Remember what I told you, though. All of my talking is going to make your ears heavy. And I guess you should know that I'm a little nervous about talking to you."

"Yeah, I kind of figured that. And I understand. So, you say as little as you want or as much as you want. It's all safe with me. You don't have to worry about me spreading your business or anything. I don't trip like that. Okay?" When Sasha nodded, she added cheerfully, "Don't look so worried. The real Miss Abbie is here. We'll have your problem solved in a jiffy."

Sasha's smile communicated doubt. "I'm going to go in the kitchen for a minute to see what I have for us to drink with that pizza."

"I assume you got to Dr. Avery in time." Zandy placed the book and tape back on the shelf and sat on the floor to remove her loafers.

"Yes. She was still in her office, but I almost missed her. She was getting ready to leave when I made it there. I turned in the paper and we walked out together. Is Sprite okay?"

"Yep." Zandy answered, walking into the small, all-white kitchen in her socks. She sat at the round glass table, pulling one foot beneath her. "What did she say? Did she get all motherly and concerned about her Sasha-dear?"

"You know Dr. Avery. She's tough, but sweet. She asked if I was feeling better and I told her that I was just a little tired and had overslept. Of course, she looked at me as if she could see straight through me and into the depths of my soul. She made me promise to come by next week to see her and have what she called a nice, little friendly chat."

"Oh, brother," Zandy said, rolling her eyes. "You know what that means – she's going to give you the third degree."

Sasha shook her head in disagreement. "She was my assigned mentor when I was a freshman last year. Ever since she found out that I was from Wisconsin and didn't have family here in Mississippi, she's been acting sort of like a surrogate mother. She just wants to make sure everything is going fine, nothing major."

"I hope so, because she can be a big bully when she wants to be. What'd she say when you told her I said, 'hello'?"

'Tell that fast Aleczandria I read her paper and if ...en I read it the second time, I just *might* give her

...*se* the one. Calling somebody fast. Girl, you should've ... ner at our freshman dance last semester. I didn't really know you then, but I don't think you were there."

"No, I didn't go."

"Anyway, she came in these skin-tight jeans and cowboy boots and she *cut up* on that dance floor. She was doing all the latest dances like she made 'em up herself. And I was right out there with her, too! We had some fun that night. Now she calls me fast and I call her Ms. Rumpshaker."

Sasha laughed at the name. "To see her in class and around campus, you wouldn't think she could get so . . . loose."

"That's what *I'm* saying. And she calls *me* fast."

They both looked toward the front door when they heard the chime. "*C'est . . . moi qui . . . offre,*" Zandy said and jumped up from the chair. She came back a few minutes later holding a medium-sized pizza box. She placed the box on the table.

"What did you say before you left?" Sasha asked her.

"I said, 'I'll get this one.' I don't know how to say, 'I'll pay for the pizza this time and you can pay for the next one' in French. Not yet anyway."

"You seem to be doing very well with your French."

"Yeah, as long as I don't have to speak it," Zandy huffed, resuming her sitting position in the chair. "I can write in French all day long, but speaking French is another story. And *this* semester, Mrs. Richards is requiring us to do more talking in French than writing. I should've taken Spanish, like you."

"Why? You'd still have to learn to speak it," Sasha said, opening one of the white cabinets with glass fronts and pulling out two plates.

"Yeah, but I would have somebody to speak it with me. Everybody speaks Spanish. I never run across people outside of my

French class who speak French. Well, except for the people w
want to hip me to a few bad words in French."

Sasha walked toward the table, carrying the plates. "You mean
profanity?"

"Exactly, and just when I was trying to give up the bad habit
of cursing *in English*." Zandy fanned the plates away as Sasha
approached the table. "Girl, keep your dishes clean. Just give me
a couple of paper towels.   I'll eat my pizza straight from the
box."

"Alright. I guess I will, too." Sasha sat at the table across
from Zandy and passed her paper towels and a glass of Sprite.

Zandy snickered. "I fell out laughing at myself the first time
I cursed in French. I just said it out of the blue. But really,
though, cursing in French doesn't seem as bad – no one knows
what you're saying. Now, I'm trying to break *two* bad habits."

"Now *that* must be hard."

Zandy shook her head. "It was at first, but not anymore. Every
now and then I let one slip, but I'm doing a whole lot better."
Reaching across the table, she threw open the lid of the pizza box
and they both whiffed in the delicious aroma of sausage, pep-
peroni, cheese, and the works. Zandy eagerly scooped up a big
slice of pizza and took a huge bite. Sasha gingerly picked up one
of the smaller slices. They ate the pizza and talked animatedly.

Picking up the conversation where they'd left off, they talked
more about their foreign language classes. Then Zandy, a psychology major, told Sasha how much she was enjoying the psychological tests they were developing in her Personality Psychology class. Sasha, a computer science major, told Zandy about a
bug in her C program that was driving her bananas because it
kept causing her program to get hung. That led to laughter-
filled conversation about some of Tougaloo's instructors — those
they liked and those they didn't like. They eagerly shared their
opinions — largely influenced by the opinions of their upper
classmen — as to which instructors should be avoided. Avoid-

'ructors, they both agreed, was no small feat since
elatively small college with a relatively small pool

_r amazement, they even discovered that they both had
_rienced the same mild shock at seeing some of the aged build-
ings on Tougaloo's campus for the first time as freshmen.

In spite of Tougaloo's less than Ivy League appearance, Sasha
stated that she'd grown very fond of its cozy college atmosphere.
She raved about Tougaloo's excellent curriculum and teaching
staff and its high academic standards. She also praised Tougaloo's
attractive new gate entrance, the new Berkshire dormitory, and
the new Fitness & Wellness Center. And she declared that
Tougaloo's African art collection was probably one of the best in
the nation. With pride in her voice, Sasha also reminded Zandy
that Tougaloo — once a huge plantation — was a historical land-
mark and that demolishing any of its buildings would be like
destroying their African-American history.

Zandy reluctantly agreed that all of that was good and fine,
but advocated that a couple of those buildings on campus needed
to be torn down or totally refurbished. She laughingly said that
if it's the history the school was trying to retain, then they should
take a picture of the buildings before tearing them down.

The next thing the two knew, they were caught up in a heated
debate about which feature was more important – appearance or
curriculum.

Sasha argued that a comprehensive curriculum that success-
fully equipped students for life and work in the real world was
more important than new buildings and perfectly landscaped lawns.

Zandy argued that both were equally important. She told
Sasha that psychological tests have proven that the senses are more
acute in aesthetic environments. "Who knows," she asked, laughing, "how much my ability to think and learn is being negatively
affected by the sight of an aging building."

The debate went on for minutes. Neither would let the other
win. Finally, they called a truce.

Zandy flung her arms in the air in surrender. "I'll drop it for now, although I still think I'm right. I like my classes because they're challenging and my instructors because they're knowledgeable, and that's very important to me. *But*," she stressed with twinkling eyes, "there are studies that back up what I say: people respond *more favorably* in aesthetically pleasing environments. So," she said, flicking a dismissive hand in the air. "I rest my case."

Sasha looked at Zandy with contrived pity and shook her head sadly. "My child, my child," she said softly, "the real world is not a huge replica of Disney World. The real world is filled with less than perfect things and less than perfect places. You must learn *now* how to not let imperfect things beset you. You must learn how to find the beauty in all that is around you, or else you will go crazy once you enter the real world. Open your eyes, my child, and look from within and you will see nothing but beauty in every crook and cranny of our beloved Eagle Queen, Tougaloo College!" Sasha finished dramatically with hands raised high in the air.

"What-*ev-er*," Zandy laughed, throwing a napkin across the table at Sasha.

Sasha grinned back. "I can't let you talk about Tougaloo. I love that school."

"Believe it or not, I love it, too," Zandy acquiesced. "I can't imagine going to school anywhere else. But you should know by now how much I like to make fun of practically everything."

"You think I *would* know that by now. I guess I'm a slow learner."

Taking in a deep breath, Zandy patted her belly with both hands. "Three slices of pizza. Boy, I'm stuffed."

"I am, too."

"I don't know how. You didn't eat anything."

"I ate *two* slices."

"You mean, you ate one slice and *messed over* the other," Zandy clarified. "That's why you're so skinny," she added with admiration.

"Skinny? I'm bigger than you are."

"That's only because I'm taller. And you're not that much bigger anyway. Probably 'cause you don't eat worth nothing. As you can see, I eat like a pig," Zandy said proudly. "But I work it off."

"Well, I can't say that I work off anything. I barely get on my exercise bike anymore. Anyway, my stomach is a little unsettled, and I don't have much of an appetite."

"Still nervous?"

"I guess so."

"Still wanna go through with it?"

"You promise not to laugh at me?"

"No," Zandy said, then laughed. "I'm just kidding. I won't laugh unless you laugh. But you can't cry either, because then I'll cry." She encouraged Sasha with a smile. "C'mon. Let's get it over with."

Together they cleaned off the table and put away the leftovers. After washing up, they settled in the front room on the sofa.

Chapter 3

Zandy slid back into a corner of the sofa and drooped down comfortably. "So, where do you want to start?" she asked Sasha.

"Oh, I don't know," Sasha replied, her voice wavering.

"Do you want me to help you get started. I can try and guess at what the problem is." Zandy's eyebrows danced. "I'm good at that."

Sasha smiled. "No, that's not necessary. Just bear with me."

"Okay," Zandy said. Wriggling her toes in her socks, she stretched her legs out over a small portion of the sofa and said, "I'm ready when you are."

"Well, let's see," Sasha began, kicking off her mules. "I told you that my father is a preacher, right?"

"Right."

"And you said that you should've known because of the way I am. Different."

"But I didn't mean anything bad by that."

"Yes, I know that. It's just that all of my life I've been a preacher's daughter, in every sense. My father and mother raised me to live a clean and holy life, and to love God and keep His commandments. If I didn't do those things, I'd open up my eyes in Hell when I died. So, for as long as I can remember, I did what I was taught. I didn't want to go to Hell, and I didn't want to disappoint my parents either, my father especially. There are many preachers who have children who do the exact opposite of what they preach. I didn't want to do anything that would shame my father or his ministry. I was, and still am, an only child, and I wanted him to be proud of me. So I made up my mind to be the best preacher's kid ever. I can't recall the exact moment that I came to that decision, but I was very young. In fact, I was seven when I testified before the church that the Lord had saved me and that I was going to be a witness for Him at school." Sasha's eyes shifted from Zandy's to the coffee table. "Hallelujah," she added dryly.

"*Seven?*" Zandy asked, her face screwed into a frown of disbelief. "Isn't that a bit young?"

"No," Sasha answered, staring out into the space of nothingness beyond Zandy's head. "At least my parents didn't think so. I didn't either, for that matter. I felt privileged to be saved at such a young age. Every chance I got, I told somebody about the Lord. If my playmates fell and hurt themselves, I told them that everything would be alright, that the Lord would heal them. Sometimes, I even laid my hands on whatever part of their bodies that hurt and prayed for them.

"If my teacher seemed to be sad about something or not feeling too well, I would tell her that the Lord was able to fix *all* of her problems. All she had to do was *give* them over to Jesus. It's so funny now, some of the things I use to say and do."

A smile briefly touched Sasha's lips, but not her vacant eyes. "When I was in the third grade, I almost got in trouble for marching up to my best friend's teacher and telling her that she needed patience and that I would pray for the Lord to give it to her, too. When my mother asked me why I had done it, I told her that my best friend, Tesha, was crying at playtime because Mrs. Loman had yelled at her for mistakenly knocking over a dish of paint. I said that if Mrs. Loman had been patient, Tesha would not have been crying.

Sasha's smile finally reached her eyes. "I said it with such conviction that my mother couldn't help but laugh. But she told me that I had to be careful about saying things that would upset my elders." Shrugging, she said, "That's pretty much how I was for the rest of my grade school years. A little missionary proclaiming the Lord in the school."

Zandy's eyes twinkled with admiration. "A seven year-old missionary. I'm impressed. When *I* was seven, I was *kicking* teachers and *throwing* paint."

Lost in thoughts of her early years, Sasha heard Zandy but continued to reminisce as if she hadn't. "When I made it to middle school," she said, her eyes drawn back to the spot beyond Zandy's head, "things began to change. I learned then that kids at that age don't care to hear all that much about the Lord and what He can do for you. I instinctively learned *not* to talk about the Lord so much.

"I also learned that, unlike the kids in grade school, the majority of the kids in middle school don't really respect others for their differences. In grade school, kids don't really care what you are — they just like you. But in middle school, you're supposed to be a part of the in-crowd, wearing the latest fashions, doing the latest dances and talking the latest talk. Of course, I did neither. I mean, my parents always kept me very well dressed, but they did *not* buy me clothes based on the latest fad. I dressed the same, regardless.

Sasha's eyes zeroed in on Zandy. "In other words, I was different — more or less a younger version of what you see now. I talked differently. I acted differently. And yes, I even dressed differently — I only wore dresses and skirts, never pants or shorts."

Again disbelief clouded Zandy's features. "You, too?" she asked.

"What do you mean, *you, too?*"

"The girls at this Pentecostal church I used to attend when I was younger — Love Alive Church of God in Christ — didn't wear pants, either. So," Zandy said, her eyes radiating keen interest, "you've *never* worn pants before?"

If there was any one question Sasha had grown to hate, Zandy had just asked it. *Why does everyone ask me that? Like not wearing pants is as freaky as having two heads.* Sasha's eyes turned hard. Without looking at Zandy, she shook her head. "No," she answered flatly.

Zandy thought she saw anger flash in Sasha's eyes. She projected her neck slightly forward to get a better look into her friend's eyes. They were void of all expression. Zandy obviously had been mistaken. *"Never, ever?"* she ventured to ask. "You never snuck on a pair at school, like some of them sanctified girls did at my school?"

Pent-up resentment threatened to spurt from Sasha's mouth, and she longed to finally scream just how much she detested the pants question and others like it. You've never said a curse word? You've never drank alcohol? You've never had sex? She'd been asked all of those questions more times than she could remember, and she was plumb tired of them. At one point in her life, the questions didn't bother her at all. In fact, she'd secretly relished them because the more she heard them, the more righteous she felt.

But, now, when one of those questions was put to her, she wanted to tell the asker to get out of her face. She was fed up with the questions. She was fed up with coming off as a goody-two shoes. She wasn't trying to be righteous anymore anyway. The questions made her sick to her stomach.

Now here Zandy was, asking her one of the same irritating questions.

But, as usual, Sasha resisted the urge to vent. She'd never attacked anyone else who'd asked her the question. She had simply swallowed her indignation and kept on smiling. Just like anyone else who'd become a pro at hiding his or her true feelings.

Sasha was better than a pro, though. She'd mastered "feeling killing." The problem was, she was getting very tired of holding her true feelings in.

Still, now was not the time let her true feelings out. Zandy was here because she'd asked her to come, because she was a friend.

Sasha looked at her and smiled evenly. "No, not ever. I was a senior in high school before I even put on a pair of pajamas."

"Sheesh," Zandy sighed, shaking her head. "I just don't understand why some churches say that wearing pants is a sin. I was about thirteen years old when I went to that Pentecostal church, and I really liked going, too. But I didn't stay long because they taught against *everything*. Wearing pants was a sin. Wearing make-up was a sin. Playing basketball and football was a sin. Going to the movies was a sin. *Everything* was a sin. You couldn't do *anything,* unless you were doing it with the church or at the church." She turned up her nose. "I left. I probably should've stayed, 'cause to tell you the truth, I eventually started doing some wild stuff after I left there. But some of the things that preacher was saying didn't make any sense to me. I had given my life to the Lord, and I was really trying to live right. But nobody could help me understand what a pair of pants had to do with my salvation."

"Well," Sasha began, "I don't know what that church told you, but I was taught that if you were a saved women you were supposed to dress modestly and not wear anything that pertains unto a man — and that meant pants."

"Dress modestly?!" Zandy fired. "Who says that I can't be modest in a pair of pants. That's what kills me about some church folks. They want to dress like they're so holy and all, but they act just like the devil. Church folks are some of the most hateful, spiteful, *and* sinful people I know. Their sins are in their heart, and they think nobody knows it. There'll be more church people in Hell than a little bit. I mean, if you don't really love God and live for Him, then dressing a certain way doesn't *make* you holy. You know what I'm saying?"

At this point in her life, Sasha didn't care one way or another. Still, she felt the need to defend what her father and the church had taught her. "Yes, but if you really are holy, and *not* a hypocrite, then you *will* dress modestly. God's people are modest in their apparel."

"And I ask you again, who says that I can't be modest in a pair of pants? Don't get me wrong. I'm not saying that *I* dress modestly. As I'm sure you already know, I like my body, and I like showing it off. I'm sure that I've made the devil himself cringe with some of the clothes I've put on. But I'm not professing to be saved, either. And if I ever *get* saved, I *will* dress more modest. But that doesn't mean that I have to stop wearing pants. Maybe I won't wear 'em as tight. Maybe I'll have to let go of my hoochie-mama dresses and my short shorts, and some of my other skimpy clothes. But wearing pants will *not* make me unholy when I get my heart right with God."

"What about Deuteronomy 22:5?"

"What about it?"

"It says — and I quote — the woman shall not wear that which pertaineth unto a man, neither shall a man put on a woman's garment: for all that do so are abomination unto the LORD thy God."

"Oh, I know what it says. I've heard it before. I used to argue that pants weren't even made back then, so God couldn't have been talking about pants. He could've been talking about a piece of armor or a headpiece or something. Who knows?" Zandy shook her head. "I don't argue that anymore because here's what I learned." She leaned toward Sasha. "Those people in the Old Testament lived under the law. But when Jesus died on the cross, the law was um . . . um . . . what's the word I'm looking for?" she asked herself.

"Fulfilled?" Sasha guessed.

"Yes, fulfilled. When Jesus came, the law was fulfilled, which means it was completed. *Jesus* completed the law. If Jesus didn't die for your sins, you could never be *righteous*. I don't care how good you live, or how many pair of pants you wear or don't wear. You could never come close to being good and holy in the eyes of God. Our righteousness is as filthy rags, the Bible says. Jesus is your righteousness and you are now complete in Him. You live by grace now, not by the law, which is nothing but a bunch of rules and regulations. With Jesus came a new commandment and a new . . . um . . . a new covenant with God. That's the New Testament. The real purpose of the Old Testament is to give us the history of God and His people. I'm not saying that the Old Testament is not important – it is, but to go back to the Old Testament and use it to determine what is right and wrong for today is *totally out of order*." She snorted. "Those people back then had to do a lot of things that we don't have to do today, like sacrifice animals when they sinned. Jesus became the consummate sacrifice when He died on the cross. People don't have to *kill* animals anymore to be saved. They just need to accept Christ into their hearts and then grow into His likeness. The Old Testament — or the Law — failed in that it could not make a man righteous. Only Jesus can do that.

Zandy leaned back on the sofa and peered at Sasha. "Let me ask you this," she said. "If you died and stood before God and He asked you why He should let you into Heaven, what would you say?"

Sasha shrugged. "I would say that I tried to live a godly life and that I tried to keep His commandments."

Zandy screwed her lips into a frown. "Wrong answer!" she declared. "If you gave that answer to God, He'd probably throw you straight into Hell. I would if I'd sent my only son who sacrificed his life for you and all you could talk about is you and your attempts at righteousness. What you *should* say to God should start out something like this: 'Father, I am not worthy to enter into the Kingdom of Heaven, but because of Jesus . . .' I don't care how old you are, how long you've been saved, or what wonderfully good things you did in this life, your answer should be the same, because it's all about Jesus making the difference."

Sasha nodded, her eyes thoughtful.

"So all I'm saying," Zandy continued, "is that you should not allow yourself to be bound by laws that don't have a whole lot to do with your faith in Christ. I can understand why things like adultery, fornication, drinking, smoking, jealously, hatred, and enviousness are ungodly — they are destructive to the body in one way or another and God wants our soul, mind, and body to be healthy in all respects. But wearing a decent pair of pants or throwing a ball through a hoop, I can't understand. Doing things like that won't put you in Heaven or Hell. The New Testament says that women of God should be modest in their apparel, and I agree, but be modest in *whatever* you put on. And, anyway, going back to the Old Testament to solely determine what is appropriate attire for you is like reading somebody else's mail. You're reading mail that wasn't even sent to you."

Sasha chuckled. "Where did you get that from?"

"What, 'reading somebody else's mail'?"

"Yes."

Zandy shrugged. "I can't remember. I heard somebody say it, and I guess it stuck." She smiled proudly. "I may not go to church often, but I used to listen to preachers all the time on the radio. I can't break the Bible down like some of them do, but I know a little bit. I know enough to hold my own."

"But not enough to want to be saved."

"Very funny."

"I'm not trying to be. It's obvious that you know quite a bit about the Bible."

"I learned a lot about the Bible from Mae Mama, too. She was a member of that same Pentecostal church. I only attended that church for about a year, but I used to talk to her all the time. Even years after I stopped going to the church. Besides my mother and my sister, Mae Mama was the only person I really liked back then. And all she used to do was talk about the Lord.

Her head bowed slightly, Zandy looked pensive. "She used to always tell me that God had His hands on me, that He was going to use me in a mighty way. It didn't matter that I was as hot as a firecracker and had a bad attitude about everything. She still said that God had an anointing on my life." Zandy laughed under her breath. "As you can see, she must have had me confused with someone else. I respect God and all, but I just can't get down with too much of the church scene. Too many hypocrites."

"That's a cop-out, Zandy. Hypocrites are everywhere."

"Yeah, you're right," Zandy said, smiling sheepishly. "I guess I'm just not ready to change my life. 'Cause you know, If I get saved, I can't keep hating my father."

"You don't hate your father. Stop saying that."

Zandy's eyes cut into Sasha like a sharp knife. *Even "hate" doesn't fully describe what I feel for the man,* her eyes said.

Sasha got the message. She cleared her throat, then asked, "Where is she now? And how did she get that name?"

"Who, Mae Mama? She's in Heaven, I'm sure. She died two years ago. Mae Mama is the mother of my mother's best friend, Mae. When T'Kara was about two years old, Mae Mama started babysitting her. The first day my mother took T'Kara over there, she said, 'T'Kara, say hi to Mae's Mama,' and T'Kara said, 'Hi, Mae Mama' and the name stuck. Mae Mama was . . . Wait a minute, now," Zandy said, shaking her head. "We're getting off track. We were talking about you, not me. We can talk about Mae Mama some other time. You were talking about not wearing pants, which, like I said, makes no sense to me."

"It's really not as bad as you think," Sasha said airily. "It's hard to miss what you've never done."

"But what did you wear in gym class?"

"The one year I did take gym, I wore a skirt."

Zandy looked at Sasha as if she'd said that she'd taken gym class naked. "Did the other kids make fun of you?"

Sasha chuckled. "A few of them talked about me among themselves, but it didn't bother me," she replied. Then making sure her emotions were in check, she added, "Most of them just asked a lot of questions. Their questions made me *feel* different. I expected to be an outcast, but I wasn't. I think my grades saved me from that. I was a straight 'A' student and most of the kids tended to respect you for being book-smart, even if you weren't street-smart or fashion-smart. And I was also, quote-unquote, a leader.

I was on this committee and that committee. I was the president of this and the president of that.

She shrugged. "So I was pretty popular without trying to be. But it wouldn't have mattered all that much anyway, me not being popular. I was a pretty independent person and didn't require approval from other people. I still witnessed about the Lord to other students, although I usually waited until they asked me questions about why I didn't do certain things. I was who I was because that's who I wanted to be. My parents' and the church's expectations had become mine, and I was content with that.

"That is, until I made it to high school. At first, it was like being in middle school. I was still popular enough, for the same reasons. And just like in middle school, I didn't attend school dances or basketball games, and things like that. I still talked about the Lord, but I was even more reserved in high school. I had only one or two close friends at school. They liked me for who I was, and even went to church with me a few times. And there were a few guys who liked me, too. At least that's what I would hear. But most of them were too hesitant to approach me. They didn't know if I would talk to them or start preaching to them."

Zandy giggled. "So you didn't have a high school sweetheart?"
Sasha shook her head bashfully.

"What about those handsome church boys?"
Sasha made a funny face, but still shook her head, no.

"I can't believe those turkeys at your school were too scared to ask you out."

"Not all of them. A few of them did try to talk to me, but you've got to understand that *church* was my life. I didn't go to movies or parties or other places where kids hung out. I went to school and church and church functions. That's it." She frowned. "And I was sort of skeptical of most of those guys anyway. I didn't know what they wanted from me. It was no secret that a lot of the girls in high school were sexually active, and I just wasn't sure if I was expected to be sexually active, too."

"You thought they were hoping to be the one to turn you out," Zandy piped in, her words laced with laughter.

Sasha nodded quickly. "Yeah. Like they thought I was a quiet devil or something — spiritual and holy in public, but a raging nympho in private."

Zandy's laugh filled the room.

"I know," Sasha said, nodding her head and smiling. "It makes me laugh, too, just thinking about some of the thoughts I had back then."

"Girl, please. I'm laughing at what you *said*. You saved yourself a lot of headache by *not* talking to them, because most of them were probably trying to do just that — get under your dress."

Sasha's eyes dropped to the floor. "Yeah, you're probably right," she said thoughtfully, then fell silent.

Zandy waited for Sasha to say something more, but Sasha remained silent. "*Qu'est-ce qui ne va pas?* — What's wrong?"

"Oh, nothing. My mind just went off on a tangent." Sasha's brow creased into a frown. "I was going to say something before my mind jumped track, but I forgot what it was."

"Well, earlier you said that things sort of changed when you made it to high school, but you never did say how."

"Oh, yeah." Sasha pulled her knees up to her chest and wrapped her arms around her legs. Underneath her loose dress, her toes dangled over the edge of the sofa. Propping her chin in the cradle of her knees, she continued. "Like I said, high school started out pretty much like middle school — I was still saved and still doing everything I thought would please my family and the Lord, too, of course." Her countenance saddened and her lips twitched sullenly. Locking her eyes with the floor, she said, "But in my junior year, I, uh . . . in my junior year, I . . ." Her voice trailed off.

Zandy studied Sasha's baby doll features, now marred with distraught. She concluded that Sasha must have done something that had really displeased her family . . . and the Lord, too, of course. *Did she jump out of her bedroom window at night to meet a boy or did she get caught under the gym bleachers kissing him?* Zandy smiled knowingly and thought, *If little stuff like that is making Sasha look this miserable, she'd fall out dead if she knew some of the things I've done.* "What'd you do," Zandy teased, "let one of those guys give you a little lip action?"

Sasha lifted her chin to look directly into Zandy's smiling eyes. She held Zandy's gaze as if it gave her the strength to say what she had been struggling to get out. "In my junior year," she replied numbly, "I lost my mother."

Zandy's eyes blinked rapidly. Her face became a kaleido-scope of emotions - astonishment, disbelief, horror, then sorrow suffused her countenance in swarming succession. "Oh, Sasha! I'm so sorry!" She scooted across the sofa to place a tentative hand on Sasha's shoulder. "You never told me that your mother wasn't living. What happened to her?"

Sasha let her feet fall to the floor. She pulled one of the decorative pillows into her arms and shrugged wearily. "My mother had a brain aneurysm," she answered in a weak voice. "Some people die almost immediately after an aneurysm bursts. My mom didn't. My father and I rushed her to the hospital, and she was in a coma for almost a week. I spent so many hours at her bedside talking to her, telling her how much I loved her and needed her. She couldn't talk or even open her eyes, but I know she heard me because sometimes she would squeeze my hand in response. I prayed so hard that week. I pleaded with God to heal my mother." She turned to Zandy with a pained expression on her face. "But He let her die anyway." Sasha sighed heavily before taking both hands and wiping determinedly at the tears that cascaded down her cheeks. "He just let her die."

"What causes aneurysms?" Zandy asked sadly. "Do they even know?"

"The doctors don't know," Sasha answered bitterly, then snapped, "but I know. I know who caused *my* mother's death."

An eerie feeling caused Zandy to shiver. *Had someone done something to Sasha's mother? Her . . . father?* Apprehension paralyzed Zandy. "What . . . do you . . . mean by that?" she asked hesitantly.

Sasha leaped from the sofa. "I'll tell you what I mean by that," she growled through gritted teeth. "I mean that *God* controls everything. He knew my mother had that aneurysm. He could've removed it. Even after it burst, He could have healed her. He's *God*, isn't He?! Instead, He let her die. He could've spared my mother's life, but He let her die! *After all I did to please Him, He let my mother die!*" Angrily, she flung the pillow to the floor. Her face ruptured into volcanic rage. "*That's* what I mean. *That,*" she snarled again, flailing a hand in the air, "*is what I mean!*" With trembling hands she covered her face and began to sob loudly.

Zandy sat wide-eyed and stunned. Sasha's outbreak had surprised her. Scared her for a moment, too. She didn't know that Sasha could look so deadly. And a minute ago, she would have bet money that Sasha didn't even know *how* to get mad. *That's one bet I would've lost big time*, she thought. *Evidently, she hasn't fully grieved the loss of her mother. It's been three years since her mother died. Shouldn't she be past this stage of rage?*

At that moment, understanding hit Zandy. Sasha wasn't angry just because her mother died. She was angry with God for letting her die. This shocked Zandy and gave her reason to be concerned.

Nothing, she thought, *makes a person more explosive than being angry with God.*

Zandy watched helplessly as the tears steadily seeped between Sasha's fingers, and her heart went out to her.

Finally, she stood and walked over to Sasha. Gently, she rubbed Sasha's upper back to comfort her. "I'm sorry about your mother, Sasha," she said soothingly, tears burning her own eyes. "I'm so sorry."

Sasha shook herself visibly and began to wipe away the tears with her hand. "Thank you," she said, her voice shaking. "I should be apologizing to you for making a total idiot of myself."

She shook her head, feeling much shame at her display of anger in front of Zandy. "I didn't mean to break down on you like that."

"That's alright. C'mon and sit down." Zandy led Sasha back to the sofa. When Sasha was seated, Zandy grabbed tissues from a box on the end table and placed them in Sasha's hand.

Sasha used the tissue to wipe at the tears that continued to flow from her eyes. "I don't cry often," she said, sniffing, "but when I do, I don't seem to be able to stop." She inhaled a deep breath and her body shook when she released it. "Where do tears come from anyway? I'd like to know so I can shut them off for good. I hate it when I cry."

"Tears are secreted by the lachrymal gland of the eye, and you needed a good cry. Here, take these." Zandy handed Sasha more tissue. "And trust me, if you didn't have tears to cry, you would go totally mad and kill up a few people."

Sasha smiled openly as she wiped away the remaining tears with the soft tissue. She looked at Zandy with glistening red eyes. "I don't know if you're more funny or more smart. *Lachrymal gland*," she repeated, shaking her head in admiration. "Either way, you always know how to make me smile."

Zandy was happy to the see the smile. It eased some of the worry she was feeling. "Most people don't see me as smart," she said, smiling back, "so every now and then I have to show off how brainy I can be." She peered at Sasha, her smile fading. She wanted to ask her about the angry statements she'd made about God, but didn't feel it would be appropriate. Sasha would talk about it when she was ready. Until then, she didn't want to chance sending her into another fit of rage.

Instead she asked softly, "Sasha, why didn't you tell me about your mother? When I saw you with your parents in that picture," she said, pointing to a large portrait over the fireplace's mantle, "I assumed she was still alive. And you let me assume."

Sasha looked up at the picture. It was one of her favorites. Almost everyone thought she favored her father, but in this picture she and her mother looked like sisters. Even her father thought so. Sasha carried a smaller version of the photograph in her wallet. "That picture was taken the year before she died."

"She was very pretty. You two favor a lot." Zandy looked from the picture back to Sasha. "So why didn't you tell me about her?"

"I don't like to talk about it. I don't like people feeling sorry for me."

"I'm not *people*, and that's your mother," Zandy exclaimed, tears forming in her eyes.

"Here," Sasha said, passing Zandy some of her tissue. She laughed softly. "You seem to need these, too."

Zandy took the tissue and patted her eyes. Pointing an accusing finger at Sasha, she mumbled, "I should be mad at you for not telling me."

"You're right. I should've told you. If I *had* told you, maybe we both wouldn't be sitting here crying our eyes out."

Zandy sniffed loudly. "You started it. I told you not to cry. And what do you expect me to do when you tell me something like that?" *And when I see you breaking down in front of me like you did.*

"I know, and I'm sorry. But," Sasha said cheerily, "enough tears. No more crying, okay?"

"Okay," Zandy said, still sniffing.

"Now where was I?" Sasha asked herself. "Oh, yes," she said, remembering where she was going with her story and blocking out everything else. "I made it through the rest of my junior year. After my mother died, the only two things that remained important to me were my grades and my father.

"My mother's death hit my father hard. He was devastated. They were so very close and still so much in love – even after eighteen years of marriage, they could barely pass each other without touching or kissing. He missed her so much. As a full-time pastor, he'd always been busy with church-related business, but not as busy as he became *after* my mother's death. When she died, he buried himself in church work, housework . . . and me. I think he was scared that he could lose me, too."

"I'm sure he was worried about you and how you were dealing with your mother's death, too."

Sasha nodded. "He was. He seemed to have a hard time letting me out of his sight in the beginning. He wanted to take me to school and pick me up everyday, instead of me taking the bus as I normally did. He wanted to take me out to eat, to the stores, everywhere, all the time. He always felt the need to talk to me, to constantly remind me that God . . . that God is omniscient and that He had a reason for taking my mother, even though we might not understand why." Sasha swallowed hard. "I assured him that I was alright and that he had no need to worry about me. Sometimes, though, I would catch him watching me with a concerned look on his face. I guess he did that because I didn't talk a lot about my mother's death."

Zandy searched Sasha's face for a sign of the passionate anger she'd shown earlier, but saw nothing. *Thank God your father wasn't here tonight*, she thought.

"I didn't want my father to be worried about me," Sasha continued. "I knew he was hurting enough already. While he was trying to be everything for me, I was trying to be everything for him. I cleaned the house. I had his clothes cleaned and pressed. I laid out what he should wear everyday. Like my mother used to do." Her eyes brightened with adoration. "Poor thing, he has no real sense of style. He'd wear blue, black, green, and orange together if you'd let him."

Zandy giggled. "He must be dressing like a clown now since you're not around to help him."

"No, he's gotten a whole lot better. I think he's memorized what goes with what. The problem comes when he buys something new. I always say, 'Daddy, when you go to the store, make *sure* you get one of those salespeople — who is not colorblind — to help you.' He rarely buys anything new, though. My mother used to buy practically all of his clothes. After she died, I found myself buying things for him, too.

"I also made sure that he ate. Getting him to eat was hard, too. Most of the time I didn't know if he wasn't eating because he was fasting or if it was because he was thinking about my mother's death. He lost a lot of weight," she said, her eyes reflecting sadness.

"Anyway," she continued briskly, "I gave up my leadership roles at school *and* at church. I spent all my time with my father and in my books. With everything else, I was just going through the motions.

"But that sort of changed at the beginning of my senior year because my classmates had chosen me to be Senior Class President, without me even running for it. I'd been the president of my freshman class, my sophomore class, and my junior class until I resigned. The class as a whole had been very sympathetic at the time of my mother's death, but I guess they felt that I needed to get back into the swing of things. Somebody had my name put on the ballet, and I beat out the other two candidates. I was amazed and touched."

"Did you decline the position?" Zandy asked.

"No, I took it. And that changed everything. During my previous years as Class President, I helped plan activities but didn't necessarily attend them. But in my senior year, I became much more involved. I attended almost every function, even if it was on a church night. I went to all the class dances. I didn't even know how to dance. I didn't even try. But I had so much fun anyway. I went to almost all of our school's football and basketball games, jumping up and down and cheering our team on like I was out of my mind. For some reason, I felt liberated.

"I was even voted Most Spirited that year. And believe me, *that* was a first." Sasha's eyes lit up. "And I can't forget about my prom. For years I'd said that I wouldn't attend it. But I did. I wore this beautiful pink gown. It was strapless, too, so I wore this short, white fur cape around my shoulders so my father wouldn't have a stroke. I went with this good-looking guy named

Robert. No, he was better than good-looking. He was gorgeous. He had transferred to West Division during his junior year and he was voted best-looking that year and the senior year, as well. He was actually one of the guys I sort of brushed off before my mother died. But in my senior year, I gave him my number.

"We weren't dating or anything, but I had been talking to him quite a bit at school and on the phone. And I was really hoping that he would ask me to go to the prom with him. Everybody liked him, but he wasn't dating anyone. So, of course, I was so excited when he *finally* asked me. He came to my house to pick me up *and* to meet my father.

"My father, he is something else. He actually took Robert into the living room and talked with him for about *twenty whole minutes*. It was just general conversation, but I had no idea what my father was going to say from one minute to the next. He can be a real comedian at times. But he didn't embarrass me, though. Thank goodness. It was the first date I'd ever had, and my father told me that he wasn't about to let me walk out of that house without him — as he put it — knowing something about the boy."

"Sounds like a scene from the Cosby Show," Zandy said with a laugh.

"I know, but that's my father. Anyway, I got Robert away from him in one piece and we drove to Red Lobster for dinner and then to the prom. Robert was driving a beautiful car that night. It was a black Porsche 911."

"It was *his* car?"

"No. I think it belonged to his father. His father owned a car dealership."

"So you guys were riding in style."

"Yes, and I had a fabulous time. I don't know exactly what it was about that night that was a turning point for me. I didn't do much at the prom besides talk and laugh and take pictures. Afterwards, a group of us — Robert, too — went to the Lake Front and did pretty much the same thing. But it was that night that I made the decision to have a talk with my father." Sasha paused, then asked Zandy. "Am I boring you, yet?"

Zandy frowned. "Are you crazy? I can't wait to hear the rest."

"Well, let me know if I start to bore you," Sasha told her, then continued. "So, anyway, a week or so after the prom, I found my father in his study, which is where he really lives." Adoration filled her eyes again. "My father is the most loving man I've ever known, and I'm crazy about him. Even before my mother died, my father was my world. After my mother died, we managed to get even closer. I guess I love him so much because he's a man of integrity and because he lives what he preaches."

"There are so many who don't," Zandy griped.

"I know, and that's why my father is so special to me. He truly loves the Lord and he strives to please Him. He wanted his family to please the Lord, too. But my father never told me to do things *just because he said so*, like a lot of parents do. He always took the time to explain to me what was right, why it was right, and why I should do right. And he's always loving and kind to me, but firm and strict to the point where he means what he says and he expects to be obeyed. He rarely makes decisions quickly; he believes in praying and thinking about things first. So usually when he said, 'No,' he meant *no*. And I really didn't know how he would respond to what I had to say to him.

Sasha's mind went back to the day when she'd walked into her father's huge study. His little house was more like it. He kept practically everything in it — sofa, table, tools, computer, papers, and books galore. Everything except food, clothing, and a bed. Sasha and her mother wouldn't allow him to do that. They'd often teased him about forgetting their existence if he had all of life's basic essentials in his study.

"My father was sitting behind his desk, reading his Bible and writing when I walked in. I stood in the doorway and watched him, praying that he wouldn't get too upset when he heard what I'd decided to do.

"Finally, he looked up and saw me. He told me to come on in and asked me what was on my mind. I blurted out that I didn't want to go to Marquette University, the Milwaukee college I'd already been accepted into with a four-year scholarship. I'll never forget how he calmly took off his glasses and laid them down on his desk. He must have looked at me for one whole minute before he asked me what *did* I want to do. He didn't appear to be upset, so I barged ahead and told him that I wanted to go another college.

"To my surprise, he started to laugh. He'd thought that I didn't want to go to college *at all*. He was relieved. I passed him a Tougaloo College brochure and told him that I had privately applied to Tougaloo College a few months back and had been accepted with a four-year scholarship there as well.

"He frowned at the brochure and said, 'Tug-a-loo. Where in the world is Tug-a-loo?' I couldn't help but laugh at the way he pronounced the name, and that was good because it helped me to release some of the nervousness I'd been feeling. I told him that it was pronounced 'Toog-ah-loo' and that it was a private, historical black college in Mississippi, just outside of Jackson.

"When he asked me why I wanted to go there and not to Marquette, I took a deep breath and launched into the speech I'd prepared months before. I told him how, for years, I'd been living a life that he and Mom had chosen for me and that I wanted to get away to find out if it was the life *I* wanted for myself. I mentioned a few more things, too, but that's about the gist of what I said."

"Oo-o-o-h," Zandy crooned, "I bet he had a Holy Ghost fit when you told him that!"

"No, he didn't," Sasha responded. "In fact, he didn't even seem surprised by what I'd said. He would have to be blind to not see that I had changed since my mother's death, but I don't think he knew the extent of the change. One thing he did know was that it had to be pretty serious for me to come to him and tell him that I planned to do something that he may not like. I just didn't have those types of conversations with my father. In the end, I think he respected me for handling it in a mature manner, even though he didn't necessary like the idea of me going off."

"So he told you it was okay for you to go?"

"Well, he had more questions about Tougaloo and wanted to see all of the paperwork and literature I'd received. But for the most part, he talked about how proud of me he was and how proud my mother would be at the beautiful and intelligent young woman I'd grown into. He told me that he was not happy with my decision, but that he trusted me to be mature enough to make my own choices in life and that he could only pray that God would keep me and direct me.

"He told me that he'd taught me the ways of the Lord and that he didn't want me to forsake them, and as much as he wanted to, he would not try to hold me back. He felt it would be a mistake in the long run. He made me come over and sit in his lap — I hadn't done that in years — and he hugged me and told me that he loved me very much and that no matter what, I would always be his little girl."

"Oh, that's so sweet," Zandy said, cooing. "He *did* tell you it was okay for you to come."

"Yes."

"And he didn't take time to go off and think about it or pray about it?"

"No, he didn't."

"Unbelievable. Most preacher-fathers would have a fit if their daughter — *their daughter*, not their son — actually told them she was going off to see if she had any wild oats to sow."

"He even flew down here with me and stayed a week to make sure I settled in okay. I'd started driving my mom's car at home, but when we got here, he bought me that Honda Accord. After that, he opened up a bank account for me and put enough money in there so that I wouldn't have to work."

Zandy laughed. "Daddy didn't want his baby working. She needs to concentrate on graduating *summa cum laude*."

"You're right. That's exactly what he said. As far back as I can remember, he's told me about how he rushed to the bank and opened up a savings account for my college education the same day he learned my mom was pregnant with me. He said he used to always tell my mom that he was going to make sure that *his baby* had enough money for college, just in case she turned out to be too dumb to earn a scholarship. Since I did earn a full scholarship, he wanted me to have the money — a portion of it anyway — to use for whatever I needed while I was in school.

"I told my father that I wanted my own apartment, but I didn't tell him it was because I was half-scared to live on campus. We found this apartment, and even though it's really too big for one person, he got it anyway. He said I needed the extra room for a study. He *believes* in having a place set aside for study."

Zandy nodded her head with a knowing look in her eyes. "Daddy was making sure you had enough room for him, just in case he wanted to drop in and check up on you," she teased.

"That's sort of what I thought, too, but he's been to Mississippi twice since then and both times he stayed at a hotel. I couldn't even talk him into staying here."

"Your father sounds like a really nice man."

"He is. I hope you get a chance to meet him."

"Me, too."

"Anyway, everything I've told you thus far is preliminary."

Zandy's brows arched. "Preliminary?" she asked laughingly. Nodding her head, she said, "Okay."

"I'll try to make this short." Sasha exhaled a brief sigh. "I spent all of my freshman year here pretty much like I did my early high school years. I'd pulled back into my shell, not that I was trying to. I think being here made me feel out of my element. I wasn't used to the campus life or the people. I wasn't going to any of the campus functions. I went to church here regularly, too, although I didn't get involved in a whole lot.

"Without even trying, I was becoming my old self, doing the things I'd been taught even though I wasn't feeling it. I was the sweet, little church girl again, and I wasn't happy about that. I came here for, you know, adventure and excitement. Not to crawl back into the humdrum turtle shell that I was starting to come out of. My purpose for coming here was failing until—"

Zandy saw the twinkle in Sasha's eyes and the twitching smile on her lips. She sat up straight. "Until what?" she asked expectantly.

"Well," Sasha said, grinning shyly, "I met this guy last semester, and I've been sort of dating him ever since."

"Really?" Zandy asked loudly. "*I knew it. I knew* there was a guy over here earlier."

Sasha laughed at Zandy's enthusiasm. "No," she said, shaking her head. "There's was no one here when you called. And stop getting excited. You're making me nervous."

"Who is he? Somebody on campus?"

Sasha spoke hesitantly. "Yes."

"It's somebody I know!" Zandy shouted, bouncing her shapely tush around on the sofa. "I can tell by the way you're looking! Who is he, Sasha?"

"Stop jumping around like that. I told you, you're making me nervous."

"Okay, I'll stop," Zandy said, still bouncing up and down. "Tell me, tell me, *tell me.*"

"Tellis."

Zandy stopped bouncing. "Tellis?" she asked herself. "Tellis? Who do I know named Tellis? I *know* I know that name. Tellis? *Tellis! Oh my goodness!*" she shrieked, jumping up from the sofa. "Tellis Jacobs! You're dating *Tellis Jacobs?!*"

"Yes," Sasha replied softly.

"*Ma foi?! –* Really?!"

"Really."

"You lie!" Zandy accused, wide-eyed.

Sasha shook her head, grinning. "No. It's true."

Zandy squealed. "How come you didn't tell me?!"

"Well, I wasn't sure —"

"Do you know who he looks like? He looks just like . . . "

"Malcolm," they said in unison. Sasha said it in a tone that was matter-of-fact, but Zandy was ecstatic.

"Malcolm, from *The Young and The Restless*," Zandy said gleefully.

"Tellis told me that everybody tells him that. I finally got a chance to see Malcolm the other day on television. I guess they do favor, except Malcolm has a chipped tooth or something. Tellis' teeth are perfect."

"I know," Zandy nodded, grinning. "I think Tellis may have a little edge on Malcolm. Did you know that he's a junior, too?"

Sasha laughed. "Yes, I know."

"Girl, I can't believe this. You have hooked yourself a good-looking older man! But let me calm down," Zandy said, falling back down to the sofa. "I'm more excited for you than you are."

"No, you're not. I just hide mine pretty well."

"I'm so happy for you. And not just because he's handsome," Zandy added, shaking a finger at Sasha. "No-good handsome men are a dime a dozen. I should know — my daddy is one," she added under her breath, then said, "From what I hear, Tellis is a pretty smart guy, with his head screwed on tight. I've seen him around with a few girls on campus, but I haven't heard any bad rumors about him. And trust me, if some of those sex-hungry twits on campus had some freak stories to tell about him, they would.

"Tellis is talented, too," Zandy continued to compliment. I remember when he recited one of his poems during one of the Wednesday assemblies last year. It was during Black History Month. Were you there?"

"Yes," Sasha replied. "The poem was good."

"Good, my foot. The poem was *deep*," Zandy corrected, then peered at Sasha. "Look at you, glowing all over the place."

"I know," Sasha said bashfully. "I'm just now starting to get used to him. At first, I was very nervous and excited around him. I tried not to show it. He thought I didn't like him, but I quickly assured him that I did. I knew that he could probably have any girl on campus he wanted, and I wasn't sure if I measured up."

"Sasha, *please*. You are *so* cute. Stop being modest. You two make a great couple. Where did you meet him? And why don't I ever see you two around campus together?"

"Tellis and I met in the library," Sasha said breathlessly. "I was sitting off in one of the corner chairs on the second floor, and he just walked up to me and started talking."

"Just like that?"

"Just like that," Sasha answered. "He told me that he'd seen me around campus. We exchanged numbers. Before I went home to Milwaukee for the summer, I gave him my number there, too. We talked almost every day. He picked me up from the airport when I came back to Jackson, and we've been seeing each other ever since. Sometimes we get together on campus, just not a whole lot. We usually get together in the evening." She shrugged her shoulders, smiling. "I'm glad we've managed to keep our relationship—"

"On the down low," Zandy interjected.

Sasha smiled. "I was thinking private, but yes, on the down low."

"So you guys are officially dating now?"

"I guess."

"What do you mean, you guess?"

"Well, he didn't officially ask me to be his girlfriend or anything, but he treats me like I'm his girlfriend."

Zandy looked skeptical. "Was it his decision to keep the relationship on the down low?"

"No. It was my decision. I didn't want us to be the topic of everyone's conversation. Not until I knew that our relationship was on a good foundation. He agreed. But all of that is changing now because we're seeing more and more of each other, which brings me to my big problem."

"Which is?"

"Well, I really like Tellis, and not just because he's nice-look-ing. Like you said, he has a great mind, too." Sasha shook her head thoughtfully. "I don't know. I just love so much about him. I love the way he looks at me. I love the way he talks to me. I love the way he . . . he makes me feel." Sasha wrapped her arms around her midriff and squeezed tight. Zandy," she blurted, "I'm thinking about sleeping with him."

Zandy's eyes bulged. "What?"

"You heard me," Sasha said softly.

"Don't you think you're moving too fast? You've only know him for what, four or five months? Have you even kissed him?"

"Yes."

"Is he pressuring you?"

"No. Not at all."

"Then why do you want to make a move like that?"

"Are you a virgin, Zandy?"

"No, but—"

Sasha looked squarely at her friend. "But what?" she asked.

"You're not like me," Zandy explained. "You're not supposed to do stuff like that. You're . . . you know . . . "

"Different?" Sasha asked, her eyes narrowing.

Zandy sighed. "Sasha, you know what I mean."

"Yes, I know what you mean. Just because I'm the daughter of a preacher doesn't make my feelings any less strong. I'm no different than you are." Sasha's eyes pleaded for Zandy's under-standing. "I just sat here and told you my whole life story be-cause I wanted you to understand how tired I am of being de-fined by my father and by the life he wanted me to live. I want to live my own life. Can't you understand what I'm saying?"

Zandy nodded her head and sighed. "I understand what you're saying, but I don't want you to do anything you'll regret later."

"I don't either, but I can't get Tellis out of my mind. All through the day and all through the night, I think about being with him. And that's frustrating enough, without thinking about my father and how it would kill him if he knew what I was planning to do. But this is *my* life. I have to keep telling myself that this is *my life*." Sasha stood and walked to stand in front of Zandy. "Shouldn't I be able to live my life like I want to? Am I not an adult, capable of making my own decisions? *Why can't I just do what I want to do?*"

Zandy looked up at Sasha's dark, troubled eyes and wondered if she was about to flip out again. When Sasha pivoted and walked off, Zandy softly asked, "Sasha, have you talked to Tellis about this?"

Sasha turned back to Zandy. Her features had softened. "A little. A few days ago. Like you, he picked up that something was wrong with me and asked what it was. It was hard for me to express my feelings to him, so I kind of beat around the bush. He finally told me to just spit it out, and I told him that I wanted to . . . you know . . ."

"What?"

"*You know.*"

"Make love to him?" Zandy bluntly voiced what Sasha couldn't.

"Yes."

"And he said what?"

Sasha's eyes turned dreamy. "He kissed me and I thought I was going to pass out. I've *never* felt like that before. *Never*. If he'd asked me to go through with it then, I probably would have." She shrugged. "But he said that we should wait a while, until we were sure of our feelings for each other."

"Well, isn't that enough?"

"I'm not sure."

"You think there's another reason why he doesn't want to sleep with you?"

"I don't know what to think. I know he's not a virgin, and I don't want him to stop liking me because he thinks I have a problem with sex."

Zandy looked puzzled. "Do you want to do it because you think it's what *he* wants or because it's what *you* want?"

"I want to do it because it's what *I* want."

"But if he's willing to wait, then maybe you should be willing to wait, too."

"I don't care if he's willing to wait," Sasha said firmly. "I want to do it now. You're still not understanding what I've been trying to tell you."

Zandy shook her head, sighing. "You may be right about that. You have quite a few issues going on here and I'm trying to keep track. But I think I *do* understand what you're saying. I can also understand why Tellis doesn't want you to feel pressured to do something you may regret."

"I could never regret being with Tellis."

Zandy grimaced. "Oh, trust me. You can regret it. Sex is not all it's cracked up to be. Let me be the first to tell you."

"What do you mean?"

"All I'm saying is, be careful. As far as I know, Tellis has a good rep but still, you need to be cautious about who you jump in the bed with. AIDS is a killer. And once you're out there long enough, you'll find that most guys are nothing but dogs anyway. They'll use you up and then kick you straight to the curb. I've seen it happen too many times. Even my doggish father did it to my mother. Guys are doing it everyday. You really need to be careful, Sasha."

"Are you careful, Zandy?" Sasha asked her pointedly.

"Yes, I'm careful."

Sasha looked skeptical. "So you're telling me that you don't have sex."

Zandy cut her eyes at Sasha. "I didn't say all of *that*," she answered, grinning mischievously.

Sasha didn't smile back. "Well, then, what makes me different from you? If you can be careful, I can, too."

Zandy stood to her feet and walked to stand face-to-face with Sasha. Looking her directly in the eyes, she calmly said, "First of all, you *are* different from me. I know that you don't want to hear that, but you *are*. We're totally different people with totally different experiences. So you've got to stop comparing yourself to me. And *second*, I understand everything you've told me tonight. Don't think that I don't. I'm feeling everything you said, right here," she said patting her chest near her heart. "What I can't understand, though, is why you're in such a big hurry to lose your virginity."

Sasha scoffed. "I'm not in a *hurry*. If I were, I would have lost my virginity the first day I stepped foot on Tougaloo's campus. Like I said before, I want to put my past in the past and do something different."

"Sasha, you *cannot* think that jumping in the bed with someone is going to erase your past and all of your problems. It just doesn't work like that. I've tried it. *It doesn't work.*"

Unruffled, Sasha replied, "That's not the only reason I want to do it, to erase my past."

"No, but it's the *main* reason you want to do it."

The two held each other's gaze, as if silently challenging each other.

Finally, Sasha sighed and looked off. "Look," she said quietly, "I want to be with Tellis because I care about him. I want to have a relationship with him without worrying about what anyone else is going to think about it. I just want to live my life for me. And right now this is what I want to do."

Zandy touched Sasha's arm. "And I understand that. I just want you to understand that I don't want you to get hurt. Why would I let you go down the street and fall into the same ditch that I fell in and not warn you? You're my girl, and I'm just trying to look out for you."

Sasha smiled at her. "I know. I appreciate it, too."

Zandy laughed out. "I can't tell. But like my Mama says, 'Keep on living. You'll learn the hard way.'" She shook her head, frowning. "I did. Guys don't care about your problems, Sasha, or what's going on in your heart. While you're looking all goo-

goo-eyed and talking about love, they're trying to figure out the quickest way to get in your pants . . . or under your dress. Squash that! When I realized that guys want sex almost more than they want to draw their next breath, I started using sex as the weapon it was intended to be, to get what *I* want. I run the show now . . . *if* there is a show."

With raised brows, Sasha asked, "Is that what you do?"

"Right. That's what *I* do, *not you*."

"You use sex as a weapon?"

"Sometimes. When it's necessary. Most of the time, though, I don't give up *nothing*. All I have to do is smile my irresistible, dogcatcher smile and wiggle my behind real nice-like and most guys come running like bulldogs in heat. And they'll do *whatever* I want them to do." Zandy's lips curled into a snarl. "They can be so *pitifully disgusting*."

"I don't think Tellis is just interested in sex. I think he really cares for me."

"Maybe he does."

"How could you be so excited earlier about the fact that I'm dating him, and now be so blasé? Before, you were happy for me. Now, it's like you're telling me not to date him because he may *dog* me out. I don't get it."

"I *am* happy for you . . . because you're happy. I'm just letting you know what I think. You asked me. I'm telling you. I'll say it again, be careful and guard your heart. *Men . . . are . . . dogs.*"

"I still say that Tellis really cares about me. And I really care about him. No, I think I love him."

Zandy threw her hands up in exasperation and rolled her eyes, hard. Shaking her head, she walked back to the sofa and plopped down.

"What?" Sasha questioned. "You don't think I love him?"

"Why y'all fall in love as soon as a guy shows you five minutes of attention, I *do not* understand."

"Why do you say *y'all,* as if you're not a woman capable of falling in love yourself?"

"I'm not." Zandy replied emphatically. "I mean, I'm *all* woman, but I'm not capable of falling in love with *no* man." She touched her chest. "This is one heart that won't get broken." *Again,* she added in her thoughts. Aloud she continued. "And I ain't into no freaky-deaky sh—, I mean stuff. So, homo-sexing is out. I don't swing that way." She rolled her eyes again. "That's why I say *y'all.*"

"*Swing that way?* What do you mean by that?"

Zandy looked at Sasha as if she came from another planet. "I'm saying that I'm not down with homosexuality, Sasha."

Sasha's mouth formed a silent 'O'.

Zandy wasn't finished. "When I *am* ready to get my groove on, I find me a nice little doggy to play around with. But trust me, there are *no* attachments." She shook her head. "I just can't get with that love thang. It's a bunch of crap. For the past twelve years, I've watched my mother pine away because she *lo-oves* my father. He cheated on her and left her for another woman — *a girl,* I should say — and she *still* loves him. She doesn't necessarily say it, but I know she does. Can you believe that? That's not love. That's stupidity. He's been with two or three other girls since then — a sugar daddy is what he is — but my mother can't seem to get on with *her* life. I wanna throw up on my father every time I see him."

"Zandy, all men are not like your father. My father was very committed and faithful to my mother."

"That may be true, but I'm not chancing my heart to find out if a guy is faithful or not. I already know that ninety-nine point nine percent of them are not."

"Well, I believe that Tellis is the faithful sort."

"I hope for your sake that he is."

Sasha sat on the sofa next to Zandy. "You're being facetious, Zandy, and I'm serious. You said so yourself that you've heard nothing but good things about Tellis. I've spent the last few months getting to know him, and he *really* is a great guy. I know you think I'm naïve — and maybe I am — but if you get to know Tellis like I do, you would know that what I'm saying is true."

"That's not possible. Tellis *is* good-looking, but he's not dark enough for me. His light skin reminds me too much of my father. I like my men choco-black."

"Zandy! I'm serious!"

"I am, too!" Zandy responded, grinning.

Sasha's lips pursed into a pout, frustration filling her eyes.

Zandy mimicked the look on Sasha's face, then laughed. "What do you want me to say? You want me to tell you that Tellis is a great guy and that you should go ahead and have sex with him?"

"I want you to help me figure out what I should do."

Zandy wanted to tell Sasha that that's not what she really wanted and that she had already made up her mind about what she should do. Instead, Zandy told her what she wanted to hear. "I can't tell you what to do, Sasha. It's your decision to make."

Sasha's eyes searched Zandy's face for any hint of facetiousness. Satisfied that Zandy was serious in her answer, she nodded. "You're right. This is my life, and I need to make my own decisions." She smiled. "I know I've thrown a lot at you tonight. Thanks so much for listening to me. There was no one else I could've been so open with about all of this."

Zandy's eyes radiated warmth. "You're very welcome. I just don't know if I helped any. I think I said some things you didn't want to hear."

"No, you were honest and I appreciate that." After pausing a second, she asked, "You don't think I'm being too silly, do you?"

Mischief danced in Zandy's eyes. "No, not *too* silly."

Sasha said nothing, just grinned.

Zandy playfully tapped her shoulder. "See? That didn't take all night."

Still grinning, Sasha replied, "That's because I gave you the *short* version, and who said I was finished?"

"There's more?"

"Not really. I just have something to ask you."

"What?"

Sasha's eyes dipped to the floor. "Will you teach me how to dance?"

Zandy laughed out. "Teach you how to *what?*"

"You said you wouldn't laugh at me."

"I'm sorry. I'm not laughing at you. I expected something more serious, that's all. Why do you want to learn how to dance?

"I don't know. I thought that maybe Tellis would—"

"I should've known that this had something to do with Tellis. Sasha wants to cut a few steps for her man. Now, I may not be the best love doctor, but *dancing?* That's something I can help you with. You want to start now?"

"No, I've bored you long enough tonight. You're spending the night, right?"

"I was, but it's not late. I'm gonna go on back home. I have to work tomorrow anyway."

Sasha had been looking forward to Zandy staying the night. She'd even pulled out a couple of her favorite classic movies — one starring Sidney Poitier and one starring Cary Grant — for them to watch. "Oh, alright," she said, her words frail with disappointment. "I guess you can teach me some other time."

"I think I should start teaching you tonight. I'm not tired." Zandy stood to her feet. "Let me run downstairs and get a tape. Unless *you* have something we can dance to."

Sasha shook her head, no.

"That's okay," Zandy told her. "I have lot's of shake-your-bootay music in my SUV." After putting on her loafers, she retrieved her keys from the pocket of her jacket and headed for the front door. Before closing the door behind her, she turned to Sasha and said, "If you're a quick learner, maybe you can show off some of your moves at this party I'm going to tomorrow night."

Sasha's eyes widened instantly. "A party? I can't go to a party."

"Why not?"

"I don't know . . . I don't have anything to wear, for one thing."

"Just throw on a pair of jeans and a shirt."

"I don't have any jeans. *Remember?*"

"Oh, that's right. You don't." Zandy laughed, then shrugged. "Well, I guess we'll just have to get you some. We're having a sale at the Gap. Come by tomorrow while I'm working, and I'll help fit you for a pair." Zandy whisked the door closed behind her.

Sasha looked at the closed door, fear gripping her. *My father will have a fit if he knew I put on a pair of pants*, she thought. Then she reminded herself, *this is my life . . . my life to live as I choose.* She smiled, her eyes bright with purpose. *Tomorrow I will wear my very first pair of pants. My wish is finally coming true.*

Chapter 4

"Be still, Sasha," Zandy gently chastised. "And keep your eyes closed."

"Can I take a quick peek in the mirror? I want to see what you're doing."

"I'm getting ready to put concealer under your eyes to hide these dark spots. And no, you can't peek. Not until I'm finished."

"Don't put on too much, Zandy. You know I've never worn make-up before."

"How can I forget? You've told me a thousand times in the last ten minutes." Zandy used the palm of her finger to pat concealer under Sasha's eyes. "Didn't you go to sleep last night after I left. You should've been exhausted after all of that dancing we did."

"Yes, I slept. Why do you ask?"

"I'm looking at these circles under your eyes."

"Those circles are from the past few weeks. Last night, I slept like a *stick*. I hadn't done that in a while. After talking to you last night, I made up my mind to stop worrying about what my father or anyone else has to say about what I do. I've been torn for too long."

Gingerly applying foundation with a sponge, Zandy said, "I guess change doesn't always come easy."

"No, it doesn't," Sasha agreed.

"I'm putting on a tiny bit of foundation now. When I'm finished, I'm going to put on some powder. It'll keep the shine off of your face."

"Okay, just don't put on too much. This is my first time wearing *any* kind of make-up. "

"Didn't I just say it was a tiny bit? You've told me a thousand times not to put on a lot. Why do you keep saying it?"

"I guess I'm just a little nervous."

"Nervous? Why? Didn't you tell me you wanted to try a little make-up?"

"Yes, I did. I keep telling myself that I shouldn't be nervous. I just can't help it sometimes, though. What do I do if I see somebody who knows that I don't normally wear make-up . . . or pants? I know saved people at Tougaloo who think that wearing make-up is wrong. Pants, too. What do I say if they ask me about it?"

Zandy stepped back from Sasha and threw her hands up in mock exasperation. "Sasha, you're killing me, girl. Just a minute ago you said that you made up your mind to not care what other people think, and now here you are, caring. *If* you see one of those *saved* people at the party and they say something to you, kindly say, 'Excuse me, but what are *you* doing at this party in the first place. Shouldn't you be at church or out witnessing or something?' And if *anyone* has a problem with the new you, tell them to go *straight to* . . . . Oh, Sasha, I'm sorry, girl" she said, leaning over to apply quick pats of powder to Sasha's face. Talking just as fast as her hand moved, she continued. "Here I am - close your eyes so I won't get this stuff in 'em — tellin' *you* to curse somebody out. Lord, forgive me. I don't want you cursing nobody. If somebody has a problem with you — tilt your face up a little bit — tell me and *I'll* curse them out for you."

Sasha smiled, keeping her eyes closed. "Zandy, you wouldn't do that."

Zandy kept working. "Oh, yes, I would. And I'll have a good time doing it, too. See, that's the difference between you and me, I don't give a . . . I don't care about what other people think about me. If a person is bold enough to let it be known that they don't like something about me, then a good cursing out won't damage their ego at all. The best thing for people to do is let everybody do what they wanna do. Nobody gets hurt. Nobody gets cursed out."

Sasha opened her eyes. "Then you must be cursing people out all the time, including your parents. Parents always tell us what to do."

"My mom, no. But my dad, yes, cause I can't stand that bast— No, I'm not going to call him that because I'm deter-mined to be like you and use good, wholesome language." Zandy repositioned Sasha's face to a half-raised angle. "Hold your face like that and close your eyes again. I'm about to put on eyeliner," she explained. Lining the tip of Sasha eyelids with the black pencil, she continued. "Anyway, when I was about fourteen, I told him to 'kiss the crack below my back.'" Zandy whooped. "Girl, my mama beat me like I stole something."

Sasha jerked her head up to look at Zandy. "I'm surprised your father didn't beat you himself. Even if you don't like him, he's still your father."

"He's a no-good cheat and I can't *stand* him. And he knew not to put his hands on me. He gave up that right when he left me and my mother to be with that *skank* girl." Placing the pencil on the kitchen table, Zandy picked up a mascara tube and pulled out the eyelash brush. "Try not to blink. I've got to put on a little bit of mascara." With expert hands, she quickly thickened Sasha's lashes with the black liquid.

Sliding the brush back in the tube, Zandy continued. "When I was sixteen, I wanted a pair of tennis shoes. I can't remember what kind they were, but they cost almost a hundred dollars. He bought me a pair that cost about fifty dollars, and I had a fit. That time, I cursed him flat out."

"Zandy, you didn't!" Sasha cried, forgetting to hold her head still.

Zandy moved Sasha's head back into position. "*Yes, . . . I . . . did,*" she boasted. "He could afford it. He builds houses, for goodness sakes! If he could buy all kinds of stuff for his girlfriend's kids, he could buy me what I wanted. I deserved more than they did."

"Zandy, you were mean," Sasha said, frowning.

Zandy smiled broadly. "I know," she bragged. "I used to go off on him or anyone else who looked at me crooked. Step my way and I'd curse you flat out. Attitude was my adrenaline. Twenty-four seven. Until I realized that I was taking my anger toward my father out on everyone else, including myself." She shook her head. "That wasn't proper. Now, I've pretty much learned how to control my anger. But when it comes to my father, I'm hopeless. I just want to kick his black . . . butt one good time. Just the sight of him turns my stomach." Running a finger along Sasha's eyebrows, she said, "Your brows are so thick. Are you sure you don't want me to pluck'em? I could give you a nice arch."

"It hurts, doesn't it?"

"Not too bad." Zandy pulled a pair of tweezers from her kit. "Here, let me show you." She plucked a hair from Sasha's brow.

"Ow! That hurt!" Sasha cried, her eye watering from the pain.

"Oh, you big baby," Zandy teased. She rubbed Sasha's brow to ease the pain. "The best time to pluck'em is right after you shower. Then, it doesn't hurt as much. But, then again, I'm probably just used to the pain. Does it still hurt?"

"No."

Zandy picked up a dark brown eyebrow pencil and proceeded to apply feather-like strokes to Sasha's brows. There," she said when she'd penciled both brows. "Now it's time for eye shadow. Anyone can put on make-up, but it takes skills to get the eye shadow right. And I got *skillz*!" she said, laughing. "Close your eyes again. I've picked colors that will go well with the new pink shirt you're wearing to—"

"Fuchsia," Sasha corrected.

"Pink, fuchsia, whatever. These colors are going to go well with that shirt. They'll bring out your eyes, too."

The room was silent as Zandy worked her magic on Sasha's eyes. Finally, she smiled down at Sasha, admiring the fuchsia-colored eye shadow she'd blended with shades of midnight black, smoky gray, and pearl white. "You're going to love the way you look when I'm done. You know what?"

"What?"

"It's a shame you were taught that wearing make-up is wrong. Jezebel's sin was not the make-up she wore on her face. It was the hatred she had in her heart toward God's prophet. What was his name?"

"Elijah."

"Yeah, Elijah. She hated him because he was a man of God and she lusted after the other guy — I can't remember his name, either."

"Um . . . I think it was Jehu."

"Whoever he was, she put on make-up to try to entice him. She used it for the wrong reason. It doesn't mean that it's wrong to wear it. Everyday people take things intended for good and use them to do bad stuff." Zandy snickered. "Ol' girl would've been just as evil if she didn't wear a drop of make-up." Stroking Sasha's penciled brows with a small brush, she said, "Make-up is meant to enhance your natural beauty, and you don't need a lot of it to do that, either. So if you're worrying about not being modest with make-up on, don't be. Because you can be."

"I'm not worried," Sasha said brightly.

"Yeah, right," Zandy said with a doubtful grin. Placing the brush on the table, she said, "As ugly as some of those women were in the church I went to, they should've been *paying and praying* for somebody to put some make-up on 'em."

Sasha laughed. "You're being mean, Zandy."

"It's the truth," Zandy said, her laughter mingling with Sasha's. "It's like they thought being saved meant looking tired, beat down, and ugly."

Sasha laughed harder. "They were just trying to look like they thought God wanted them to look. Chaste and holy."

"No, that's not it. Tell the truth and shame the devil, Sasha. You know looking all plain-jainy makes y'all *feel* holy. Hmph," she grumbled, "Mae Mama told me that years ago the sanctified church didn't even allow women to get their hair relaxed or wear shoes with the toes out? They couldn't even wear the color red!"

Sasha was surprised. "I knew about the shoes, but not about getting your hair relaxed or wearing red."

"Well, it's true. Mae Mama told me. I guess red was too much like the devil and relaxed hair was too much like the world."

"We can get our hair relaxed — mine is. And we can wear red and any kind of shoes we want to wear."

Zandy put her hands on her hips. "Which goes back to what I was saying last night about the pants. Just like somebody in the church finally realized that getting your hair relaxed wasn't going to send you to Hell, somebody in the church will realize that a pair of pants won't send you to Hell, either. Maybe you'll be that somebody in your father's church."

Sasha shook her head. "Not if I can help it. And anyway, what makes you think the church will listen to me."

"Start with your father. He's the pastor. He'll listen to you."

"Oh, I'm supposed to go to my father and say, 'Daddy, those things you've been preaching about wearing pants is wrong.'"

"What's wrong with that?" Zandy questioned, her face a mask of frowns as she searched her make-up kit for a blush that would accentuate Sasha's rounded cheekbones. Choosing one called Pixy Pink, she said, "You can tell him the story about the ham. You ever heard it?"

"No."

"See, this woman cooked a ham for her husband one day. The ham was good but she had cut off both ends of the ham before she cooked it. The husband didn't see anything wrong with the ends, so he asked his wife why she cut 'em off." Zandy hunched her shoulders. "The wife said, 'I don't know. I cut 'em off because my mother used to cut'em off before she cooked *her* ham.' So the husband decided to call his mother-in-law to see why *she* cut the ends off the ham. He asked his mother-in-law," Zandy continued, hunching her shoulders again, "and she said, 'I don't know. I cut'em off because *my* mother used to cut'em off.' So then the husband decided to call his *mother-in-law's mother.* He asked her the same question, and do you know what she said?"

"What?"

"She said, 'I don't know *why* they cut the ends off *their* hams, but I cut the ends off *my* ham because it was too big to fit in the only pan I had to cook it in back then." Zandy laughed out. "You get it?"

Sasha laughed, too, nodding her head. "I get it."

Zandy began to blush one of Sasha's cheekbones. "Tell your father that maybe he's preaching against *some* things because he heard someone else preach against them, not because the Bible says they're wrong. Like nothing is wrong with eating the ends of a ham."

"I don't plan to tell my father or anyone else anything contrary to what they believe. They can believe what they want to believe. Can we change the subject?"

"Don't go gettin' all crabby on me, now. I'm just tryin' to help a sista out." Zandy moved to Sasha's other cheekbone and blushed it. "We can talk about whatever you want to talk about."

"Can I see my face now?"

"Nope. Wait 'til I'm finished."

"How much longer do I have to wait?"

"Until I'm finished," Zandy replied sweetly. "It won't be much longer."

Sasha sighed impatiently. She could only imagine what she looked like. A clown, or even worse, a prostitute. She sighed again, but kept her mouth closed.

Zandy stood back and surveyed the work she'd done so far. *I'm so good, I should start charging*, she thought appreciatively.

Before, Sasha's eyes were just pretty. Now, thanks to her, they were dark and sultry, two bottomless pools of alluring innocence. She smiled and gave herself a mental pat on the back. She had transformed Sasha into the exotic beauty she was. It hadn't been hard to do, she admitted. Sasha's facial features were very attractive and nicely proportioned. The perfect playground for a make-up connoisseur. *Like myself*, she thought gleefully.

Zandy's eyes dropped to Sasha's full lips, crying out for a little bit of pampering, too. She'd work her magic on the lips as well.

Sasha looked up at her and made a face. "Will you stop looking at me and finish?"

"Oh, hush," Zandy snapped playfully. "Relax your lips. I'm about to turn them into a pair of succulent smack-a-roos." With A-one dexterity, Zandy outlined Sasha's lips with a Punchy-Pink lip liner, then smoothed the color out some with a sponge tipped pencil. "Loosen your lips just a little bit, just enough for a small opening." Putting the sponge tip aside, Zandy opened a small container of frost-colored lip gloss. She lightly glossed Sasha's lips with a lip brush. "Hold still. I'm almost finished."

Sasha frowned, but still said nothing. She was trying her best to be patient.

"Open your mouth and tighten your lips. I need to put the lipstick on."

Sasha opened her mouth very wide.

"I wanna put lipstick on you, Sasha, not *feed* you. Here, do like this." Zandy showed Sasha how to hold her lips. When Sasha's lips were poised correctly, she laughed and said, "*Merci* — Thank you." She began to polish Sasha's lips with the closest shade she had to the color of fuchsia. It was perfect.

"That color is too loud, Zandy."

"Sasha, you can't talk while I'm doing your lips. You're making me mess up. Pass me a tissue." Removing a smudge of lipstick from Sasha's face, Zandy continued, "And it's not too loud. It's gonna look good with your new shirt. Here, smack your lips on this tissue."

"Why?"

"To remove the excess lipstick."

"Why do I need to do that if you didn't put on too much in the first place?"

"It's procedure, that's why. And stop asking so many questions."

"Are you sure it's not too much?"

Zandy replied, "You tell me." She picked up a large hand mirror from the table and stood with it in front of Sasha. "*Voilà!* — Look!"

Sasha took hold of the mirror and looked at her reflection. A light "Oh" was all she could manage to get out. Words were stuck in her throat. She stared wide-eyed at the person in the mirror. *Is that me?* she asked herself. Timidly, she touched her cheek, lightly swept with blush. She pouted her full glossy, colored lips. *Yes, that's you*, her thoughts answered. Keeping her eyes on the mirror, she turned her head slowly to the right and then to the left. *It's really me.*

She smiled shakily, raising her eyes above the mirror to look at Zandy. "I can't believe that's me. I look like . . . a supermodel. You *are* good."

Zandy grinned. "I wish I could take all the credit, but I can't. You already have attractive features — flawless skin, pretty eyes, nice lips, a cute little button nose. The make-up just brings them out more."

"I *see.* And I guess this hairstyle does, too." Zandy had taken Sasha to Rob's salon during her lunch break. She'd practically had to strap Sasha down in Rob's chair, promising her that he wouldn't cut off any of her hair or put it in some wild-child hairstyle. To Rob, she'd simply said, "hook her *up*", and then floated out of the salon to return to work. Sasha had sadly watched her go. Since she'd been in Mississippi, she'd been going to the same hair salon, getting the same simple style — a head full of bouncing tresses.

She'd had no idea what Rob was going to do to her head. Frightening visions of shock-straight hair assaulted her mind's eye, even when Rob leaned her head back into the sink and said in an effeminately throaty voice, "Relax, sweetie. You're in *very* good hands." He'd been right. He had styled her hair beautifully. Looking in the mirror, she reached up and touched one of the lustrous curl-loops at the top of her head. She smiled. Her fears had been pointless. "What do you call this style, Zandy?"

Zandy shrugged. "*Je ne sais pas* — I don't know. That's a French Roll in the back. And these," she said, pointing to five braid-like rows of hair, "are called flat twists. And then those big curls at the top are called barrel curls. Together, I don't know what you call it, but it's *tight*. You like it, don't you?"

"I *love* it," Sasha answered softly, still looking at her reflection.

"So, is it too much make-up? I can take some off, if you want me to."

"No. I've got to get used to it, but it's okay. I look like I've been to a professional."

"*What-ever*, girl. I *am* a professional. Don't you know who I am? I am Mademoiselle Davis, Connoisseur of Beauty. At your service." Zandy bowed dramatically before Sasha.

Sasha batted her lashes coyly. "Thank you, Mademoiselle Davis. You have done a *splendid* job."

In a voice dripping with sweetness, Zandy said, "You're welcome, Your Majesty." "Now stand up," she said, changing to a brusque tone. "It's time for you to put your clothes on. It's almost nine o'clock and the party starts at ten."

"What about *your* make-up? I want to watch you put it on."

"You've already showered, Sasha. I haven't. I'll do my make-up after I shower. And you know you don't really care about my make-up. You're stalling."

"Yes, I do care. I want to watch you so I can learn how to put it on, too."

"Maybe, but you're still stalling. Do you want to wear the jeans or not? I saw how uncomfortable you were when you tried 'em on. You don't have to wear 'em, you know."

"I didn't say I didn't want to wear them."

"Well, c'mon and get up. I'll let you watch when I put on my make-up." Zandy took the mirror from Sasha's hand and laid it on the table. Reaching to pull Sasha up from the chair, she said, "But right now, you need to go in your bedroom, take that robe off and put on your new shirt *and* your new black jeans. Girl, you gonna be turning all kind of heads tonight."

"That's not what I want to do." Sasha frowned, flopping back down into the chair.

"The way you look in *those* jeans, you won't have a choice. Look out you fine, black brothas! Sasha Lindsey is in town! *Tonight* is gonna be your night, girl. You're gonna go to this party, meet a few people, and have a good time. Even do a little dancing." Zandy started popping her fingers and shouted in a singsong voice, "Hey-y-y. Ho-o-o. Hey-y-y. Ho-o-o." She nudged Sasha playfully. "C'mon, girl. Do some of them moves you were doing last night. You already knew how to dance. You just needed somebody to show you some moves. How you do that move, Sasha, when you twist all down to the floor?" Zandy popped her fingers rhythmically to the music in her head and dropped to a squatting position and proceeded to bounce her behind around in the air. "Hey, now!" she shouted as she danced. "I think I got it! Yeah, that's it! Hey-y-y-y. Ho-o-o-o. Hey-y-y-y . . ."

Sasha burst into laughter. "That's not what I was doing. I can't even do that. You know I can't. You're so silly."

Zandy stood fully upright. "Look at you, trying to be all shy. It might've taken you a while to forget about that shyness last night when you were dancing, but you did. Now look, it's back again. C'mon," she said, pulling the reluctant Sasha from the chair again. "Didn't you say you wanted a change?"

"Ye-es."

"Then you're gonna get a change tonight. Stop looking so scared, 'cause you can't chicken out on me now. We gotta do the Booty Call dance routine I taught you, too, even if I have to drag you out on the dance floor. C'mon, you're gonna have fun.

"I know you were worried about people drinking and stuff, and like I told you before, you don't have to worry about that. There won't be a lot of drinking at this party. I know the girls throwing it. They're good girls . . . for the most part," she added mischievously. "They're gonna have mostly soft drinks in the can and bottles of flavored water. They're throwing the party to have a good time, not to get people drunk and stupid. Everybody who wants to drink will have to bring their own beer. That's what some people do, and sometimes they manage to sneak in something a little stronger than beer. That's why you should never drink from a punch bowl. Only from a can. That *you* open. And if you leave your can for a while to go dancing or to the bathroom or something, don't drink from it when you come back, unless you had someone you can really trust watching it for you. Otherwise, get another one. People have been known to slip some serious stuff in other people's drinks. Are you taking this all in?"

"Yes."

"I don't drink, and I don't hang out too tough with people who drink. So even if everybody else wants to drink like hogs, you and me - we gonna be cuttin' up on the dance floor. Alright?"

"Alright."

"You haven't forgotten the dance steps, have you? First, you walk four steps to the right, then shake your booty," Zandy said, walking through the steps. "Then walk four steps to the left and shake. Then you walk backwards two big steps, then you do a *big* shake, like that, and then you jump up—"

"Zandy, you don't have to show me. I remember the steps."

Zandy laughed. "I don't know why I'm worried. The way you were rumpshaking last night, people are gonna think *you* taught *me* how to dance. Now go in there and put your clothes on so we can go and get our groove on. Hey-y-y-y. Ho-o-o-o . . ."

Chapter 5

Sasha was one big ball of nervousness and excitement, all rolled into one. She'd had mixed feelings all day about coming to this party. And now that she was here, she wasn't sure just how to act. A small part of her wanted to jump up on a table and dance 'til she dropped. Maybe that would help her release some of the excitement that was stirring in the pit of her stomach. The larger part wanted to drag Zandy off the dance floor and demand that she take her home, right now.

Drag Zandy is exactly what she'd have to do. Zandy was out on the dance floor, obviously having a good time. At the moment, she was dancing with a pint-sized guy who looked young enough to still be in high school, but moved like he was born on Soul Train. He was the sixth or seventh person she'd danced with already tonight. From the moment they'd walked through the door, all sorts of guys, offering compliments and extending invitations to dance, had swarmed Zandy like moths do a flame. Sasha had literally seen heads turn and mouths drop open when Zandy passed by.

Sasha was sure it had a lot to do with the sparkly, orange two-piece number that clung to Zandy's body like spandex. It was a definite eye-catcher. The skimpy top was halter style with two strips of material that barely covered the fullness of her breasts. The bottom was a seamless pair of knickers that fell low on her hips and hugged her shapely bottom and thighs. Around her midriff she wore a thin, gold chain adorned with a heart-shaped charm, which dangled enticingly at her navel. On her feet she wore orange, platform-heeled sandals that strapped her thin ankles and lightly clicked the floor as she sailed around the room, greeting her peers with a bright, friendly smile and eagerly introducing them to Sasha.

Most of the students at the party attended Tougaloo, and Sasha recognized many of them by face, if not by name. Still, some of the students attended Jackson State, and Sasha didn't recognize any of them. But Zandy knew them. She seemed to know every single person at the party — by name — and she was determined to acquaint Sasha with as many of them as possible.

For the first forty-five minutes after they'd arrived at the party, Sasha had reluctantly followed Zandy around the room meeting and greeting tons of students. The students kindly welcomed her to the party, without any obvious regard to the makeup or the pants she wore. To her surprise, she'd even received a considerable number of invitations to dance as well. Still, she'd turned them all down. In her mind, she was too much of a novice to be dancing with strangers — the chances of being laughed at were too great. She preferred to watch those who were far more adept at doing what she'd learned to do only last night.

Once again, her eyes picked out Zandy on the crowded floor. Sasha was amazed at the rhythm and agility that Zandy possessed when she moved. She was in definite command on the dance floor, and she and her partner flowed well together as they danced the intricate routines, their passion for dancing evident in each motion.

Soon Zandy would be running over to try — once again — to get Sasha out on the dance floor. Each time she'd come, Sasha had said that she'd wait for the next song.

They'd been at the party for almost two hours now, and Sasha hadn't danced once. In fact, she'd gotten as far from the dance floor as she could. She'd found a secluded spot behind the table section where she could virtually go unseen in the large rectangular room. Except for the scattered beams of colored light that poured from the ceiling and the small flames of candles that flickered on the few tables, the room was considerably dark, which was fine with Sasha. A dark room made it just that much easier for her to hide out.

Still, she couldn't hide from the smell of popcorn that permeated her nostrils and caused her mouth to water. Not willing to unglue herself from the wall, she resisted the urge to walk across the room to the refreshment area and get a bag of the buttered morsels. Inwardly, she criticized the hosts for not having the popcorn ready at the start of the party. *If they'd had the popcorn ready when I first came, I could've gotten some then, when I had Zandy with me. The popcorn is clear on the other side of the room, and that's too far for me to walk by myself in these jeans. Now I'll have to send Zandy over there to get the popcorn for me.* Resigning to be content with the Sprite she held, she took a small sip from the can, and chills broke out over her entire body. The room was morgue cold. *Somebody was determined to not have a hot and sweaty dance party in here tonight.* Shivering slightly, she turned her attention back to the jammed-packed dance floor.

She marveled at the rigorous dancing of some and the highly sensual moves of others. Things had certainly changed since her high school dance days, or so it seemed. She didn't want to join the dancers out on the floor, but every now and then, she found herself tapping her feet to the rhythm of the music. Each time, she'd stopped the tapping and silently chastised herself. *This is so ridiculous. I don't have any business being here. But isn't this what I wanted? To hang out like everybody else and have a good time. So why am I holding back?*

Maybe it's the jeans, she thought. Her very first pair. She certainly hadn't gotten used to wearing them. Her eyes, like clockwork, kept straying down to the full hips that surged from her sides like small mountains. *These jeans make my hips look so . . . curvaceous. I should've worn a big shirt to cover them.*

She thought about pulling her shirt out of her jeans, but decided against it — the shirt wasn't long enough to cover her hips anyway. She groaned, then laughed at herself. Who was she fooling? She kind of liked the jeans, in spite of the awkwardness she felt wearing them. They were a little tight — thanks to Zandy, who thought Sasha should be a little daring in her first pair of pants — but still Sasha liked the way the jeans molded her frame and how the legs flared out over her black high-heeled boots. The jeans made her feel stylish.

They also make me feel a little . . . sexy. Was that a bad thought? Sasha's eyes darted around the room, as if searching for someone who could've tapped into her private thoughts. *You're becoming wicked*, she scolded herself. But it was the truth, she felt sexy for the first time in her life. Well, maybe not the *first* time. The first time was when she'd kissed Tellis in her apartment the other day. She'd kissed him a few times before, but those kisses didn't even compare to the last kiss they'd shared. She felt giddy just thinking about it. *I wonder what Tellis would think if he saw me in these jeans? Would he think I looked sexy, too? Or would he think I'm trying to be someone that I'm not?*

Sasha hadn't told Tellis that she was going to a party. If he hadn't had to work, she would've felt compelled to invite him along. But he did have to work, and she'd been relieved. She'd told him that she was going to spend the evening with her friend, Zandy, and left it that. She didn't know how he would take the idea of her going to a party, and she wasn't quite ready to find out. Until she'd made a few groundbreaking changes in her life, she wouldn't give Tellis all the gory details of her past church life and religious beliefs. *Nothing can make a guy run away faster than a sanctified girl*, she thought wryly.

She hadn't kept everything from Tellis, though. He knew that her father was a preacher and that her mother was dead. With all the questions he'd asked her about her life, her family, her hopes and dreams, she'd had no choice but to tell him. Questions were his way of getting to know her, he'd said. They were his way of discovering what made her tick.

Sasha had loved the way he'd inquired about her heart's desires. Still, she couldn't bring herself to tell him how uncommonly strict her spiritual upbringing had been, how confused she'd often felt because of it, and how desperately she needed to get away from it. For fear of coming off as the she-can't-do-anything girl of her youth and losing him to another, she did her best to project the image of an everyday, ordinary person. *I'll make sure Tellis doesn't run,* she told herself. *I'll be the kind of girl he's used to dating, and I'll give him the kind of pleasure he's used to getting. Then we'll both be happy. He'll have a girl who satisfies him in every way, and I'll be well on my way to a brand new life.*

"*What'z up?*" a voice roared in Sasha's ear. Startled, she jumped slightly and almost dropped the Sprite can she'd been clutching. She'd remembered Zandy's words and hadn't parted from the can since she'd first opened it. She swung her head toward the voice and saw an unfamiliar guy standing beside her. He was brown sugar black with a freshly cut fade and muscular biceps. And he was staring at her with a lopsided grin on his face.

"Yes?" she asked with a hesitant smile.

"Sorry if I scared you," the guy yelled in her ear. "I spoke twice, but I guess the music was too loud for you to hear me."

Sasha recognized the beat of the song being played by the hefty, but spirited DJ. It was one of the songs she and Zandy had danced to last night.

"That's okay," she said. "I was lost in thought."

"What was that?" he questioned loudly.

Sasha raised her voice. "I said, 'that's okay.'"

"I'm Eric," he said smoothly in her ear. "And your name must be Angel because you look *so* heavenly." He raised a cup to his mouth and slurped loudly from it. His tongue teased his wet upper lip as he leaned his face closer to Sasha's.

Sasha frowned. She might be naïve, but she wasn't stupid. The come-on line sounded ridiculous to her ears.

"My name is Sasha," she said, stepping away from him. She reached out to shake his hand. He looked with surprise at her outstretched hand, as if he wasn't sure what she wanted him to do with it. Then, grinning broadly, he moved the cup to his left hand and gripped hers. He didn't release it, but held it firmly in his own. He seemed totally unaware of Sasha's uneasiness.

She pulled her hand out of his grasp and smiled apologetically.

"So-o-o-o," he said, moving his body closer to Sasha's. He stretched his arm out to place his hand on the wall just beside her head, blocking her in on one side. Then he leaned over and spoke seductively in her ear. "You go to Jackson State?"

His eyes strayed down the full length of her body and back up again. He then let his eyes drop down to rest on her bountiful chest. The shirt Zandy had picked out for her was made from a rayon-polyester blend, and it fit snuggly around her upper body. By the time his eyes came back to hers, they were filled with an exaggerated, smoldering look. His tongue flicked out and over his upper lip.

Sasha wanted to be polite, but his closeness was suffocating. She turned her face from his and casually stepped beneath his arm and away from him. She crossed her arms over her chest. "Uh . . . no . . . I attend Tougaloo College," she told him, looking out over the room in desperate search of Zandy. *Where is she?*

"Eric! What you want now?" Zandy had appeared out of nowhere, and Sasha could've fallen over with relief. "Why you always up in somebody's face, running yo' game. Everybody knows you're a *play-ah*, Eric, so stop sweatin' her." Zandy playfully pushed him away from Sasha and stood in between them.

"Yo, Aleczandria! What'z up, girl!" Eric said, taking his hand from the wall and standing straight. He paced a little and quickly ran his thumb and forefinger twice down the bridge of his nose, as though embarrassed at being caught running his game on a new, unsuspecting victim. Smiling his crooked grin at Zandy, he said, "I didn't know you were here, girl!"

"Yeah, right." Zandy laughed knowingly. "What you *didn't* know was that Sasha was here with me. You thought you found somebody who was gonna listen to those tired lines you be droppin'."

"See now, Aleczandria. Why it's gotta be like that?"

"Because you're a true bug-a-boo," Zandy said, nudging him away. "Go on, now, Eric."

Eric openly appraised Zandy. He slowly wrapped an arm around her shoulder and leaned down to whisper in her ear. "You lookin' good, baby," he said. "You know orange is my favorite Popsicle flavor and when I see you in this gear, baby, I just wanna lick you *up and down*." His tongue glided over his upper lip. "I saw that big booty of yours out there on the dance flo' shaking like a big water balloon. When you gonna let me —"

"I thought you didn't know I was here, Eric," Zandy said, pushing him away from her.

Eric gripped his side. "I like love taps, baby, but you're a little too rough on a brotha."

Zandy rolled her eyes. "Bounce, Eric," she said, dismissing him.

You gonna dance with me tonight?"

"I'll think about it."

"Yeah, you will," he said with confidence and walked off.

Zandy turned her eyes — thickly lined with a black eye-smoker crayon and shaded with dark, glitter-based eye shadows — toward Sasha and burst out laughing. "Sasha, why didn't you tell Eric to get out of your face?"

"I didn't want to hurt his feelings."

"Girl, *p-lease*, I saw him when he first came over to you. I was hoping he would at least get you out on the dance floor. I should've known that Eric would come on too strong, though. I saw you turn your head away when he leaned over to you, and I said, let me get over there and get that boy away from Sasha. He's a nice guy and fine as all get out, but he's one of Jackson State's biggest players, so you can't take anything he says seriously. Didn't I tell you that most guys are dogs?" She looked off in the direction Eric had departed and saw him making his move on another innocent-looking prey. She shook her head. "Look at him."

Sasha spotted Eric. "Look at *her*. She seems to like what he's saying."

"Yeah, well, I hope she can handle her own." Zandy flicked a dismissive hand in the air. Anyway," she said, looking again at Sasha, "it's about time you get your groove on. It's time for you to get on the dance floor."

Sasha was instantly attacked with anxiety. "I'm not ready yet."

"At the rate you're going, you'll never be ready."

"I'll dance the next song. I *prom—*"

"There you are, Aleczandria! I was looking for you!"

Both Sasha and Zandy turned toward the girl who'd spoken. She was petite, with a narrow face and a short spiked hair cut. And she was white.

"Hey, Brandi!" Zandy greeted loudly. "I had to run over here to get my friend." Pointing to Sasha, she added, "This is my friend, Sasha — the one I was telling you about. She still doesn't want to dance. I was just getting ready to drag her out there anyway." To Sasha, she said, "This is Brandi. She's the exchange student from Brown. You've probably seen her around campus."

Sasha nodded her head, yes. She'd seen Brandi around campus a lot this semester. It was hard to miss her, being the only white student on campus. Sasha shook Brandi's hand. "It's nice to meet you," she said, smiling. In her head, though, she wondered how she'd overlooked Brandi in the sea of black faces at the party.

Brandi looked at Sasha with friendly eyes and smiled back. "Still kinda nervous?" she asked her.

"Ye-es," Sasha answered, pumping her head up and down.

"It won't be so bad," Brandi assured her. "Aleczandria and I will be out there dancing with you."

"And she can dance, too," Zandy piped in. "And I ain't talking about no square-dancing, either. Ol' girl got some moves!"

"See," Sasha said, frowning. "Dancing with you two will make me look goofy."

"Too bad," Zandy said and took hold of the can Sasha was gripping with both hands. She pried it from Sasha's hands. Sitting the can on one of the nearby tables, she told Brandi, "Were gonna have to drag her out there."

Brandi shrugged, smiling. "If that's the only way to get her out there, then I guess we have no other choice."

Zandy grabbed Sasha by one hand and Brandi took the other, and they both proceeded to pull her through the table section and onto the crowded dance floor. They stopped about one-quarter of the way onto the floor, just far enough for them to be swallowed up by the throng of dancers. Only then did they release Sasha's hands.

"C'mon, Sasha, girl. Just start moving like this and before you know it, you'll get your groove back from last night." Zandy started popping her fingers to the upbeat tempo booming over the room. She then began to sway her upper body to the rhythm of the music. Brandi did the same.

Sasha just stood before the two of them, laughing nervously and throwing quick looks around the room. *Somebody is bound to see me make a fool of myself out here.*

"Sasha!" Zandy shouted her name over the music, grabbing her attention. "Are you going to dance or what?"

Sasha swallowed deeply and nodded her head. Slowly, she raised her hands to pop her fingers, mimicking Zandy. She tried to sway her body like Zandy and Brandi so easily did theirs, but her movements were stiff and off beat.

Zandy laughed out and then shouted encouragement. "Yeah, girl! That's it! C'mon with it!"

Brandi danced on the opposite side of Sasha and shouted encouragement as well.

As she continued to move, Sasha felt the tension draining from her body. She began to sway her body in sync with the music, which made Zandy yell with even more excitement. Twirling her hips from side to side, Zandy grinned and popped her fingers more enthusiastically. Brandi threw her hands above her head and waved them wildly in the air. Their excitement was infectious and Sasha grinned as her own movements became more pronounced. Throwing her hands above her head, she popped her fingers as she danced to the bounce of the music. The anxiety she'd felt earlier began to dissipate and was quickly replaced with a feeling she couldn't readily ascertain. But as she dipped down to the floor, following Zandy's adept movements, the nature of the feeling dawned on her. She'd danced enough times in church to recognize this overwhelming feeling. It was the feeling of release, the feeling of liberation, the feeling of letting go. Many times she'd given over to the praise music at church and danced before the Lord with all her might, and she'd been infused with this same feeling. How odd that she would experience the same feeling of exhilaration on the dance floor. *But I would never do these moves in church.* With that thought, she laughed out.

Zandy, interpreting the laughter as Sasha's expression of excitement, challenged Sasha with some steps a little bit more intricate than what they had been doing. Brandi easily picked up the moves. Sasha knew that she could never dance as smoothly as these two, but she also knew that she possessed an innate rhythm that allowed her to emulate their moves to some satisfaction. After she'd mastered the steps as much as the novice dancer in her would allow, she got that feeling again. Release. Liberation. Maybe it was this feeling that caused so many to love this way of dancing and this type of music, both of which she had been taught were worldly and of the devil. How could you tell anyone that this was wrong when it came with such feelings of freedom? Maybe the answer lay in what her father once told her: Expression in the form of dance was meant to be good for the body and soul. Your dance, he'd said, is meant to be in praise unto the Lord for all His goodness and mercies toward you. So, it's the reason for and the object of, your dance that makes the difference. Sasha's pondering of her father's words was short-lived. Zandy was trying to tell her something, so she leaned her ear closer to Zandy's mouth.

"You keep dancing with Brandi," Zandy shouted. "I'm going to tell the DJ to play the song we danced the Booty Call routine to last night." When Sasha nodded, she headed off toward the DJ's platform. After she'd gone a short distance, she swiftly turned back to Sasha. "And don't try to be sneaky and leave this dance floor. I *will* find you," she promised loudly. To Brandi, she said, "Keep a close eye on her."

They all laughed and Zandy half-danced and half-shuffled her way through the not-yet-tired dancers.

Sasha danced on with Brandi. She didn't feel like a fish out of water anymore. As long as she was dancing with Zandy and Brandi, no one would pay any attention to her anyway. Not as long as they continued to dance in the erotic clothing they were wearing. Brandi wore a black, leather short set that was similar to the outfit Zandy wore. *And she has a pierced navel,* Sasha thought happily. *Nobody cares about what I have on. Jeans are normal. Shirts that look like bras are attention-getters. I could've been out here dancing and having a good time way before now.*

Sasha felt her energy level surge. She was really ready to get her groove on now.

"He's going to be playing our song in a minute." Zandy said, dancing up to Sasha and Brandi. "So get ready, Sasha."

Adrenaline was pumping through Sasha. This party was supposed to be her outlet to a good time, so a good time was exactly what she'd have. She'd deal with any forthcoming regrets later. Much later. Tonight, from this point on, she would banish all inhibitive thoughts from her mind and enjoy whatever lay on the horizon. With a confidence she hadn't possessed all evening, she shouted, "I'm ready!"

As if the DJ had been waiting to hear her speak those exact words, he faded out the music and spoke into the microphone. "This next one is for three special ladies on the dance floor tonight. For Miss Aleczandria, who we all know and love. For Miss Brandi who came all the way from Rhode Island to party with us. And for Aleczandria's good friend, Miss Sasha, who is partyin' with us for the first time. Let's show Sasha some love."

All heads in the huge room began a gradual spin toward the threesome. Everyone seemed to recognize Zandy and Brandi, so it was only expected that they'd guess Sasha to be the other "special lady." The crowd began to clap loudly and yell words of welcome to Sasha.

Sasha almost keeled over with embarrassment. "Zandy, why did you do that?" she demanded to know through gritted teeth, her eyes wide with mortification. Her lips formed a nervous smile as she noticed that many were throwing welcoming smiles her way, but her eyes threw miniature daggers at Zandy.

Zandy, as expected, burst into laughter, and Brandi laughed with her. "I didn't tell him to do that," Zandy tried to explain. "I just—"

Zandy was cut off by the booming introduction of their song, but the vivaciousness of her laughter was again infectious, and Sasha found herself smiling genuinely at some of those nearby who still greeted her.

With the song in full swing, the crowd quickly forgot the three. The selection was evidently an all-around favorite because loud whoops and yells filled the room and tables were left empty as everyone found partners and ran to the dance floor. Zandy gave Sasha's arm an encouraging squeeze, and they gleefully began to dance again with the others.

Zandy and Brandi led out in the Booty Call dance routine. Sasha joined in slowly, taking special care not to miss a step. Zandy's moves, for Sasha's sake, were at first moderate and encouraging. Once she saw that Sasha easily recalled the steps and that she was actually getting into the dance, Zandy moved more passionately, adding more zest to the routine. All reservation gone, Sasha was once again infused with sensations of freedom. She gave herself over to the feeling and she forgot about all else, but having a good time.

The song seemed to go on forever, but that was fine with the threesome. They were totally engrossed in their dancing, so much until they were surprised to look up and find that some of the other students had joined them in the routine.

The DJ saw the large group dance and fed their fusion by masterfully launching into another jam just as lively as the former. The dancers became ecstatic. Electricity generated by the dancing and the music filled the building.

Sasha and Zandy danced on with the others, neither of them showing signs of fatigue. Through the hustle of dancers, their eyes met briefly and they grinned happily. Together, they were finally on the verge of finding what they had come in search of — a good time.

Sasha had problems falling asleep. Her heart was still pounding from the excitement of the night. The group had danced together through three straight songs before everyone returned to the normal routine of one-on-one dancing. But sparks continued to fly on the dance floor throughout the night.

To her delight, she'd even danced with a fair share of guys, including a couple of slow dances. The guys had complemented her and even threw a few admiring glances her way, but none of them found it necessary to come on as strong as Eric had. They were pretty cool and laid back, and that helped her to relax even more.

She'd sat and talked and laughed with some of the girls at the party, too. She didn't feel like the oddball of the dance. She was just another college student out on a Saturday night, having a good time.

When Zandy had tapped her on the shoulder and told her that she was beat and ready to go, Sasha had been disappointed. She'd been thoroughly enjoying herself.

Zandy had said it would be fun, and it was. I had a good time. Now if I can only get some sleep.

She glanced at her clock on the bedside table. It was 3:15 a.m. She'd been home for almost an hour and she was still too excited to sleep. If she didn't fall asleep soon, she'd be too tired to get up for church.

Church. She groaned loudly. She'd almost forgotten that it was Sunday morning, and Sunday morning always meant church. She kicked at the covers and groaned again. She could feel the excitement seeping out of her and the guilt seeping in.

How many times had her father preached about those sinners who partied on Saturday night and shouted at church on Sunday morning? Hypocrites, he'd called them, and Sasha had always backed him up with a hearty "amen."

Annoyed with the onslaught of guilt that suffused her, she flipped over on her stomach and punched her pillow. *Forget it, then. I just won't go to church today.*

Chapter 6

Sasha was groggy with sleep when she reached over to the nightstand and blindly picked up the receiver of the ringing telephone. "Hello," she mumbled.

"Good morning. How are you, besides sleepy?"

There was something about that serene, not quite baritone voice that moved her like no other. Sleep left her instantly, and her toes tingled.

Sasha smiled and answered, "Good morning, Tellis. How are you?"

"Great. I'm sorry for waking you. But I was thinking about you, and . . . "

"And?" Sasha slowly prompted.

"*And* so many things, like I really wanted to call you at one o'clock this morning when I made it in from work, but I didn't want to wake you. So I had to settle for lying awake almost half the night thinking about the many things I find attractive about you, and why. Do you want to hear my list now, or can you wait until later?"

Sasha stared blissfully at the ceiling. Tellis never wasted any time getting to the point. She liked that. Her heart had expanded with every word he spoke, and now it seemed to be on the verge of bursting. It was almost painful. She sighed to release the tension.

"Did I say something wrong?" He laughed. "I think I heard a heavy sigh."

"No, Tellis, you didn't say anything wrong." Sasha needed to give her heart time to settle before Tellis said something else that would send it into a pitter-patter frenzy. Changing the subject, she softly asked, "Why did you make it in so late?"

"I stayed in the lab with Dr. Omwe, testing chemicals."

Sasha raised a brow. "Until one o'clock in the morning?"

"Yeah," Tellis answered. "We'd planned to wrap things up by seven, but ended up working through the night because we were making good progress." Deep laughter rumbled in Tellis' throat. "Dr. Omwe gets really excited when we're making headway. I guess I do, too. I'm glad he chose me to work with him. It's a great opportunity that should get me the internship with DuPont this summer."

"That would be great."

"It would be, but I'd miss you," he said smoothly. "The internship is in Boston, and I can't take you with me.'

Sasha's heart was flip-flopping again. She sighed heavily.

"I heard that sigh again. Sighs tend to mean that something is wrong."

"The sigh wasn't meant to imply that at all."

"Then what did it imply?" he asked, unruffled.

Sasha didn't wait to think over her words before speaking. "Tellis, you know how I feel about you. I tried to tell you the other day how much my feelings for you have grown, although I don't think I did a good job of it. I guess I was too giddy with emotion to find the right words to express myself." She laughed nervously, then said, "But just to hear that you reciprocate my feelings makes me want to laugh and scream at the same time. This is all so new to me. I'm happy and scared at the same time."

"What scares you?"

So many things scared her when it came to her feelings for Tellis. Where should she start? She sat up in the bed, propped her pillow up against the engraved, whitewashed headboard that extended almost to the ceiling, and leaned back.

"Well, it scares me that I like you so much. I'm scared that you may find that I'm not all you expect me to be and that you'll decide that you no longer like me as much. I'm scared that . . . that I may lose you, and that I'll be hurt deeply because of it."

"I promise you that you and I are going to have a really good talk the next time I see you," said Tellis. "I know that you're attracted to me and I'm attracted to you, too, but we need to have an open and honest discussion about what we want from this relationship. But for now, I want you to know that I understand your fears. I guess I have them, too. I would like to be able to tell you that you don't have to fear that I'll stop being attracted to you or that you'll lose me and so on. But I can't. Just like you can't promise me that I won't lose you. We're still just getting to know each other. So you can't promise me that you'll feel the same way about me three months from now. There's still so much we need to learn about each other. You know what I mean?"

Yes, I know what you mean, Sasha thought. *If I don't turn out to be the girl you want me to be, you'll break up with me.* Aloud she said, "Yes. I understand."

"So, all I want from you right now is for you to promise me that you will give us a chance to discover each other. Let's not take things too fast. Isn't it more important to be friends first?"

That wasn't exactly what Sasha wanted to hear, but she quietly replied, "Yes. Being friends first is important."

"So we're going to talk later?" Tellis asked her.

"Mm-Hmm," she affirmed.

"And you're going to let me tell you everything I'm liking about you right about now?" he asked flirtatiously.

Sasha heard the huskiness in Tellis' voice and her toes began to tingle again. "Yes," she replied softly.

He chuckled lightly. "Everything?"

"Yes."

"Then I guess I need to take my cold shower now."

They both laughed.

"And what will you tell *me*?" he asked in a seductive tone.

"Everything, of course." she replied smoothly.

"You're too sweet for words."

Before she realized it, Sasha's voice had taken on the same husky and seductive tone.

"So are you," she said.

"Oh, so I'm sweet to you, Sasha?"

"Yes."

"And what else am I to you?" he asked daringly.

Sasha heard the sensual flirtation dripping from her own words when she replied, "I don't think I should respond to a question like that over the phone. Anyone could be listening in, and I wouldn't want to offend their ears. I'll tell you *everything* when I see you. When *will* I see you?"

"When do you want to see me?"

"Always."

"Always?"

"Always."

"Even now, while you're in bed in probably your most provocative nightgown?"

"Why? Would you find that tempting?"

"Just the thought of it is tempting."

"You're a big boy. You can handle it."

"Maybe . . . maybe not. It all depends . . ."

"On what?"

"On you."

"Oh, I see. You're going to follow my lead on this? I thought you were a leader."

"One of my greatest assets is that I can follow just as well as I lead, especially when the destination promises to be so . . . desirable. Following you would be worth the journey."

"But I want *you* to lead, Tellis."

"Why?"

"Because you're so good at it."

"And you re not?"

"In this case, not as good as you."

"I'm not sure I agree with that," he said, laughing. "You were pretty aggressive the other day when you laid that kiss on me."

Sasha's face burned with embarrassment and she cried out, "Tellis!"

"Don't *Tellis* me. You know what I'm talking about. I usually have to almost tie you down for a kiss, but not the other day when I was at your apartment. No-o-o-o. That was a different story, a different day. And your leadership skills didn't seem lacking to me. I had no problem understanding what your lips were saying."

"I can't believe you—"

"What? Am I embarrassing you?"

"Yes!"

"You don't have to be embarrassed. I enjoyed every bit of it."

"I bet you did!"

Sasha heard him chuckle.

"Stop laughing at me. I think I'm blushing." She touched her warm cheek.

"Oh, really? I'd like to see that. I'll let it slide for the moment, but I may have to bring it up again when I see you. I need to see what a blush looks like on you. You're really very pretty, you know."

Sasha heard the seriousness in his voice and she exhaled deeply.

"I *have* told you that?" he asked her.

"Not in those exact words, but, yes, you have. Twice."

"Are you counting?"

"Only because it's important to me that you think so."

"Well, I do think so."

"And you, sir, are very gorgeous. But then I'm sure that all the *ladies* have told you that before."

"At this moment, I'm only interested in what one lady thinks."

Sasha smiled broadly and laughter slipped through her lips. "Why the laugh?" he asked.

"Oh, I'm just happy, that's all."

"Well, good. I'll leave you on a happy note. Call me when you return from church. I'll come over and we can have our talk. Or better yet, why don't you just invite me to church with you and save yourself a call?"

Sasha was flabbergasted. She sat stunned and immobile on the bed. This was the last thing she'd expected, especially when she'd already decided to skip church service today. She massaged her temple to ease the tension that gripped her.

"So, is it okay for me to go to church with you?" Tellis asked, as though he sensed that something was wrong.

Sasha gritted her teeth. "Yes," she managed to say. She didn't want to lie to him, so she added, "I think so."

"You *think* so?" he asked quietly. "What does that mean?"

"I'm not really sure, so can we talk about it later? You know, when we come from church?" Her voice pleaded for his understanding.

He understood. "Alright," he said, then added, "Do you realize that you just said when *we* come from church? I want to go with you. I don't understand why you wouldn't want me to go with you, but if you don't want me to go, I won't."

He is so understanding, Sasha thought. She felt ashamed of her negative reaction to him going to church with her. *To church of all places. What girl wouldn't be happy that her boyfriend looked forward to going to church with her? I should be whipped.* "Tellis, I want you to go with me," she said evenly. "How soon can you be ready?"

"What time do you want me to be there?"

Sasha looked over at her desk clock. It was fifteen minutes before ten. They wouldn't make it in time for Sunday School. She'd missed it for the past month anyway. She was feeling less and less guilty about that. "Worship Service starts at 11:30, so if you get here around that time, that'll be fine."

"Sasha, we have enough time to get ready and be on time for Worship Service," he stated gently, but firmly. "I don't go to church as much as I should, but when I do go, I don't like to be late if I can help it. Why don't I pick you up at 11:00? That way, we'll make it by 11:30. Alright?"

Sasha knew he was right, but she felt like she'd been chastised. There was a time when she'd made every effort to be on time for church. Even for Sunday School. Now she was on time for everything but church. Tellis had just reminded her of how guilty she used to feel about being late for service.

"Is that alright with you?" he asked again.

"Yes. I'll see you when you get here."

"Alright," Tellis said, then hung up the phone.

Sasha hung up her end and fell back onto the pillows. She'd been elated only a few short minutes ago. Now, she felt almost depressed. *What happened?* she asked herself. *How did we end up talking about church?* Leaning over, she grabbed the receiver and punched in Zandy's number.

"Hello," a voice growled into the phone after the first ring.

"Hello. May I speak to Zandy, please."

"Look, I'm still in the bed, and I don't feel like getting up. Call back and let the phone ring until she answers." Click.

Sasha stared at the receiver in her hand, amazed that Zandy's roommate could be so unnecessarily rude. Sasha hung up the phone. She'd just wait and talk to Zandy later. No, she couldn't wait. She grabbed the receiver again. She needed to talk *now*. She redialed the number. The phone rang four times before Zandy answered. "Hey," she said as if expecting the call.

"Hi. This is Sasha. Are you up?"

"Hey, Sasha. Sort of," Zandy said, yawning. "Was that you who called a few minutes ago?"

"Yes, that was me. Your roommate — what's her name?"

"Kayla," Zandy said with distaste. "Why?"

"She was rather rude when she answered the phone," Sasha stated without offense.

"What'd she do?" Zandy demanded to know. When Sasha explained what happened, Zandy exclaimed, "She can be such a— Hold on a minute, Sasha," and before Sasha could stop her, she was gone.

Sasha could've kicked herself for even mentioning Kayla. She hadn't wanted to start an argument.

Zandy must have been very upset because Sasha could hear her shouting in the background. Sasha pressed the phone closer to her ear. Evidently Zandy had forgotten her vow to stop cursing because she could hear a few of the expletives Zandy yelled at her roommate. She was cursing up a storm. Her cursing had a rhythmic flow, as if it was an art she'd mastered. Sasha strained her ears to hear Kayla's response, but she didn't hear one peep from the rude roomy. *Zandy must have scared her speechless.*

"Hey." Zandy was back on the line. Her voice held no signs of anger. "That girl is a trip," she said.

"Zandy, I'm sorry. I didn't mean to cause an argument."

"You didn't cause anything," Zandy said, her voice rising. "She's just trippin'. Let me tell you what happened. Last week I finally told her that her man keeps trying to get with me. He came by here when he knew she was at work, talking about he'd left something over here he needed to get. The whole time he was here he was all up in my face. Kayla and I have been roomies for almost a year and I thought we got along alright. So when ol' boy tried to run his game on me, I told her about it. I felt bad about telling her, but I figured she would appreciate the tip. At least I know *I* would want to know if *my* man — if I had one — was scheming on *me*.

"Anyway, this stupid girl gets mad and wants to fight me! Can you believe that? I'm looking out for her and she turns and wants to jump me. Some girls are so simple in the head, and she's one of them. She has to be twisted if she thinks I want that hood rat. The boy is as ugly as sin. He may *have* a tight body, but that doesn't mean I want to get with him. I literally laughed in her face when she said that I've been after Kelvin the whole time.

She said that he already told her that I was playing up to him. The boy's not in school. He doesn't work — she practically takes care of him, giving him money all the time. I don't know where he lives, but at one point it looked like she was trying to move him up in here and I wasn't having that. He doesn't have a ride, either — he's always driving her car, dropping her off where she wants to go and then off he goes with the car. Can you believe that?

"I have no idea what she sees in him. One day I heard her on the phone telling one of her girls how good he is in bed. I guess that's what she sees in him. She's a stupid fool, and that's exactly what I told her when she stepped to me about *her* man. I told her she had best be getting out of my face and the next time she stepped to me that way, I was going to body slam her. I should've slapped her right then and there for being so stupid." Zandy exhaled a deep sigh. "Anyway, girl, don't worry about Kayla. What's up?"

All of a sudden what Sasha had to say didn't seem important anymore. "Oh, I didn't want much."

"You must have wanted something, else you wouldn't have called back after Kayla hung up on you. C'mon, what's up?"

"Well, I don't have long to talk — I've got to get ready for church. Tellis is going with me." She paused, expecting a response from Zandy. When none came, she continued. "He invited himself," she said, as if it was supposed to explain everything.

"Is that one of the Ten Commandments I never learned — Thou shalt not invite thyself to church?" Zandy asked.

"See, you're trying to be funny again, when I'm really serious."

"I don't mean to make fun of you, Sasha. But why does that bother you? He wants to go to church with you. You should be happy."

"I know I should be happy, but I'm not. I told you the other night, I want a life outside of the church. I don't want Tellis to be eager to go to church when I'm trying to leave it."

"You're being paranoid. He just wants to be with you."

"We can be together without going to church."

"Going to church today is not going to hurt anything."

Sasha sighed. "Yes, it will. It's like he's coming into my world – the world I'm trying to put behind me – and he'll see how different I am, from him and other girls."

"You know what?" Zandy asked. "I think it's about time we take the word different out of any sentence that applies to you. In the beginning I did say that you were sort of different, but I'm reneging on that statement right now. I'm starting to go a little bunkers with you always saying how different you are. Like you're stricken with some kind of incurable disease. So can't we just forget about all of our differences and let's all just . . . get along." Zandy laughed at her own little pun.

"See, there you go again," Sasha retorted. "Being facetious."

"No, Sasha, I'm not being facetious — I really meant what I said. I hear and understand all that you're saying, but in my humble opinion, you may be taking things a little bit too far. Just relax and stop your worrying. The worst thing that could happen is that Tellis gets saved and God calls him to be a preacher." Zandy giggled. "Now how bad would that be?"

Sasha stiffened. Zandy had spoken her fears, and she didn't like it, even if Zandy was only joking. This was serious business. "I'm going to stop talking to you, Zandy," she said bitingly. "You're no help to me right now."

"Well, here's what I'll do. I'll pray that Tellis *doesn't* get saved, and I'll tell God that he'd make a lousy preacher."

Sasha could hear Zandy's laughter floating through the line. "Bye, Zandy!"

"I'll stop, Sasha. Don't hang up."

"You're not going to stop, Zandy. Good-bye!"

"Don't hang up, Sasha! I promise to stop!"

Sasha threw back the covers and scooted to the edge of the bed. "I'm hanging up anyway. I've got to get dressed before

Tellis gets here, and I've wasted enough time talking to you already. Some help you are."

"You're welcome. Next time, I'm charging you by the minute." Zandy said, laughing. "I'll see you in a few."

"What do you mean, *you'll see me in a few?*"

"With all my great counseling skills, I can understand why you must think I'm perfect, but even *I* need Jesus. So I'm going to church with you, too!"

Sasha groaned. "No. Not you, too."

"Yep. Me, too. I'll be there in a jiffy. Bye."

"Wait, Zandy!" Sasha cried. "Zandy? *Zandy?!*"

The line was dead.

Sasha hung up the phone. Frowning deeply, she slid off the bed and stalked over to her closet.

Things weren't looking as good as she was starting to think they were.

Chapter 7

"Hey! Tellis here yet?" Zandy asked, strutting through Sasha's front door.

"Not yet, but he should be here in a few minutes," Sasha answered. "He called to say he was on his way."

"That suit looks good on you," Zandy said, admiring Sasha's lime green suit. The suit's short, double-breasted jacket and its straight, full-length skirt gave Sasha an elegant appeal. "I like it. It goes well with your new hairdo."

Sasha had wrapped her hair in a silk scarf before going to bed. She wanted to keep the style looking fresh as long as possible. "Thank you," she replied, limping across the living room towards her bedroom.

Zandy closed the front door. "Where's your other shoe?" she asked.

"I'm not sure," Sasha shouted from the bedroom. "I was searching for it when you started pounding on the door. Was there a fire out there or something?"

"Very funny. Can I come back there?"

"Sure."

Zandy stood in the doorway of the bedroom.

"Haven't you noticed the doorbell out there?" Sasha asked, smirking. She was still a little put out with Zandy for teasing her so much on the phone.

Zandy ignored the smirk. "Yeah, I've seen it."

Sasha entered her walk-in closet. Dropping to a squat, she searched rows of shoes for a high-heeled pump swirled with various shades of pinks, purples and greens. Finding it at the back of the closet, she slipped it on her foot and walked out of the closet. "Why don't you use it then?" she asked Zandy.

"That's what's wrong with the world today — everybody wants to take the easy way out. They push little, dainty doorbells and wait quietly at the door. Well I'm an old-fashioned type of girl. I prefer doing things the old-fashioned way, when there was no such thing as a doorbell. I pound."

"Well, hand over the keys to that nice little Jeep you have out there—"

"*Excuse me*, but that's a Kia Sportage, baby. There *is* a difference. Call it a sports utility vehicle or a truck, but *never* a Jeep."

"What-*ev-er*," Sasha said, using one of Zandy's expressions. "Hand me the keys to that *Kia Sportage*. I'm sure you would love to walk home, you know, the *old-fashioned way*."

"See, there you go. Just like black folk. Always trying to twist a sista's words around and taking stuff out of context. Doorbells have *nothing* to do with cars."

They both laughed.

Zandy sat on the edge of Sasha's unmade bed. "I'm glad you invited me to church today," she said.

"I did *not* invite you to church. You invited yourself."

Zandy giggled. "You're right. I did. And I can tell that you're not happy about it, either. Looking at me with your face all screwed up like you drank some castor oil. That's why I *will* be praying for you at church today."

Sasha couldn't resist smiling. "Don't forget to pray for yourself, too. Tell the Lord to teach you how to be serious *sometimes*."

"I'm not gonna bother God with such nonsense — He's probably tired of people being stuffy all the time anyway." She waved a dismissive hand in the air. "I plan to have me a shoutin' good time today."

"That would be a sight to see."

"What? Me shouting?"

Sasha nodded, yes.

"Girl, I told you I used to go to church when I was younger," Zandy said. "I know how to shout, and I know how to do the sanctified dance, too. Watch, I'm gonna show you today at church. But, then again," she added, walking over to Sasha's full-length mirror hanging on the wall, "I'm not sure if I can do much of anything in *this* dress." She turned from side to side, looking at her reflection in the mirror. The dress she wore was a simple, but fashionable one. Navy in color with a classic A-line cut, the short-sleeved, collarless mini-dress perfectly outlined the shapely contours of her figure. On her long legs shimmered ultra-sheer navy stockings, and on her feet she wore the latest navy square-toed, squared-heeled pumps. Tiny pearl earrings and a thin pearl choker completed the outfit.

Zandy stood facing the mirror and raised both hands straight up in the air. "Look a there, Sasha," she said, frowning. "Even if I tried to raise my hands to the Lord, everybody in church will practically be able to see all my stuff!"

Sasha choked on unanticipated laughter. "You should've known not to wear a mini dress to church."

"Oh, my goodness!" Zandy continued, turning her back to the mirror and looking over her shoulder at her reflection. "You can almost see the curve of my butt from behind when I raise my hands like this! Look at that, Sasha!"

Sasha was shaking with laughter.

Zandy, very serious about the unsuitableness of her dress for church shouting, jumped and clapped her hands experimentally in the mirror, watching the hem of her dress obsessively as it dipped up and down. "Glory! Hallelujah! Thank you, Jesus!" she yelled, jumping up and down and waving her hands in the air.

Tears of laughter filled Sasha's eyes. She could remember many times when she herself had tested the suitability of her clothing for church by dancing in front of a mirror. But had she looked as ridiculous as Zandy now looked? The thought threw her into another fit of laughter.

There was a knock at the front door, and Sasha, not daring another look at Zandy, walked quickly to the door. She flung the door open, her face still suffused with laughter.

Tellis stood there, looking as debonair as they come. Sasha's sparkling eyes glided quickly over his impressive form, clad in a greenish-gray suit, white shirt, matching print tie, and black, slip-on leather shoes. In his hand he held a large black Bible.

"You look very nice," Sasha said, stepping aside to let him enter. "I notice you don't use the doorbell, either."

"I always forget it's out here, it's so low on the wall. I'll remember next time, though. Why are you smiling like that?" he asked, stepping into the apartment.

"Zandy," Sasha replied, as if the name itself served as explanation. "She's in the bedroom. Close the door and have a seat. We'll be out in a minute." She turned toward the bedroom.

Tellis closed the door, then cleared his throat.

Sasha turned back to him, a questioning look on her face.

"Don't I get hug, a kiss, or something? Even a friendly hug will do."

Sasha smiled shyly.

He laid his Bible on the end table and pulled her into his arms. Planting a soft kiss on her forehead, he whispered, "Hello."

Sasha wrapped her arms around him. She wanted to be as passionate with him now as she had been on the phone, but one look in his dark eyes left her flustered and speechless.

He smiled down at her. "Not as bold as you were on the phone, I see."

"Don't tease me, Tellis."

"So that's what a blush looks like on you. I like it." He lightly touched her hair. "I like your hair, too."

"Thank you."

Tellis released her from his embrace. "Zandy's probably waiting for you back there."

Sasha could've stayed in his arms all day, but she did need to check on Zandy. "We'll be right out."

Tellis moved to the sofa to sit down and wait. Just as he squatted over the sofa to sit, Sasha was back with Zandy following reluctantly behind. Tellis resumed his standing position.

"Tellis, this is Zandy. I think you two have met before."

"We have met," Tellis said, smiling at Zandy. "I remember you telling me how much you enjoyed my poem during one of the Wednesday assemblies. I see you around campus, but we've never really talked. It's good to meet you again." He extended his hand toward Zandy.

Zandy placed her hand in his. "It's good to meet you again, too," she said smiling and shaking his hand.

Tellis' gaze became thoughtful. "For some reason I thought the name was different. Alexandria or something of that nature."

"Yes, Aleczandria," Zandy said, stressing the correct pronunciation of her name. "My friends call me Zandy. I've been hearing some great things about you," she added, glancing at Sasha.

Tellis followed her eyes to Sasha. "I've been hearing a lot about you, too, Aleczandria," he said, pulling Sasha into the circle of his arm. He smiled at Zandy. "I hope we can be friends as well."

"Me, too. So call me Zandy."

"Sure," he said. "Are we ready to go?" he asked Sasha.

"Yes," Sasha croaked. His display of affection in front of Zandy had surprised her, and she fidgeted with her Bible and purse strap as she moved out of his arms. "Ready, Zandy?" she asked weakly.

Zandy noted Sasha's nervousness, and her smile grew to a grin. "I think so.

"Alright," Tellis said, smiling charmingly at both ladies. "Let's go, then."

Zandy was right behind Sasha as she trailed Tellis out the door. She whispered in Sasha's ear. "Do you think angels in heaven look that good?"

Chapter 8

Sasha drove onto the church's large parking lot, almost filled to capacity. She swerved easily into a space close to the street and all three moved to vacate the car. Each one of them lost in thought, they walked in the glare of the sun toward the church's large, white double doors.

Tellis admired the red brick church and the well kept grounds adorned with a massive array of colorful flowers. The small billboard standing in the midst of the flowers proclaimed the church's name — The Garden of Prayer — and Tellis thought the name very befitting. The size of the church appealed to him as well — not too large, like the enormous Baptist church his parents attended, but not too small, either.

Sasha walked beside Tellis. She quietly prayed that absolutely nothing would happen in service today that would embarrass her in front of Tellis. Like someone calling her up to have words or to sing a song. She had no idea what was on today's program, but she had no desire to be a part of it. She prayed that the kind members of the church, who often tried to include her in many of the church's programs and activities, would not feel led to call her out for anything today. She just wanted to go in, hear the message for the day, and leave.

Zandy followed close behind Sasha and Tellis, tugging at the hem of her dress. She didn't know what had possessed her to put the dress on in the first place. She'd been to church enough to know that you could go in with no intentions of praising God, and before you knew it, you'd be up and shouting all over the place like somebody set fire to you.

I knew that before I put this dress on, she thought. *So why did I put it on? Nothing but the devil. At least that's what Mae Mama would say. That snake had me thinking I was looking oh, so fine in this short number. Now I feel like a slut.* "Uggh," she groaned, pulling once more at her dress. She closed her eyes and raised her face heavenward. "Ple-e-a-a-se, don't touch me, Lord," she pleaded under her breath. "Not today. I'd be too shame to shout."

"You okay, Alecz . . . Zandy?" Tellis asked, concerned.

Zandy's eyes snapped open. She barely avoided colliding into Sasha, who now stood beside Tellis at the church entrance. They both looked curiously at Zandy. "What?" she asked both of them, her eyebrows raised high. "Haven't you ever seen a person pray before? We *are* going to church, you know."

Tellis grinned. "I do apologize, but I could've sworn you were growling."

"Me, too," Sasha agreed, smiling. "It must be that dress again."

Zandy crossed her eyes and screwed her lips into a funny face. "Can we *please* go in church, Mr. and Mrs. Smarty Pants. It's evident that both of you need to learn what it means to pray."

Tellis turned to open the door of the church, and they all walked in with smiles on their faces.

The congregation was standing and joyfully singing the opening song of praise:

> *What a mighty God we serve!*
> *What a mighty God we serve!*
> *Angels bow before Him!*
> *Heaven and earth adore Him!*
> *What a mighty God we serve!*

In likeness of the welcoming Spirit that enveloped the three as they entered the house of the Lord, the usher greeted them with a welcoming smile. Her eyes sparkled when she saw Sasha and she hastened forward to give her a bear hug and then her two guests.

The usher spoke into Sasha's ear. "It's good to see you, Sister Lindsey. I've been missing you."

Sasha offered no explanation, only a smile — a guilty one. It didn't daunt the bright smile of the usher. Directing her smile once again toward Zandy and Tellis, she led them all down the middle aisle to sit in the fourth pew from the front of the church.

As soon as their bottoms hit the pew, Zandy was mumbling in Sasha's ear. "Did she *have* to sit us so close to the front? The preacher will be able to look right into my eyeballs."

Sasha smiled knowingly. "I know how you feel," she said.

Zandy screwed up her lips into a brief pout. She looked as if she was going to say something else to Sasha, but decided against it. She clapped her hands in rhythm with the music and joined in the singing. She knew the song quite well from her younger days in church.

Sasha felt some of her tension ease as she clapped and sang, too. Still, her eyes slid covertly to the left to check out how Tellis was fairing. He looked fine so far. At least he wasn't looking all over the place, goggling everyone. As far as she knew, Tellis had grown up in a quiet Baptist church that didn't encourage shouting and dancing. She cast another glance at him. This time, his eyes met hers. He smiled as he attempted to sing the words to the song. By the way he hesitated over some lyrics and totally missed others, she knew he didn't really know the song. Sasha smiled back and resumed singing a little more lively than before. She simply had to believe that everything would be alright.

Long after the singing had ended, the music and hand clapping continued. Some even danced for a while. Eventually, when most were able to find their seats, one of the young deacons shared a scriptural reading. Jeremiah 6:16-19:

Thus saith the Lord, Stand ye in the ways, and see, and ask for the old paths, where is the good way, and walk therein, and ye shall find rest for your souls. But they said, We will not walk therein.

Also I set watchmen over you, saying, Hearken to the sound of the trumpet. But they said, We will not hearken.

Therefore hear, ye nations, and know, O congregation, what is among them.

Hear, O earth: behold, I will bring evil upon this people, even the fruit of their thoughts, because they have not hearkened unto my words, nor to my law, but rejected it.

There were many 'Amens' to the reading. Then someone in the congregation began to sing another song:

Were you there when they crucified my Lord?
Were you there when they crucified my Lord?
Sometimes it makes me tremble, tremble, tremble.
Were you there when they crucified my Lord?

The singer's voice was rich and clear and filled with passion. Zandy strained her neck to see who owned the voice. "Who is *that*, Sasha?"

"She has a beautiful voice, doesn't she? That's Mother Hensen. She's the church mother." Sasha pointed out the sixty-nine year old lady dressed in white sitting on a front pew.

"Ol' girl can blow!"

Sasha playfully reprimanded Zandy with a slight shove of her shoulder. "*Ol' girl can blow?* Don't you mean, *Mother Hensen* can really sing?" she whispered.

"Must we get technical at a time like this?" Zandy whispered back. "They both mean the same thing." She held a finger to her lips. "Shhhhh. I can't hear."

Were you there when they nailed Him to the tree?
Were you there when they nailed Him to the tree?
Sometimes it makes me tremble, tremble, tremble.
Were you there when they nailed Him to the tree?

Were you there when they pierced Him in His side?
Were you there when they pierced Him in His side?
Sometimes it makes me tremble, tremble, tremble.
Were you there when they pierced Him in His side?

The pain and agony that floated on the words that Mother Hensen sang caused the church to envision what Christ's death on the cross must have been like. They thought of the harsh cruelties that Jesus had suffered on their behalf. The song moved some to tears. Some stood and began to worship the Lord.

The song moved Zandy, too. Before she knew it, she was up on her feet shouting, "Sing that song, Mother Hensen! Sing that song!" She flung her arms in the direction of the Mother for emphasis and up went her dress. She quickly found her seat.

Sasha looked at her wide-eyed, trying not laugh.

Tellis couldn't hold back his laugh. He chuckled, but quickly checked himself.

Zandy's brows furrowed. "What?" she asked looking from one to the other, as if she had no clue what they were laughing at.

"Nothing," Sasha said, smiling.

"Well, stop looking at me like that," Zandy said with an exaggerated roll of her eyes.

Still smiling, Sasha turned her eyes toward the front of the church, where Mother Hensen had now stood and bellowed the last verse of the song:

Were you there when they laid Him in the tomb?
Were you there when they laid Him in the tomb?
Sometimes it makes me tremble, tremble, tremble.
Were you there when they laid Him in the tomb?

The church clapped vigorously and waved their hands wildly in the air when the Mother eventually took her seat. Sensing that the saints were itching to praise the Lord, the organist, a middle-aged gentleman with a shiny bald head, immediately picked up the beat of the song and carried the congregation into worship and praise. A young girl, who looked no older than thirteen, jumped on the drums and began to play with skill and excellent timing. Somebody began to beat a tambourine loudly. Together, the instruments produced glorious music that was just right for hand-clapping, foot-stomping praise. Some begin to shout. Some began to dance. Some began to run around the church. Some began to speak in tongues.

Sasha sat still as the people around her praised God. Even when Tellis and Zandy stood to their feet and clapped their hands, she remained seated. She didn't want to be hypocritical. How could she honestly praise God when this was the last place she wanted to be?

By the way the rest of the congregation was jumping and shouting, church was *not* the last place they wanted to be. The organist continued to play swiftly, his fingers dancing across the organ's keys and his bottom practically bouncing across the bench as he played. And the saints continued to praise God. It was not until Elder Earl, the senior pastor of the church, began to make his way to the microphone in the pulpit that the organist slowed the tempo of the music.

Elder Earl, a giant of a man with short, curly black hair and graying sideburns, shouted praises unto the Lord as he stood at the microphone.

"If we keep on shouting like this," he said with a wide grin, "we won't get a chance to hear the man of God speak today. Hallelujah!" he roared, throwing a hand in the air, "We're gonna let the Lord have His way in this church. He can take all the time He wants. Hallelujah!"

Now that the pastor was up, the church slowly began to quiet down as the saints found their way to their seats, still praising the Lord.

"He's so worthy to be praised!" Elder Earl shouted.

"Amen!" the church shouted agreement.

Elder Earl lowered his voice to a moderate tone. "We do give thanks unto the Lord today for His many, many blessings," he said, still excited. "His blessings are countless and His mercies are endless. We just can't thank Him and praise Him enough. So I just want to encourage each of you to praise God. Regardless of where life's challenges may find you, if you can remember to praise God, there's a breakthrough ahead for you. Stay encouraged. Saints of God, stay encouraged.

"I'm so happy to have each of you in the house of the Lord today," he continued with a wide smile. His eyes roamed the full congregation. "Praise God. I see some familiar faces, and I see some not so familiar faces," he said, his eyes lighting on the pew where Zandy, Sasha, and Tellis sat.

Sasha went rigid in her seat. *Please don't embarrass me*, she pleaded silently.

The pastor's eyes moved on. "And I thank God for each of you."

"Amen!" someone in the congregation yelled out.

Elder Earl cleared his throat. "Most of you know that the Church of Deliverance is having their tenth year church's anniversary today, and we are invited to attend. The program starts at two o'clock, so I'm hoping to end service early today so that we can be a part of that service this afternoon. Now, I know that some of you are going to leave and go straight to where you can get something to eat."

Elder Earl smiled as laughter spread over the congregation. "And that's alright. I like to eat, too." He placed his hands on his slightly protruding belly. "I told Sister Earl just this morning that she's going to have to stop feeding me all of that good food she cooks. I'm almost fifty years old now, and I can't work off them black-eyed peas and butter beans like I used to when I was a young man. Praise the Lord." Elder Earl rubbed his belly. "I believe I heard myself grunt this morning when I reached down to tie my shoes. My belly was in the way."

The church roared with laughter. When the laughter subsided he continued. "So, go ahead and eat if you want to, but don't eat too much. We don't want you to be too weighted down if the Holy Ghost wants to come in and have His way. Amen?"

"Amen!" the congregation laughingly chorused.

"Also, since we're going to be in service this afternoon, we won't be having service here tonight. The young people were going to be in charge of the service tonight, and I understand that our very own Minister Makil Thames was supposed to bring the word of God tonight," the pastor said, turning to nod at a young man sitting in the pulpit.

The congregation began to clap and many of the young people began to whoop and cheer.

"For those of you who don't know," Elder Earl explained to the congregation, "Minister Makil is a saved young man, filled with the Holy Ghost, and he has been *anointed* to preach the Word of God. You only have to look out over the congregation at the many young people here to see that God is using him to draw young souls to Christ. He's a kind young man with a humble spirit and I thank God for him. And since he won't be speaking tonight as planned, I want him to come and have a few words. Say, 'Amen' for Minister Makil as he comes."

Zandy had begun to fidget. She'd been thoroughly enjoying the church service — watching everyone praise the Lord took her back to her childhood days when she'd praised the Lord, too — but now her dress was starting to get on her last nerve. She sat tugging at the dress' hem, which came shamefully high up her thighs. She placed her Bible over her lap, hoping it would help. The small Bible barely covered a single thigh.

I should've borrowed one of Sasha's sweaters, or something, to throw over my legs. The sound of applause snapped Zandy back to attention. She preened, as everyone else did, to see the young man who stood up in the pulpit and approached the rostrum with a Bible in his hand. He shook Elder Earl's hand in passing, laid his Bible on the rostrum, and stood poised before the congregation. His smile was almost shy, humble to be exact.

"Praise God, Saints," he said in a mild, tenor voice, just loud enough to be heard over the church.

"Praise God!" the congregation echoed.

"*Praise God!*" Zandy said with emphasis, her praise more for the young minister than for God. In a split second, she'd sized him up. Tall, basketball-player thin, hershey dark, and baby-faced handsome. *He gets an 'A' for looks.* Her eyes then scanned his clothing. Charcoal brown vest, matching pants, cream-colored shirt, and brown silk tie with soft yellow, orange, and beige prints. *And he gets an 'A+' for style.* She leaned over and whispered to Sasha without taking her eyes off the young minister. "Is he a preacher?"

"Yes," Sasha whispered back. " Didn't you hear what Elder Earl just said?"

Zandy ignored the question. "He's cute and *tall*. I like his style, too."

Bumping Zandy slightly with her elbow, Sasha whispered, "Zandy, you need to pay attention to the *Word* of God, not the *man* of God. I thought you didn't like guys anyway."

"I never told you any such thing. I like guys. I just don't love 'em. He looks like someone I'd like to get know."

"Did you forget that he's *saved?*"

"Shhhhhhhh," Zandy whispered back, smiling. "I'm trying to hear what he's saying. Pay attention," she said, pointing a finger toward the pulpit.

Sasha could do nothing but smile. She did as she was told and turned her eyes again to the young preacher in the pulpit.

The look on the young minister's face had become sincere, causing him to look older than his seventeen years. "I want to thank God for being the awesome, *awesome* God that He is," he said. "I thank Him for sending His Son, Jesus Christ, who endured the weight and pain of my sins on the cross that I might have life. And I especially want to thank God for saving me in my youth. There are many young people who really feel that they can't live a saved life." He shook his head slowly. "They're wrong. There are young people all over the world proclaiming their love for God, and they are living victorious lives in the Lord. And while there are many young people who *are* saved, there are countless young people who are not. They're lost to drugs, alcohol, sex, gangs, you name it.

"But God wants to save them, and if you're not saved," he said, peering out over the congregation, his eyes touching on some of the many young people in the church, "He wants to save you. He wants to heal your brokenness. He wants to deliver you from your addictions. He wants to have a relationship with you. It may seem like a crazy thing to say, but I *really* don't think young people know just how much God loves them and how much He wants them to know Him as the loving God He is. Young people need to know that God is not a myth or the figment of someone's imagination. He's very real, and He's waiting to be invited into their lives. That's where I and other saved young people come in. Our purpose is to reach those lost souls and share the love of God with them. For who can draw a young soul to Christ better than another young soul?

"If you're a young person in this room right now and you're not saved — it doesn't matter how young you are — I want to urge you to give your life to the Lord. Not only do we need you on the battlefield fighting to win souls for Christ, but I also guarantee you that once you give your life to the Lord, you will never be the same. Nothing compares to knowing the Lord. Nothing."

His eyes roamed the congregation that listened intently to his words. "I'm not even eighteen yet, and before the Lord saved me just over a year ago, I was into all kinds of illegal stuff — robbery, selling drugs, money laundering," he said, his voice quivering slightly. He swallowed hard, then cleared his throat. "Anything that would put money in my pocket, I did it. I was probably one of the wealthiest teenagers in this state, but I was living a dangerous life. One night, I sold drugs to an undercover cop. Just as I was taking payment for the drugs, it dawned on me that I was dealing with a cop. Like lightening, I started running. He fired shots at me left and right. I don't know how I got away, but I did, unharmed. I'd been shot and almost killed in a gang fight when I was fourteen, so I knew what bullets ripping into my flesh felt like. That night, after running from the police, I was shook up." Minister Makil's eyes filled with unshed tears. "I was scared to death. I cried for the first time since I was a young kid. All of a sudden, I was tired of the life I was living. I knew that I would eventually end up dead. I was supposed to have been dead *that night*, and I wasn't ready to die. I was too young to die. I went home that night and told my mother that I was through with the street life, that I was going to change.

I came here to church the next night, a Friday night, and I've been changing for the better ever since. My mother and my sister are sitting right over there," he said, pointing to a plump, petite woman and a young lady who looked so much like him, she had to be his twin sister. Both mother and sister wiped teary eyes with tissue as they listened to Minister Makil's testimony.

"Both of them can tell you that I was a real-life menace to society, and that no man could tame me. But when Jesus got a hold of me, He flipped my world upside down. When my mother and my sister saw how the Lord had changed my life, they gave their lives to the Lord, too. I praise God for saving them. I praise Him for saving *me* and for giving me what I had been missing.

"I never had a father in my life, and all my life, I was searching for my father's love. I didn't realize it at the time, but I was trying to fill a void in my life, a huge hole in my heart. All of that changed when I gave my life to the Lord. The love of God filled my heart and made me whole, and He became a Father to me. And the Lord also gave me a father in Elder Earl," he said, turning to look at the pastor in the pulpit, "and I thank Him for that."

Turning back to congregation, Minister Makil continued. "So, you see, it's my endeavor to share that same love of God that changed my life with every young person that I can. Yes, I'm concerned about adults being saved, too, but my calling is to reach lost young souls. I pray that each of you young people will give your life to the Lord and accept the calling He has on your life."

Minister Makil scanned the crowd and chuckled lightly. "Some of you here today don't have a choice in the matter. You're not ready to give your life to the Lord, not even thinking about being saved, but the Lord is about to change your life. You don't know it, but the Lord's got your name on His hit list and He's coming after *you*. He's about to upset your world, just like He did mine. I had no thoughts of getting saved when I did. But God saved me because He loves me, and because He has a work for me to do. A year ago, it was my time. Now it's your time. Some of you are coming to the Lord whether you like it or not. He's about to snatch you out of your sin and rearrange your life for the better. God has a work for you to do. He has a plan for your life. Accept His calling."

The congregation stood to its feet, clapping and cheering, as Minister Makil made his way back to his seat.

During the drive back to Sasha's place, Zandy talked non-stop. Sitting in the back seat of the car, she rambled on and on about the church service. "I just felt good in there today," she said. "I wanted to run and jump all over the place. But I couldn't, you know, because of my dress. But the Holy Ghost just didn't want to let me go. I'm ashamed to say that I really had to fight it off, because I didn't —"

"Him," Sasha interjected.

"Him what?" Zandy asked, leaning up toward the front seats.

"The Holy Ghost is a He," Sasha explained. "You said 'it'."

"Oh, that's right," Zandy said, excited. "I remember that now. The Father, the Son, and the Holy Ghost." She leaned over and tapped Tellis, who was sitting quietly in the front passenger's seat, on the shoulder. "You can't sneak nothing by Sasha — she *knows* her Bible."

"Stop saying that," Sasha said, frowning.

"Well, it's true," Zandy replied, undaunted.

Tellis looked at Sasha with interest. "Is that so?" he asked Zandy.

"Yes, it is," Zandy answered firmly.

Sasha groaned inwardly. She continued to drive, locking her eyes on her road. All of her life people had been trying to make her into a Bible scholar, a little missionary, and she'd thought that she'd gotten away from that when she'd left home. Evidently she hadn't.

And it's my own fault, she thought. *How can I expect people to forget my past life if I keep reminding them of it? Why can't I just keep my mouth closed?*

Zandy leaned back on the seat. "Anyway, I was about to cut up in there. Didn't you see me cut a little step, Sasha?"

"Mm-Hmm," Sasha mumbled absently.

"And I really enjoyed Minister Makil. He can minister to my needs *any time*."

"Zandy!" Sasha shouted, nailing Zandy with her eyes in the rearview mirror. "You ought to be ashamed of yourself. Lusting after the man of God!"

Tellis laughed, but said nothing.

"I know," Zandy snickered. "The devil must be losing his touch because God's gettin' all of the good ones"

Tellis nodded in agreement, fastening his laughing eyes on Sasha. "I know what you mean, Zandy."

Sasha ignored his admiring gaze. *If he only knew.*

"You're right, though, Sasha," Zandy acknowledged. "I need to do like Mae Mama used to do and tell that devil to *get behind me, Satan!*" She laughed out. "I really did enjoy his testimony, though," she said sincerely. "He said some very interesting things." She looked thoughtfully out the window. Huge magnolia trees blurred her vision as the car whizzed down the street. "He really got me to thinking."

"Me, too," Tellis agreed softly.

Sasha was irritated. The last thing she needed to hear was that her friends — the friends she needed to help her cross over to a new life — had been touched by the Word of God. She sighed with frustration. *At least neither of them gave their life to the Lord during the altar call.*

Chapter 9

*T*he wind jerked the branches of the large oak tree like they were mere twigs on a bush. Refusing to snap, the branches retaliated with ferocious swipes at the turbulent wind. Sasha lay in bed, surrounded by the dark of the night, and watched the struggle between wind and tree through the pane of her window.

The stormy scene reminded her of the vicious fight that had been taking place within her. Her desire to live a life outside of the church fought strongly against everything she'd ever been taught.

As far as she was concerned, though, the fight was over — her desires had triumphed with a knock-out victory. She refused to deny herself any longer. She'd spent all of her nineteen years denying herself, trying her best to please God. And what did that get her?

A dead mother, that's what it got me.

Didn't I do the things I was taught to do? Wasn't I faithful to You? Didn't I serve You?

Didn't I keep my head up high when kids whispered comments about me?

"She's *sanctified*," Sasha mimicked aloud. "She can't wear pants. She can't do *anything*."

I never let their sneers get me down. I was so proud to be saved, so proud to be a child of God.

But that wasn't enough, was it?

Why wasn't it enough? I don't understand.

Didn't I go to church every time the church doors opened? Didn't I spend hours studying my Bible? Didn't I fast and pray? Didn't I testify of Your goodness?

Still, it wasn't enough. It wasn't enough for You to answer my prayer.

Why wasn't it enough?

Didn't I remain faithful to the church when other young people left by the dozens? Didn't I abide by the rules of the church, regardless of how strict they were? Did I wear pants? Did I cut my hair? Did I wear make-up? Did I go to the movies? No! No! No! and No!

I didn't do any of those things. I wanted to please You.

But still, You let my mother die.

Sasha flipped her body over to lie on her stomach and slammed her head into the pillow. A grimace on her face, she mocked the teachings of her church. "God doesn't want you to cut your hair. Your hair is *your glory.* What woman in her right mind wants to cut off her glory?"

For all the good not cutting my hair did me, I could've cut my head bald, she thought derisively.

As far back as Sasha could remember, she'd never gotten the urge to cut her hair. Growing up, she'd seen a few cuts that might have looked attractive with her face, but she'd always been satisfied with the styles her long hair permitted her to wear. For her, not being able to get a haircut had never been an issue.

But it had been an issue for some of the other girls in her father's church.

Nashon instantly popped into Sasha's head. Nashon was fifteen when she asked one of her cousins to relax her long, thick hair. The cousin forgot to use a neutralizing shampoo, and Nashon's hair fell out by the handful. In the end, Nashon had to get a haircut to restore her damaged hair. Sasha had liked Nashon's shorter hairstyle, but the church hadn't liked it, at all.

One of the other young girls, begrudging Nashon's new hair-style, complained to her mother about it. The girl's mother then took it upon herself to complain to Sasha's father about it — if her daughter couldn't cut her hair, then Nashon shouldn't be getting hers cut, either. Trying to keep peace in his church, Sasha's father had asked one of the church mothers to take Nashon aside and talk to her about the importance of obeying the rules of the church. Afterwards, one missionary after another subtly threw off on Nashon's haircut during the lessons they taught during church services.

Even then, Sasha felt that Nashon, one of the young, dedicated members of the church, had been treated unfairly. Sasha had always respected the teachings of the church, but in her seventeen-year old eyes, the church was stripping Nashon's faith because she'd gotten a very much-needed haircut. Sasha had told her father that no one had even stopped to consider why Nashon had gotten her hair cut in the first place, that the church had just criticized her and condemned her to Hell. It wasn't right, she'd said. Was Nashon supposed to walk around with her head messed up just to remain in line with the church's teaching against women getting their hair cut? Sasha hadn't thought so. If a woman's hair is her glory, she'd said in Nashon's favor, then a woman should do whatever is necessary to make her hair *look* like it's her glory, even if it meant cutting it. The Bible, she'd argued, says that a woman's hair is her glory — it never said that she shouldn't cut it.

Her father had said that he understood her viewpoint, but as far as Sasha could tell, nothing changed. The church continued to rebuke and chastise anyone who stepped outside of its rigid doctrinal teachings.

The church talked about all that you couldn't do more than they talked about Jesus, she thought, her lips curling into a sneer. *They were just waiting for someone to break one of their rules.*

Sasha was sure that no one in the church had noticed the damaged ends she'd clipped from her relaxed hair. She was about to graduate from high school at the time and well on her way to being dead tired of the church's rules and regulations. Sick of the split ends that were causing her hair to shed, she'd marched into the bathroom, scissors in hand, and began to defiantly clip off the dead ends of her hair. When she'd finished, the length of her hair was one inch shorter. Turning from the mirror, she'd strutted straight to her father's study and told him what she'd done and why.

Her father had sat at his desk and looked at her hair, in wild disarray from the unprofessional trimming. Then he'd looked her directly in the eyes.

Defiant when she'd first entered the study, Sasha felt a sliver of fear run up her spine at her father's steady gaze and dead silence. With a little less boldness, she'd explained again why she'd clipped her ends.

Her father's response had surprised her. "Everyday you're looking more and more like your mother," he'd said, smiling. "Did you forget that we were going out for dinner?" When Sasha had numbly shook her head, no, he'd told her to hurry up and do something with her head so that they could leave.

Sasha had turned like a zombie and walked out of her father's study. She'd never understood her father's nonchalant response. She'd assumed it was because he'd been really missing her mother. Whatever the reason, she was happy that he hadn't yelled at her. Her father didn't get mad often, but when he did, it wasn't a pretty sight.

Sasha had known that, as the pastor's daughter, she was more subject to scrutiny than any other young person in the church and she'd been prepared to defend herself if anyone in the church confronted her about her clipped ends. But no one had said anything. No one had noticed the difference in her hair.

It's a good thing, too, she thought angrily. *I would've given them a piece of my mind.*

Her mother's death had been the last straw. Up until then, she'd accepted whatever the church taught. After her mother's death, she didn't care what the church taught or thought. She'd been determined to leave and do her own thing.

She'd done it, too. She'd left her father's church and she was putting its teachings behind her. Moving on had been more difficult than she'd expected, but she was determined to reach her goal. She'd get church and God out of her system, if it were the last thing she did.

And I'm going to be with Tellis, too. Nothing and no one will stop me.

All of the contempt and cynicism she'd been feeling about the church left at the thought of Tellis. He'd promised that they would have a heart-to-heart talk after church, and they had. But not before he'd given her the kiss of her lifetime. It was better than the one before. She vividly recalled how he'd grabbed her in a tight embrace as soon as Zandy had walked out the door and said, "I thought she'd never leave." He'd kissed her with so much passion, she'd been dizzy with emotion. That same emotion gripped her now. *Tellis might have said that we should take things slow and get to know each other as friends first, but his kiss said that we're already past the friendship stage.*

Smiling broadly, Sasha wrapped her arms around the pillow, a poor substitute for her soft, warm Tellis. He was all she thought about until sleep crept in and stole her thoughts, more than one hour later.

"I was wondering if you were going to drop in to see me," Dr. Avery said, pointing a well manicured finger to the leather chair that sat in front of her large, mahogany desk. "Have a seat," she said. She unbuttoned the thigh-length jacket of her brown, wool suit before sitting down. "How are things with you?" she asked, smiling at Sasha.

"Pretty good, I guess," Sasha responded, settling down in the chair. She rubbed her neck.

"Problem with your neck?"

"Hmm?" Sasha asked absently. "Oh, no, my neck is okay. I just have a slight crook in it."

The professor's eyes perused Sasha's face. "Otherwise, you're feeling better?"

Sasha didn't understand the intensity of her instructor's gaze. "Excuse me?" she asked.

"Aleczandria said that you missed class last week because you weren't feeling well."

Sasha smiled. "I know, but I told you on Friday that I was okay. I was just a little tired, that's all."

Dr. Avery continued to study Sasha. "So, what is it that has you so tired, young lady?" she asked. "So tired that you'd miss one of *my* classes."

"You know," Sasha said, trying hard not to squirm in her seat. "The same old stuff — studying late, etcetera, etcetera."

Dr. Avery raised a thinly arched eyebrow. "Really? Well, I already know about your study habits, so tell me about the etcetera, etcetera part."

Sasha was used to Dr. Avery's concern. She wasn't used to the intense scrutiny, though. She began to feel uneasy. "There's nothing to tell. I just need to start going to bed a little earlier."

Dr. Avery leaned back in the leather, high-back chair and crossed her arms and legs all in one motion. She studied her student, her eyes speaking what her mouth didn't say.

"What?" Sasha asked peevishly. "Why are you looking at me like that?"

Dr. Avery shook her head slightly.

"You look like you don't believe me."

"How *could* you tell?" Dr. Avery asked.

"I can see it in your eyes."

"And I can see in your eyes that you're not telling me the whole truth." Pointing at Sasha's head, the instructor asked, "Who put your hair in that ponytail?"

Sasha had slept fitfully, ruining her sleek hairstyle. After brushing her hair out, a quick ponytail was all she could manage before rushing out for class. She raked a whimsical hand over her unruly head. "I did."

"I see," Dr. Avery said. "I was thinking you'd let the Rugrats do it. I guess they didn't dress you, either?"

Sasha glanced down at the washed out cotton shirt that used to be a deep pink and the long, faded blue jean skirt she wore. She shook her head, no.

"Well, I have been totally off base." Dr. Avery shook her slowly with a look of feigned confusion. "By the way you've been looking the past couple of weeks, I was sure that you'd hired the Rugrats as your personal hair stylists and wardrobe assistants. And don't think I haven't noticed how you've been dragging into class and dragging out lately, either." Dr. Avery's accusing gaze fell to Sasha's clothes. "Look at you," she chastised gently. "Your hair is a mess and you look like you dressed in the dark. I thought I knew what happened to my beautiful, immaculately dressed student, but I was wrong. The Rugrats are not the culprits. And since I evidently don't have a clue as to what has happened to the real Sasha, why don't you fill me in with the truth."

Sasha was not offended by Dr. Avery's words. She grinned at the professor. "You make me sound like a bag lady."

"That's because you look like one."

"It took me a while to fall asleep last night. I was tired when I got up this morning, and I didn't feel like dressing up today. I wanted to be comfortable, so I threw on some comfortable clothes." When Dr. Avery shook her head and murmured under her breath, Sasha added, "It's true that I've been in a little bit of a slump lately, but that's because I've been swamped with class work . . . and stuff. But everything is better now." Sasha's eyes drifted from Dr. Avery's to the floor. She wondered whether she should tell the professor about the "stuff" that was going on in her life.

Dr. Avery spoke before Sasha could form a decision. "I called your father."

Sasha went rigid in her chair. Her bulging eyes questioned Dr. Avery.

It was Dr. Avery's turn to grin. "Don't look at me like that. I didn't say anything to your father about your slow demise. I was only making sure that he was not the cause of it. I was glad to hear that he's doing quite well." Seeing that Sasha continued to look uneasy, she added, "I didn't even talk about you, except to say that you're doing very well in my class."

"Well, what *did* you talk about?" Sasha asked, not quite ready to believe Dr. Avery.

"Pearson, and how he's doing."

"Pearson?!" Sasha asked, surprised. "Since when did you start calling my father by his first name?"

Dr. Avery smiled slowly. "Your father said that 'Elder Lindsey' was too formal, seeing that I am the instructor and very dear friend of his daughter. He said that I should call him Pearson. And," she added, "I told him to call me Kinsari."

Dr. Avery's real name — Theola — slid through Sasha's mind. Any other time, she would have teased the instructor about the name, but at the moment, she didn't care what her name was. "Is something going on between you and my father?" she asked, her look skeptical.

"No."

Sasha's eyes searched Dr. Avery's pretty, dark-skinned face. It was blank. "Are you sure?" she asked.

Dr. Avery pulled her chair closer to the desk. She reached down and picked up a gold-plated letter opener and a large envelope. She ripped the envelope open and pulled out its content. "Your father is a preacher, a man of God," she said, her eyes on the papers.

"That doesn't answer my question."

"Yes, it does," Dr Avery said, shuffling through the papers. "What would a preacher do with me? Your father needs a nice, gentle, soft-spoken woman by his side." She chuckled lightly, lifting a steady gaze to Sasha. "I'm sure that I'm much too wild and spicy for the likes of your father."

Sasha looked at Dr. Avery and felt a warmness infuse her insides. She really liked this strikingly chic and widely celebrated instructor who had befriended her when she was a mere rookie on campus. She admired the professor's flawless appearance – the head full of dreadlocks that fell just below her jawbone, the carefully made up face that enhanced her undeniable, dark beauty, and the narrowed, up-turned eyes that shone bright with vivacity, compassion, and the wisdom of her forty-four years.

She'd probably make a great stepmother, Sasha mused.

"Hello-o-o," Dr. Avery crooned, tapping the letter opener on the desk.

Sasha's eyes blinked rapidly.

"Are you alright?" the professor asked.

"Yes," Sasha replied, rubbing her stiff neck again. "I guess I got lost in thought."

Dr. Avery studied Sasha. "I guess you did. I thought I was going to have to break my letter opener to get you back."

Sasha smiled warmly at the instructor. "I'm sorry, Dr. Avery. What were you saying?"

Dr. Avery pushed her chair back, stood, and walked around the desk to where Sasha sat. She perched a slim hip on the desk. "That crook in your neck still seems to be bothering you. Why don't you ask Tellis to massage it out for you."

Sasha's mouth dropped open.

Dr. Avery had been watching closely for Sasha's reaction. She stood, smiling down at Sasha. "It's about time you know that on this campus, I'm like God — I know everything." She pulled Sasha to her feet and embraced her. "Bring Tellis to my house for dinner. Thursday night. Seven-thirty. Don't be late."

Sasha drove home in a daze. It seemed that someone had been talking to Dr. Avery about her. *Who would be talking to Dr. Avery about me?*

Zandy, who else?

Sasha was almost positive that if Zandy had spoken to Dr. Avery about her, it could only have been out of concern. But still, Sasha's business was Sasha's business, and no one else's. She'd confided in Zandy because Zandy said she wouldn't tell anyone. Dr. Avery was a dear friend, and Sasha had to admit that she was growing very fond of the instructor. That, however, did not give Zandy the right to talk to their instructor about her love life.

Zandy had to have said something. How else would Dr. Avery have known about Tellis?

Zandy told me that she wasn't a gossiper. She lied to me.

Unmitigated anger caused Sasha's feet to jam the gas pedal and her Honda Accord quickly excelled to five miles over the speed limit. Normally not one to speed, she didn't care if she got a ticket this time. She was in a rush to get home, and she would be calling Zandy as soon as she got there, too. She gave the gas pedal another push and the car sped down the busy two-lane street.

The stoplight just ahead of her turned red, and it was by the sheer grace of God that she looked up in time to avoid going through it. Her car came to a screeching halt, just beyond the white pedestrian line.

Sasha's fingers tapped the steering wheel as she waited impatiently for the light to change. "I refuse to take Tellis over there so she can pry into my business some more," she mumbled. "If she wants to find out about what's going on with me and Tellis, let her find out like she does everything else, from blabbermouth!"

I wish people would just stay out of my business!

The blaring horn from the car behind brought Sasha out of her reverie. The light had turned green. Sasha glared at the driver through her rear-view mirror before pressing heavily on the gas and speeding off again.

She was mad enough to hurt somebody.

Chapter 10

*T*he telephone was ringing when Sasha threw open her front door. She stalked across the room and snatched up the receiver, daring it to be Zandy on the other end. "Hello," she growled through clenched teeth.

"Hi, Lovely."

It was her father. He had started calling her by that nickname many years ago. The name still had a way of melting her heart. Immediately, the steam went out of her and tears pricked her eyes. "Hi, Daddy," she whimpered.

"Are you alright, baby?" Her father asked, his voice deepening with concern.

Now was not the time to have her father overly concerned about her. The last thing she needed was for him to come down on one of his just-wanted-to-make-sure-you-were-okay visits.

Sasha steadied her voice. "I'm fine, Daddy. I'm just coming in from class, had a tiring day." She dropped her keys at the base of the phone and fell onto the sofa.

"You're not working too hard, are you?"

"No, Daddy, I'm not working too hard. How are things with you?"

"Good. Good. God is just doing great things at the church."

Sasha smiled. Her father never seemed to be able to separate his own welfare from that of the church.

"During service last night," he continued, excited, "Brother and Sister Kaley's son was filled with the Holy Ghost!" His voice rumbled with laughter. "I tell you, it was a sight to see. God's glory was all over that young man."

Sasha's eyebrows shot up. "*Jo-Jo* was filled with the Holy Ghost?" Sasha couldn't believe it. Jo-Jo had been one of her high school's most frightening students. Whenever he went to school, that is. Only nineteen, he'd been in and out of juvenile institutions for everything from car jacking to aggravated assault.

"Yes, Jo-Jo," her father confirmed. "Just last month, I called him up during service to pray with him, and the young man looked at me like he wanted to pound my face in." Elder Lindsey chuckled. "I think I embarrassed him. I prayed for him and told him that we loved him and to keep on coming to church. Well, he kept coming and last night the Spirit of the Lord fell on the young man after I preached, and he began to speak in tongues. We all began to praise God, including Brother and Sister Kaley. Sister Kaley did more crying than anything. I tell you, it was enough to bring tears to a dead man's eyes. That old devil lost another one. Praise God! Glory to His name!"

There was never a time or place when her father was not subject to praise God, and nothing made him praise God more than a soul being saved. "That's good news, Daddy."

"It is, Lovely. Hallelujah! It's very good news."

"Sounds like the church is doing well." Sasha could hear the dryness in her words as she spoke them. She hoped her father hadn't heard it.

He hadn't. "The church is doing fine, Lovely." He coughed, clearing his throat. "I've put Elder Simmons in complete charge of church matters for a while."

Sasha jerked forward on the sofa. "Why, Daddy?" she asked fearfully. "You're not sick or anything, are you?"

"No-o-o," he quickly assured her. "I'm fine."

Elder Simmons was the Assistant Pastor of her father's church. He'd been her father's right hand man for a number of years, and her father loved him dearly. But never had he given Elder Simmons complete reign of the church. Her father was too wrapped up in every aspect of the church to do that. Something had to be wrong. "Then why did you put Elder Simmons in charge?"

"Well, I've been troubled in my spirit lately about some things concerning the church, and I've decided to take some time off to shut in and seek God about it. I sense in my spirit that God wants to take the church to another level. I don't fully understand the direction God is leading me, but I know that if I seek Him, He'll give me a vision concerning the church."

"Where are you going?"

"Nowhere. I'll be here at the house. Unless the Lord leads me to do otherwise."

"For how long?"

"How long will I shut in?"

"Yes."

"As long as it takes, Lovely. Until I hear from the Lord."

"You won't be fasting the whole time, will you, Daddy?"

"I expect to be fasting a large portion of the time, yes." He chuckled. "But I'll make sure that I don't waste away."

Sasha didn't particularly like it when her father went on extended fasts. He always lost so much weight while fasting, and when he did eat, he didn't eat much. His tall, lean frame only became more lean, skinny almost. If she were there, she could at least prepare hearty, hot meals for the times he did eat. She wanted to tell him not to do it, to just shut in and pray, but skip the fasting.

That's like telling the sun not to shine, she thought. *He'll never listen to me.*

"Alright, Daddy, but please make sure you don't push yourself too hard. Okay?"

"I won't, Lovely. I'll be fine." He laughed. "You can always come home and check on me. I miss you. I'm still not used to you being away from home."

"I miss you, too. Very much. It won't be long before I'm home again. Thanksgiving is just around the corner."

"I know, and I can't wait to see you."

"And when I see you," Sasha playfully scolded, "I want you to be looking as good and handsome as you did when I was at home for the summer." Her father had been in tip-top shape, especially for a forty-seven year old. When they'd gone out together, his lean physique and chiseled features had attracted more attention from women than he ever wanted to receive. He'd found it embarrassing. "How else am I going to get you married off to another lady as beautiful as Mom?" she teased. Instantly, an image of Dr. Avery appeared in her mind. Thinking that Dr. Avery may not be a good stepmother after all, Sasha gave the image a hard mental kick out of her head. "I don't like you being alone all the time," she said to her father. "You need a companion. You need someone to make sure you're coordinating your clothes right."

Elder Lindsey laughed, then said, "Did you receive the package I mailed to you?"

Whenever she got on the subject of remarriage, her father always changed it. "Yes, I received the check," she answered. "I didn't need it, you know."

"Buy yourself something nice."

"No, I'm going to buy you something nice."

Elder Lindsey knew it was futile to try and dissuade his daughter. He was always receiving one thoughtful gift after another from her in the mail. "Well, I should let you go now. I'm sure you have some studying to do."

This was the moment Sasha dreaded — the moment of good-byes. Her father never said good-bye without having prayer with her first. Before her mother's death, she'd relished their family prayer times, especially when it was her turn to lead prayer. Prayer had been an integral part of her own daily walk with the Lord, too. She'd taken everything to God in prayer.

But that was then. Now, when she closed her eyes to attempt to pray, she only saw the face of her dead mother. She had no real desire to pray anymore. In spite of the many things she was thankful for, she could never bring herself to tell God. Angry words and accusations were all she had for Him. And she didn't consider that praying. Blasphemy was probably more like it.

The lack of a prayer life didn't condemn her any longer. The guilt was all gone. That is, until she had to pray with her father. When it was her turn to lead prayer, she barely managed to get through it, mumbling and stumbling her way through from beginning to end. It was obvious that her prayer life was suffering substantially. Her father would have to be deaf, dumb, and stupid to not know it. And she knew that he was neither. But still, he continued to ask her to lead prayer. She wished he would just stop. But she knew that he wouldn't, so she waited, cringed and breathless, to hear the dreaded words from her father, because this time was her time to lead prayer.

She didn't have to wait long. "Let's have prayer, Lovely, before you go."

Sasha's chin drooped down to her chest. She closed her eyes and tried to conjure up a sweet and simple prayer that she could zoom through without stumbling. Maybe she could recite the Lord's Prayer and be done with it.

"I'll lead prayer today," her father said.

Sasha almost slid off the sofa in relief. She liked it much better when her father prayed. All she had to do was throw in an occasional "Yes, Lord" here and a "Thank you, Lord" there. Prayer was a breeze when her father was doing the praying.

Like always, Sasha was the center of her father's prayers. She closed her eyes and listened as he prayed for God to shield her from the snares of the Enemy and to "bind the Enemy on every hand" in his daughter's life. He even rebuked the Enemy, himself, telling him that he couldn't have his daughter, that she was a highly favored and precious child of God. His daughter, he kept repeating, belonged to God. He then asked God to strengthen her in her walk with Him, to increase her faith, to keep her in good health, and to bless her in her studies.

"And, Father," he said, ending the prayer, "I thank You for the angels that you have encamped around my daughter, to protect and guide her. In Jesus' name we pray, Amen."

"Amen," Sasha said.

"Well, baby, I'll let you go now. I could talk to you all day, but I know you have work to do. I love you, and I'll talk to you very soon."

Sasha told her father that she loved him, too, and promised to call him in a few days. As soon as she placed the receiver on the hook, fresh tears sprang into her eyes. Hearing her father's voice always made her feel good, but his prayers made her feel like a devious monster.

Sasha was restless and bored. Tellis had just called to say that he'd be working with Dr. Omwe this evening. He wasn't sure if he'd be able to come by, but he'd call her when he made it home. She was disappointed. He usually spent his Monday evenings with her, and this was one Monday she needed him with her, to hold her. His comforting arms would've helped to relax the edge off of her nerves.

If Zandy hadn't told all of her business to Dr. Avery, Sasha would call her. She'd decided against calling Zandy earlier, figuring that talking to her might make the situation worse. Sasha wasn't as mad at Zandy as she had been earlier, but she was still too ticked off to talk to her. Calling her was out of the question.

I need to buckle down and work on that C program, she told herself.

She still hadn't found the bug in the program, and it was due this Friday. But she just didn't have the concentration required for the program. The seven-page program would only agitate her more.

She rolled from her prostrate position on the bed to her feet. *At least Tellis had liked the idea of having dinner with Dr. Avery,* she thought as she walked down the short hall of her apartment. *That was one good thing he said, if nothing else.* Stopping in the doorway of her study, she leaned into the doorjamb. She loved this room because it was so different from the soft pastel colors that decorated the rest of her apartment. Almost everything in this room was black. Her eyes took in the black IBM computer, the black laserjet printer, and the large, black desk they both sat on. The tall bookcase filled with all sorts of books was black. The four-drawer file cabinet was black. The desk lamp was black, as well as the two-line phone that rested beside it.

Her eyes swept over the white walls covered with artwork colorfully bedecked with vibrant oranges, yellows, reds, and blues. A mixture of the same colors danced with splashes of black in the large, designer rug that lay in the middle of the white carpeted floor. The colors were electrifying. And whenever she walked into the room, their radiating warmth would quickly embrace her and prodigiously ease all worries from her troubled mind.

She stepped into the room. Hugging herself, she closed her eyes and let the peacefulness of the room infuse her. She thought back on the time when she'd just moved into the apartment and how her father had walked through every room praying, calling forth God's spirit of love, protection and peace. She remembered how he'd prayed longer in this room, consecrating it as her room of prayer and meditation. She quickly opened her eyes, dismissing the thought. She much preferred the idea of the stimulating colors being behind the room's tranquility.

She walked over to the desk and picked up a small book. It was her thesaurus. She'd used it to write the paper for Dr. Avery. She sighed deeply. She couldn't understand why she'd been so upset with Dr. Avery earlier. It wasn't as if she didn't occasionally invite Sasha over for dinner. She and Sasha dined together at least once every month or so. A couple of those dinners had even been at Sasha's apartment. Naturally, she would want to invite

Tellis over, too. She'd have to call Dr. Avery and apologize for angrily stalking away from her office as she had.

The thesaurus in hand, Sasha walked over to the bookshelf and slid the book into its slot. Near the bookshelf was a half wall of empty space. Her keyboard used to be there. She walked to stand in the space. Raising her hand, she gently touched the small tambourine and violin-sized guitar she'd mounted on the wall just above the keyboard. Up until a few months ago, this small space had been her music corner. This was where she'd come to sing and create songs. This was where she'd found release in the musical notes she'd played day after day for hours on end.

When she'd returned for classes this semester, she hadn't enjoyed the keyboard as much. Every note she'd played and every word she'd sang was tied to spiritual songs she'd learned or written before, songs she preferred to forget. As much as she'd tried to sing about finding sweet love or loving the man of her dreams — anything but the love of God — she'd hit a brick wall. She'd taken the keyboard down and put it away.

Sasha walked over to the study's closet door and opened it. The huge, leather keyboard case lay on the floor of the closet as if calmly waiting for the day she'd return for it. Why she suddenly felt compelled to pull out the keyboard, she didn't know, but she reached in and gripped the heavy case by its handle and dragged it out of the closet. She opened the case and within minutes had the Yamaha keyboard back in its original place, hooked up and ready to go. She pushed the power button. The panel lit up with a myriad of features. Her small fingers raced over the keys as she played her customary warm-up scales. It was like riding a bike. Her fingers never forgot the feel of the keys.

The scales always reminded Sasha of her mother. It was she who was Sasha's first piano instructor. At first, Sasha had hated piano practice, but it was one of those things she'd never complained outwardly about for fear of displeasing her parents. But within six months of sitting down at the piano for the first time at the age of eight, her once clumsy fingers had become one with the piano keys. Playing, then, was no longer a chore, but a gift.

By age eleven, Sasha had required teaching more advanced than her mother could provide. It was then that she began piano lessons with the incomparable Mr. Johnny Green, the fifty-two year old multi-instrumental musician. He skillfully played the piano, the saxophone, the trombone, and the guitar. But the piano was his favorite.

The things Mr. Green could do with a piano were almost sinful, she thought, shaking her head.

His high-energy style of playing was eclectic — fusing jazz, blues, gospel and classical rhythms — and mind-boggling. Her eyes mesmerized by the alacrity of his fingers, the eleven-year old Sasha came to the sudden realization that she was only a beginner, with a long way to go. He'd convinced her that pianos could talk, and she wanted to learn their language.

Under his tutelage, she developed into a masterful piano player. The proof of her mastery saturated the den of her parent's home in the form of first-place ribbons and trophies. In her junior year of high school, she'd been rigorously training with Mr. Green and one of his equally talented peers for a highly competitive international competition. She'd practiced relentlessly, determined to place among the top three performers of the competition. But when her mother died, she'd lost all interest in the competition.

Sasha's hands fell flat on the keys, bringing her reminiscing to an abrupt halt. *This keyboard's going right back in the closet.* She reached over to power it off, but the chiming of the doorbell distracted her.

Who could that be? she wondered, making her way quickly to the front door. *Maybe Tellis was able to come over after all.*

A smile on her face, she stood on the tip of her toes and looked through the peephole. It was Zandy. Sasha stepped away from the door, her smile gone. She thought seriously about not answering the door at all, but Zandy pressed and held the doorbell like someone was chasing her. Sasha unlocked the door and opened it. Placing her body in the small opening, she looked at Zandy with void eyes.

"Hey, girl," Zandy said, strolling in, almost pushing Sasha out of the way. "I saw your car outside, so I knew you were here. What took you so long? I rang the doorbell this time like you told me to. Aren't you proud of me?" she asked happily.

Without responding, Sasha closed the door and walked past Zandy to the sofa. Picking up the remote control, she flicked on the television and sat down.

Zandy walked over to Sasha, her forehead knotted in a frown. "Excuse me, but did I miss something? Is this the type of greeting I get when I drop by to see a friend?"

"When you come by uninvited, yes." Sasha answered dully, her eyes focused on the television.

"Granted, I should've called first," Zandy said, grinning sheepishly and playfully flipping the long hair falling from Sasha's ponytail. "But you know how bad I am about doing things at the spur of the moment."

Sasha jerked her head away.

Zandy's grin faded. "Okay, so this is *not* about me coming over without calling first. What is it about, then?" She waited for Sasha to answer her. When no answer was given, she moved to stand directly in Sasha's line of vision, blocking her view of the television. Crossing her arms, Zandy began to tap her foot. She stared down at Sasha as if she had all the time in the world.

Sasha thought about waiting Zandy out. *If I don't say anything, maybe she'll just leave.*

"I'm not leaving here until you tell me what's going on," Zandy said firmly, still tapping her foot.

Sasha knew she meant it. "I went by to see Dr. Avery today," she said flatly, as if her statement explained everything.

"*And?*"

Exasperated, Sasha turned hard eyes on Zandy. Going straight to the heart of the matter, she said, "Evidently you two have been discussing my relationship with Tellis. And I don't appreciate it."

Zandy's foot went still. "What?!" she exclaimed.

Sasha just looked at her. *You must think I was born last night,* her eyes said.

"What are you talking about, Sasha? I haven't been talking to Dr. Avery, and no one else, about you and Tellis."

"Well, how else would she know about us?"

"I don't know. All I know is that I haven't told her anything. I told you, whatever you said to me would remain with me. Is that why you're acting like you got a stick up your rear end? You think I talked to Dr. Avery about you and Tellis? Did she tell you that?"

"No, not real-ly," Sasha answered, her voice faltering.

"Well, then, what made you think I did?"

Sasha eyes pleaded with Zandy for understanding. "I don't know. She started asking me all of these questions about why I was looking all washed out and why I was . . . why I was . . . she called my father!"

Zandy hands went up like she was a traffic cop. "Hold up. I'm confused. What are we talking about here? Me talking to Dr. Avery, you talking to Dr. Avery, or Dr. Avery talking to your father?"

Sasha threw the remote control on the sofa and gripped the sides of her head with both hands. Massaging her temples, she said, "I'm confused, too. What I was trying to say is that while Dr. Avery was asking me tons of questions about why I've been looking so down and out lately, she mentioned that she'd called my father."

"Called him for what?"

"Just to make sure that he was doing fine and to make sure that he wasn't the reason for my *slow demise,* as she put it."

"But what made you think that I talked to her about you and Tellis?"

"She told me to get him to massage the crook out of my neck."

Zandy frowned. "*And?*"

"And she invited us over for dinner."

"Listen to me closely, Sasha. I'll talk *very* slowly. I want you to tell me what happened to make you think that I told Dr. Avery something about you and Tellis."

Sasha felt like an idiot. "I told you."

"That's it?! She mentioned a crooked neck and dinner, and you got mad at me?!"

Sasha's eyes begged for forgiveness. "I'm sorry."

Zandy dropped down on the sofa, close beside Sasha. "Dr. Avery probably saw you and Tellis together somewhere or heard some tidbit about you two — probably from one of those jealous skeezers on campus who wished she had him — and she was just trying to get the scoop right from the horse's mouth. Did you give her the cold shoulder like you did me?"

"No. To tell you the truth, I didn't know I was so angry until I was leaving her office. I was too busy daydreaming about her being my stepmother," Sasha added thoughtlessly.

Zandy jerked forward. "Your *stepmother?!*"

Sasha raised a hand to calm Zandy. "It's not what you think, so you can stop those ears of yours from twitching."

Zandy tentatively touched an ear and leaned back. "What am I supposed to think when you're fantasizing about Dr. Avery as a mother?"

"Nothing," Sasha answered, then returned to her original train of thought. "When she first mentioned Tellis, it was like she was teasing me, telling me that she knew my secret. I know now that I overreacted, but I left her office in a huff. On the way to my car, my mind starting racing and I started to put two and two together—"

"And came up with sixteen," Zandy interjected.

"The more I thought about all that I shared with you, the angrier I became," Sasha continued. A look of confusion clouded her features. "It was like I was out of control. I wanted to hit somebody—"

"Dr. Avery," Zandy interrupted once again. "I know at the time you thought you wanted to hit me, but it was that meddling woman you really wanted to hit."

Sasha turned somber eyes toward Zandy. "I'm serious, Zandy. Even if what I was thinking about you was true, I should never have gotten so angry and so . . . so . . . cocky. Many people have done things that I didn't like in the past, but I never got *that* angry with any of them. I don't usually act like that. I'm not the temperamental type."

Zandy obviously didn't feel that this was the time for Sasha to fall into a state of melancholy because she continued to be mischievous. "You know, I'm glad *you* said it and not me, because I happen to agree with you. A few minutes ago you wanted to scratch my eyes out, and I couldn't understand it, either. You're normally so *sweet* and so *kind*."

Sasha knew Zandy was teasing her, but she really wasn't in the mood for it. She rolled her eyes upward. "This is serious, Zandy. I don't like the person I'm becoming."

Zandy raised a hand, as if to defend herself. "No, don't misunderstand me. You're right. This *is* serious. *Real* serious," she said, standing to her feet. Her tone became intentionally proper and contemplative. "So I think that, right here and right now, we need to get to the bottom of this. We need to find out what's behind this impetuous change that has overtaken you and has caused you to become so angry and deranged and furious and paranoid and just down right *non compos mentis* — that's Latin for crazy."

Sasha crossed her arms and tightened her lips. She refused to join Zandy in her folly.

Zandy paced the floor, her eyes squinted in deep thought. "It's very important that we get to the bottom of this before something happens and you crack up — that's a psychological term — and kill somebody. Aha!" she said, whirling around to face

Sasha with a gleam in her eyes. "A suitable approach may be to begin by first eliminating what definitely is *not* the cause of your problem."

Sasha smirked and tightened her crossed arms. She fastened her eyes to the television screen, trying to tune Zandy out.

"Well, it looks like I'm going to have to figure this one out by myself." Undaunted, Zandy continued to pace. "I have got to figure out why your behavior patterns are changing so drastically." Suddenly, she stopped and turned toward Sasha. With exaggerated sincerity she said, "It can't be because you ain't gettin' none, because you ain't never had none."

Zandy's words slowly registered in Sasha's ears and her eyes grew as big as saucers. Pointing an accusing finger at Zandy, she spluttered, "You . . . ought . . . to be . . . ashamed!"

"What?" Zandy asked, looking as innocent as a two-year old.

Sasha blushed profusely. "You know exactly what I'm talking about!" she accused and picked up a pillow from the sofa and threw it at Zandy. She missed. Frowning, she lunged at Zandy, but Zandy moved quickly out of the way.

"What did I say?" Zandy asked innocently, standing safely on the other side of the sofa. "It's a well known fact that once you've had sex and go an extended period of time without sex, you can go mental! I thought you knew!" The veneer of sincerity that Zandy had donned gave way to boiling laughter.

"That's not true, and it's not funny, either!" Sasha started to laugh, despite herself. She threw another pillow at Zandy, who deftly dodged its blow as well.

"It *is* true, too! It's on page one of my psychology book!"

"No, it's not!" Sasha refuted and ran around the sofa toward Zandy.

Zandy, roaring with laughter, dodged Sasha and ran down the hall and into the study. Just as Sasha was approaching, she tried to slam the door closed.

Zandy wasn't quick enough. Sasha burst through the door and crashed into Zandy, toppling them both to the floor.

"That's not true!" Sasha still challenged

"Yes, it is!" Zandy yelled.

They both began to laugh so hard, tears rolled down their cheeks. A full five minutes later, they were still sprawled on the floor, exhausted from simply too much laughing.

Sasha sat stunned at her keyboard. "You didn't tell me you could sing like that!" she accused Zandy. "I heard you singing a little bit in church, but . . . wow!"

Zandy had just finished crooning her own jazzed up version of "This Little Light of Mine." The room still reverberated with the colorful sounds of her high-pitched voice.

"*You* didn't tell me you could play like *that!*" Zandy quickly countered, thrusting a finger down at the keyboard. Sasha had skillfully played along as she sang, instinctively knowing when to fade in and out. "You have a great ear."

Sasha shrugged off the compliment.

"I don't remember seeing this keyboard in here before," Zandy said. "Did you just get it or something?"

"No," Sasha answered. Casually, she began to play a one-hand melody on the keyboard. "It was in the closet."

Zandy gave Sasha a playful shove as she sat down beside her. "I wish I could play," she said. "I'm jealous." She watched in fascination as Sasha's fingers whizzed over the keys. "I bet you can blow, too."

"I do sing, but *you* blow."

"Let me hear you sing."

Sasha brought the melody to a sudden end. "Maybe some other time. I'm not up to it right now. Besides," she smiled at Zandy, "my singing pales in comparison to yours."

Zandy ignored the compliment. "What-*ever*, Sasha. I know you can sing. I can tell by lookin' at you. You're always so modest."

"You can't tell if a person can sing just by looking at them."

"I know *you* can sing." She flicked Sasha's ponytail again. "C'mon, sing me a song. I'll play for you, like you did for me."

"You play the keyboard, too?" Sasha asked, excited.

"Not a lick. But I'll try if it'll get you to singing."

"It's been a long time since I've sung, and I don't really feel like singing right now."

"Sasha, I know that I teased you quite a bit tonight, but I wasn't trying to be insensitive. You were upset and I just wanted to sort of, you know, lift up your spirits a little bit."

Sasha nodded her head. "I know."

"I really should be mad at you for thinking that I would go talking to Dr. Avery about your personal business. I wouldn't do that, even though I know that she has a genuine concern for you."

"Thanks for being so understanding. You had every right to be upset with me."

"You gotta do something worse than throw a few accusations to get me mad at you. If you can forgive me for teasing you, I can forgive you for getting upset."

The two embraced warmly.

"Zandy, what you said earlier — you know, about going without sex — that's not true, is it?"

"I know you don't believe me, but it's true. It's one of the first things I learned in my psychology class. Studies have shown that sixty-nine percent of patients in mental hospitals are there because they were sexually active at one time and then became celibate. Without sex, they just went crazy. It's in my book. I'll bring it with me the next time I come over and you can read it for yourself."

Sasha shook her head sadly, her eyes so wide she looked scared.

Zandy's lips began to twitch with laughter. "Naw girl, I was just kidding. You know that's not true. You're just *too* easy."

Sasha smiled. "One of these times you're going to say something very important, and I'm not going to believe you."

"I know," Zandy said, grinning. "I need to stop teasing you

so much." Cocking her head to the side, she said, "You're smiling again. Are you sure you don't want to sing with me? I love to sing, and I love to hear other people sing."

"You sing, and I'll play."

Zandy thought for a few seconds, then said, "Okay. I'll sing this song I wrote a couple of years ago. It's called "In Your Presence"."

"It's a gospel song?" Sasha asked, surprised.

"Why does that surprise you? I'm not the gospel-singing type?"

"No, that's not it. I was thinking earlier today just how tired I was of singing gospel."

"I don't care what anybody says, gospel is the best kind of music. I wrote "In Your Presence" when I was really depressed and down about everything. I always felt better whenever I sang it."

"Go ahead and sing it. I want to hear it. I'll join in with the keyboard once I pick up the melody."

Zandy raised a hand to her mouth and began to lavishly throw kisses out. "Thank you all for coming to hear me sing tonight," she bellowed to an invisible crowd of screaming fans. "I would like to dedicate this next song to my dear friend, Sasha Lindsey. She's down in the dumps, and I hope this song will lift her up."

Sasha shook her head, smiling. "Just sing the song, Zandy."

"Alright," Zandy said, clearing her throat. In a soprano voice that was resonant and balladic, she sang:

In Your presence when I am sad, I find joy.
In Your presence when I am broken, I am made whole.
Only You can shine in me, a love that wondrously makes me
complete.
Only You, only in Your presence, Lord.

In Your presence when I should fear, I'm not afraid.
In Your presence when I have doubts, they're wiped away.

Only You can shine in me, a love that wondrously makes me complete.
Only You, only in Your Presence, Lord.

In Your presence is everything I need.
No good is withheld from me.
In Your presence is where I live to be.
No other can fulfill me.
Lord, it still amazes me just how Your love makes me complete.
Only You, only in Your presence, Lord.

"Zandy, that's a beautiful song," Sasha said, interrupting. "The melody. The words. It's just beautiful."

"Thank you. I like it a lot, too. It's very comforting."

"It is," Sasha agreed, peering at Zandy as if seeing her for the first time. "Maybe you can teach me the words."

"Yeah, girl. We can sing it together."

"Alright," Sasha said, playing an introduction to the song. "Take it from the top, and I'll play along with you."

"Oo-o-oh, girl!" Zandy exclaimed, watching as Sasha's accomplished fingers moved over the keys. "That sounds good. Better than I ever imagined it would."

Sasha smiled. "Just sing the song, Zandy."

So Zandy opened her mouth and the room was filled with her song.

Chapter 11

Zandy's mind was on Sasha as she drove home that evening. They'd spent over two hours at the keyboard singing and clowning around. She'd taught Sasha the lyrics to her song, and Sasha had taught her how to play "When The Saints Go Marching In" with a few simple chords. It was after eight o'clock before they realized the time. Zandy had hastily said her good-byes and left. She hadn't been ready to leave, but her books were calling her. She couldn't afford to put off reading the African American History chapters any longer.

Sasha seemed to be in better spirits by the time Zandy left. She'd even told Zandy that she was going to work on her gruesome C program. Zandy had left feeling glad about the teasing she'd done at Sasha's expense throughout the evening. The teasing had worked – it kept Sasha laughing, in spite of herself, and it kept her mind off of Tellis. Zandy had even persuaded Sasha to sing one of her own songs. "Destiny," it was called, and Zandy had loved it. She'd loved Sasha's singing voice, too.

I knew she could blow, Zandy thought, smiling.

Once she'd heard Sasha's voice, Zandy had insisted that they do some harmonizing. With Sasha's soul-stirring alto voice and Zandy's wide-ranging soprano voice, they produced harmonies worthy of a record deal. Zandy had always loved to sing and had always longed for somebody to sing with. Her mother sounded like scratches on a chalkboard, and her sister couldn't carry a tune if you tied it to her. Her father sang like a mockingbird, but she wouldn't sing with him if he were the last person on earth. Her other friends didn't sing, either. In high school, she'd had a friend who had a pretty good singing voice.

Now why did I have to start thinking about her? Zandy asked herself, frowning.

She hated it when her thoughts got snagged on Tali. If she never thought about her again, it would be too soon.

Zandy reached down and flipped on the radio switch and a thumping rap song poured through the speakers. She turned the volume up, blasting the sound. Bouncing to the music, she hooked a right and made her way to Interstate 55 South. When she merged with the interstate traffic, Tali was still in her head. Zandy turned the music down. It wasn't helping her forget the girl.

Zandy and Tali had been friends for two years when Tali started dating Zandy's ex-boyfriend. Two weeks after Zandy had broken up with Darian, someone dropped a buzz in her ear – her bestfriend Tali was dating Darian. Zandy had been blown away. Where she came from, friends didn't date each other's exes. That was a no-no. No if, ands, or buts about it. Tali would never do anything like that, Zandy had insisted. She'd been convinced that the source of the information was wrong.

Zandy had called Tali up and told her what she'd heard. To her eye-popping surprise, Tali told her that she hadn't meant for the relationship with Darian to happen, but it had and that Zandy shouldn't care anyway, being that she hadn't been in love with Darian when they broke up. Zandy was too shocked at first to be angry. Even when Tali had cut the conversation short and hung up the phone, Zandy had still been at a loss for words. For days afterwards, she tried to contact Tali, but to no avail. She left messages for Tali to call her so they could talk the matter through, so they could save their friendship. Tali never responded. It was obvious that Tali was avoiding her, even at school, and Zandy slowly became bull-fighting mad.

She worked hard to suppress her anger. Why should she be upset about the loss of a friend who obviously wasn't a friend? She was the one who had befriended Tali, the transferred mulatto student with cat-green eyes, when she'd been shunned by many of the other girls primarily because of her striking beauty. Zandy had never cared a whole lot about physical beauty — not even her own — so she made every effort to show herself as a friend to Tali. And Tali had clung to her like white on rice. They became quick friends, and it wasn't long before Tali was accepted as a part of the in-crowd.

But she messed up and committed the cardinal sin of friendships, Zandy brooded, her blood pressure rising an inkling. *That bratty, backstabbing slut. I let her off too easy,* she thought, remembering the fight she'd had with Tali.

It happened at a post-graduation house party. Zandy and Tali were juniors, but Zandy called the host of the party and learned that Tali was expected to attend. Zandy had sorrowfully told the host that she would be unable to make it to the party. That was a lie. She'd had every intention of going to the party. And she'd had every intention of slamming her fist upside Tali's head. Figuring what goes around eventually comes around, Zandy had tried to move on and forget about what Tali had done, but she found that hard to do when Tali kept downing her real bad around the school. Zandy couldn't wait any longer for the you-reap-what-you-sow principle to validate her. Her fist in Tali's face was all the validation she needed.

Dressed for action in T-shirt, jeans, and tennis shoes, Zandy had gone to the party. She pasted a smile on her face and con-gratulated her graduating friends. But she never strayed far from the front door, neither did her eyes. She didn't like the idea of fighting at the party, but she didn't have much of a choice if she was going to confront Tali. School had already been let out for the summer break and she didn't know when she'd see Tali again, if not at the party. And she was not going to wait until school started again. If Tali had known that Zandy was waiting for her, she probably wouldn't have attended the party. But Zandy hadn't told anyone that she was coming. She didn't want to risk Tali finding out.

Zandy had been at the party for almost an hour when Tali and Darian walked through the door. Within seconds, Tali spotted Zandy. Their eyes locked across the room. Then, Tali flipped her long black hair in the air and rolled her eyes away from Zandy's. Hot anger blazed through Zandy and she marched across the room, her fists balled tight. Without saying a word, she punched Tali squarely in the face.

The surprise of Zandy's attack, as well as the force of her tae kwon do punch, sent Tali, dressed in a green, skintight jumpsuit and three-inch heels, flying backwards. Darian quickly kneeled to aid Tali, who was holding her broken, bloody nose and screaming curses at Zandy. While Darian kneeled beside Tali, Zandy rushed over and kicked him as hard as she could in his side, cursing him and telling him that he was just as no-good as Tali was.

The kick lifted Darian in the air, and he landed with a loud groan on top of Tali. Tali screamed louder, pushing and kicking Darian off her. Anger and humiliation caused Darian to spring to his feet and lunge at Zandy, but he couldn't get to her. Two bouncer-looking guys held him back. Zandy wasn't afraid of him. Bouncing around on her tiptoes with her fists raised for fighting, she begged the two guys to let Darian go. She screamed that she wanted to whip a fit on the punk.

One of the guys finally grabbed her bouncing body and pulled her through the awestruck crowd and out the front door. On the porch, he told her to take a few breaths and calm down. She did, then examined herself. Nothing was torn, broken, or bleeding. She started grinning. She'd kicked both of their behinds.

Just as Zandy stepped off the porch to leave, Tali ran to the door and flung more curses at her. Zandy had turned to Tali and silently beckoned her to come on outside. But Tali stayed behind the screen door, yelling at the top of her lungs. Zandy smiled wickedly at her and then walked off down the street, grinning and congratulating herself for a job well done. The knockdown punch she'd given Tali was so sweet, she laughingly thought about getting in the ring with Mike Tyson.

Since Tali, Zandy had kept her distance from clingy girlfriends. She just didn't want the hassle. Even when she'd been looking for a roommate and Kayla had moved into her apartment, Zandy had treated it all as if it were a business deal. She had no intentions of having a live-in best friend.

And as much as I try to keep my distance from her, Zandy thought as she sped down the highway ten miles over the speed limit, *she still thinks I want that rodent of hers.*

Zandy shook her head in disbelief and looked out the passenger window. She'd been so lost in thought, she missed her exit. Rather than looping back around, she decided to drive further down the interstate to the exit that would take her to her mom's house.

Thinking about Kayla reminded Zandy that she had one month to find another roommate. That's how long she'd given Kayla to find somewhere else to stay. She didn't need all the drama Kayla was putting her through.

I have no idea where I'm going to find another roommate, Zandy thought. *Too bad Sasha already has her own place.*

Zandy's instincts told her that Sasha would make a great roommate: for one thing, she wasn't clingy. Nowhere near it. If it hadn't been for Zandy, they never would've become close friends. After they'd turned in their assignment to Dr. Avery, Sasha had remained friendly toward Zandy, but that was it. No more calls to discuss the assignment. No more meetings in the library to work on the assignment. Not even one I'm-just-calling-to-see-how-you're-doing phone call. Zandy had been surprised to know that she missed talking to the cute, soft-spoken girl who always wore dresses. She caught up with Sasha one day after class and invited her to lunch with her. Sasha accepted and from then on, their friendship began to flourish.

Zandy laughed as she exited the interstate. *Now I'm the clingy one. I just keep trying to hang on to this friendship, and I don't know why. Especially with the attitudes and accusations she's been throwing my way. If she was anyone else, I would have dropped her like a hot potato a long time ago. But, for some reason, I feel drawn to her. I feel like our friendship was meant to be, like meeting her will be a . . . a . . .*

"Life-changing experience," a small voice said.

Zandy snatched her eyes off the road and whipped her head toward the passenger seat. The voice had come from that direction, but she didn't see anyone. Zandy's forehead creased into a mass of frowns. She'd heard a voice, and it hadn't been her own. She gripped the steering wheel, her heart racing in her chest.

The stoplight ahead turned red. Slowing to a stop, she threw the gear of her SUV in park. She flicked the interior light switch on and slowly turned around to peek into the back of the vehicle. It was empty. She settled down in her seat and breathed a sigh of relief.

"I am truly *buggin*," she said.

The light turned green and she drove off, slightly shaken. She kept telling herself that she hadn't heard anything, but she knew she'd heard something.

A life-changing event, the voice had said. She was sure of it.

Zandy drove into her mother's driveway and parked in front of the brick, three-bedroom house. Before she could even remove the key from the ignition, T'Kara threw open the front door and rushed out. Zandy watched as her sister's long legs leaped over the four steps of the porch to the ground.

Quickly covering the short distance to the driveway, T'Kara threw her arms open wide and crashed into Zandy's body. Unaware that she'd knocked the wind out of Zandy, T'Kara gripped her big sister with a tight hug. "Where have you been?" she asked, loosening her hold on Zandy. "I've been calling you all day, and you didn't call me back."

Zandy looped her arms around T'Kara's neck and they walked toward the house. "Hey, T.K. Where's Mama?"

"You promised not to call me that anymore. It's T'Kara, remember?"

"Oh!" Zandy exclaimed, slapping her forehead. "I keep forgetting. Well, hey there, T'Kara. Where's Mama?"

T'Kara ignored Zandy's question. "Why didn't you call me back, Zandy?"

"Have you forgotten that I'm in college and that I have classes to attend?"

"Not all day," the twelve-year old pouted.

Zandy smiled. She was used to playing Twenty Questions with T'Kara when she came home. "I stopped by a friend's house."

T'Kara stopped in her tracks, her eyes wide. "Was it a boy's house?"

Zandy faked astonishment. "How did you know?"

"Who is he?" T'Kara asked, her body twitching with excitement. "Tell me. I won't tell anybody. I promise. It'll be our secret."

"Alright, but don't you tell a soul." Zandy looked around, as if to see if anyone was looking, then pulled T'Kara's eager ear close to her mouth. "Sike! It was a girl's house!" Laughing, Zandy bounded up the stairs and into the house. Her grinning little sister was close behind.

"Hey, Mama," Zandy spoke, walking into the kitchen her mother had recently painted and wallpapered in soft yellow and white. "I see you've finally finished the kitchen. It looks nice." Zandy placed her keys on the large, white table, then walked to stand just at the back of her mother.

"Hey, baby. How are you?" her mother responded, rinsing a pot and placing it in the dish rack.

Zandy should've been used to the veil of melancholy that sometimes shrouded her mother's face, but she wasn't. Seeing her mother like this always made her think of her father's betrayal. "I'm doing fine," she answered, resting her chin on her mother's shoulder.

"We haven't heard from you in a few days. Everything alright?"

Before Zandy could answer, T'Kara butted in. "That's what I wanted to know. I called her a thousand times today, Mama, and she didn't even call me back. She had more time for her *friend* than me," she complained, sticking her tongue out at Zandy.

"Have you finished your homework, T.K.?" her mom asked quietly.

"Mama, you said you would stop calling me by my nickname."

"I said that I would try. Now, have you finished your homework?"

"No ma'am," T'Kara mumbled.

"You need to go and finish it then."

"That's what you get," Zandy mouthed to T'Kara, then made a face.

T'Kara scowled at Zandy before walking out of the kitchen.

"Yeah, everything's okay," Zandy told her mother. "I had a couple of tests to study for, that's all. I was on my way home from Sasha's to do some more studying, but I missed my exit. So I came on over here."

"How is she doing? I still haven't met her."

Zandy walked over to the stove and lifted the lid of a large pot. Spaghetti and meatballs. T'Kara's favorite dish. "She's fine," Zandy answered perfunctorily, retrieving a bowl from the cabinet and spooning out a large helping of the spaghetti. "Hopefully, you'll meet her soon." As Zandy leaned against the refrigerator and ate the spaghetti, she peered at the back of her mother's head. "You been doing okay?"

"Yeah, baby." Her mother said with a sigh. She pulled the sink plug, and the pipes loudly slurped the dishwater down the drain. "I'm a little tired, but I'm doing fine."

Zandy expected to hear the lie. It's what her mother always said. But people who are doing fine don't look so lifeless. And they don't lose pounds of weight for no reason at all. Her mother looked almost frail in the two-piece cotton pant set.

"So," she asked her mother airily, "how's Steve doing?"

Zandy's mother kept her back to her. "I haven't talked to Steve in weeks," she answered evenly, drying off a pan with a large dishtowel.

"So you're not dating him anymore?"

"I never was dating him. I was only seeing him . . . occasionally."

"So you're not *seeing* him anymore?"

"No."

That figures, Zandy thought. *When will the cycle end?*

A registered nurse at St. Dominic's Hospital, her mother was always meeting men. Nice, successful, attractive men. She administered to them a little tender care and smiled at them with warm, concerned eyes, and they were hooked. Good men obviously got sick like everyone else, because over the years Zandy had watched some *"fi-ine"* brothers walk into her mother's life. And one by one, she'd watched her mother give them the boot right out of her life, for no apparent reason.

"Why not?" Zandy asked, slightly irked. "He was a nice, stable guy. And I know he was really into you. You date him — I mean, *see* him — for almost a year and then it's just over? What happened?"

"Nothing happened."

"Something had to happen, Mama. You don't just stop *seeing* the VP of a telecommunications company who is trying his best to love you without something happening."

Her mother stooped and placed the pans she'd dried off in one of the lower cabinets. "T.K. didn't like him," she said, resuming a standing position before the sink.

Zandy twirled the spaghetti around her fork, shaking her head. Her mother was starting to recycle her excuses. The T.K.-didn't-like-him excuse was the one her mother used a few years ago when she was dating Daniel. Now it was back. "T.K. loves you, Mama, and she wants you to be happy. And she *did* like Steve. She told me she did. She just didn't like him as much as she likes her *daddy*." Her voice tinged with deliberate cynicism, she added, "I get the feeling that that's your problem, too."

Zandy's mother whirled around to face her. "I'm a grown woman, *Aleczandria*," she said defensively. "And like I've told you before, my love life, or lack thereof, is none of your business." Turning back around, she gripped the edge of the sink and exhaled quick, deep breaths. "Now, your father will be here in a few minutes and when he gets here, I don't want you to sass him in the way that only *you* can do. He is an adult and he is your father, and you will respect him as such."

Zandy's appetite was shot. She practically threw her plate on the counter, spaghetti strings leaping from the plate to the countertop. "What's he coming over here for?" she demanded to know.

"He's coming by to drop off some money for T.K." Her mother's voice had returned to its usual, placid tone.

"What you need to do is slap him with child support, and none of us would ever have to see his cheating behind again!"

"Shut up, Aleczandria! I mean it. Just shut up!"

Zandy had long ago found out that when her mother called her by her Christian name, she wasn't going to take much more back talk. She'd be flailing curses and slapping faces in a minute.

T'Kara popped into the kitchen, smiling broadly. "Zandy, did Mama tell you that Daddy is on his way over here? He's bringing me money for a new violin. My other one is broken. I dropped . . ."

"Get outta here, T.K.!" Zandy and her mother yelled in unison.

T'Kara looked from one to the other, her smile turning into a sad frown. Pouting, she stalked out of the kitchen.

"Mama," Zandy said in a much lower tone, "Why do you keep doing this to yourself?"

"Doing what, Zandy? The man is coming over here to bring his daughter some money. It has nothing to do with me."

"We both know that that's not true. Maybe he *is* coming to see T.K., but you really wish . . . he was coming to see you. Better yet, coming to stay."

"Zandy, I have moved on with my life," her mother said in a tight voice. "And your father has moved on with his. So I don't know where you get all this nonsense you're always talking."

"I get it from you, Mama," Zandy replied. "Can't you see the pattern in your life? You keep letting good men slip through your fingers, as if they're not an endangered species already. You seem to like them a lot, but then poof, they're gone! Like magic, they vanish out of your life. Richard wanted to marry you, and Simon, too. What?" she asked, walking to stand near her mother. "Are you afraid of commitment? Are you afraid that they're gonna do the same thing to you that my doggish father did? Mama, all men are not like him," she said softly, recalling Sasha's words. "And it breaks my heart to see you shutting happiness out of your life over and over again. And you know I'm telling the truth, too. That's why you have those dark circles under your eyes. That's why you're losing weight. It's what you do every time you break it off with one of those guys. You know that you deserve to be happy, but for some reason, you won't allow yourself to be happy. The only reason I can come up with is that you're still in love with that crazy man you call my father."

Her mother turned to face her. In an evenly-modulated voice, she said, "I *am* happy. When I make decisions that are in the best interest of my child, that's makes me happy. Now, however you choose to see it, is *your* business. You have a right to your opinions, however ridiculous they may be."

Zandy hated it when her mother spoke to her in that tone of voice. It made her feel like she was immature, with no idea of what she was talking about. But Zandy knew she was hitting the nail right on the head. She'd watched her mother do the same thing too many times. Shaking her head sadly, she said, "You're in denial, Mama. T.K. will love anyone that you love, and you know that. But every time you kick a man out of your life, you're just giving her more reasons to believe that there's hope for you and Walter, that her trifling daddy is the only man that can make you happy. So she keeps on wishing and hoping that her mother and father will get back together. Don't allow her to keep doing that. It can be unhealthy for her in the long run."

"T.K. loves her father very much and she's bound to have hopes of us getting back together. She's a child, and children do that. But I do *not* encourage her, in any way, to think that her father and I will be reunited. She is very much aware that her father has his own life, and I have mine."

"Mama, give me a break. You're still carrying the man's last name. After all these years. What's up with that?"

"Changing my name will only complicate things for T.K. No child wants to be questioned about having a name that's different from her mother's."

Zandy threw her hands up in exasperation. "You've got to be kidding me. Do you really think that T.K. is that shallow? T.K. doesn't give a flying flip about what other people think. You're hiding behind her, and you know it." Frowning, she said, "Fine. If you want to keep on loving a man who ripped your heart apart and then left you, then you do it. But don't ask me to respect him, because I won't. I don't care if he is my father. He doesn't deserve my respect, and *I hate his guts!*"

Zandy was consumed with anger, but when her mother glared at her with deadly eyes, she took two steps back. "Go home, Aleczandria," her mother said evenly. "Go home *now* before I hurt you."

Zandy wanted to tell her mother that she was sorry, that she wasn't trying to upset her, but she didn't. Instead, she walked over to the table and snatched up her keys, then turned to leave out the door. But her father's tall muscular frame filled the doorway, blocking her exit. Zandy grimaced. She'd wanted to be gone by the time he arrived.

Her father greeted her kindly. "Hello, Zandy," he said, his eyes fixed on her.

His endearing, puppy eyes had captured Zandy's heart as a child. She'd always liked the way they sort of drooped on the sides, making him look sad even when he was rolling with laughter. As a child she'd often played with those eyes, wishing that she'd been born with a pair just like them. Those eyes, so full of gentleness and love, especially when they'd been directed at her. Those eyes, always telling her that she was daddy's little girl.

Those eyes that lied to me, she thought, staring at him with hardness in her own eyes. *Thank God I wasn't born with his eyes.*

"That's *Aleczandria* to you," she said, her voice rough with indignation. "Only family and friends can call me Zandy, and you're neither. Now, will you move out of my way?"

"So you hate my guts?" he asked quietly, his sad-looking eyes searching her face.

Distaste filled Zandy's mouth, and her lips twitched in a sneer. "That's exactly what I said," she answered boldly. "And I don't recall stuttering when I said it, either."

"What did I ever do to you that would cause you to hate me? What happened between me and your mother is between me and your mother. How many times do I have to say that? I wish you would stop shutting me out of your life. Don't you think we've been at odds long enough?" He held up a hand, as if to touch her.

Zandy's eyes shot daggers at the hand until it fell heavily to his side.

He stepped aside to let her pass by.

T'Kara had been standing behind him. She stared at Zandy through eyes that were just like their father's, silently pleading for Zandy to be nice to him.

Zandy stopped long enough to give T'Kara a hug. "I'll see you later," she told her, then stalked through the living room and out the front door, slamming it shut on T'Kara's cries for her to come back.

Resisting the temptation to slam a brick through the window of her father's four-wheel drive, she jumped in her SUV and slammed the door. Throwing the gear in reverse, she burned rubber out of the driveway, her eyes stinging with anger and unshed tears.

Chapter 12

Zandy walked across the park's lawn, her hands balled tightly in the pockets of her windbreaker. She was still seething from last night and she wasn't happy about it. If there were a pill or potion she could take that would stop the anger she felt toward her father from eating away at her, she'd take it. In a heartbeat.

Since no such remedy existed, the anger ate away at her appetite, her sleep, her concentration, and her peace of mind. She'd gone to her nine o'clock history class, but she hadn't heard one thing the instructor said. And the instructor had been reviewing for next week's test.

It'll be my own fault if I flunk the test, she thought. *I shouldn't keep letting him get to me the same way every time I see him.*

Desperate to calm her raging nerves, she'd skipped her next class to seek the solace of the park's large pond. The soft ripples in the water and the concerted sounds of nature usually helped to ease any tension she felt.

As she approached the bench where she always sat whenever she visited the park, she looked up to see a man already sitting there. *Drat. He's sitting in my favorite spot.* That bench faced the best view of the pond and trees. Now, she'd have to walk around the pond to the other bench. Fearing that she'd scowl at the man if he looked at her, she avoided eye contact with him as she passed him.

"You are most welcome to sit here," the man said, his voice pleasantly mild. "It will not be long before I am gone."

The man had to be speaking to her. No one else was around. Slowly, Zandy turned back to him. With a polite smile on her face, she said, "Thank you, but I'll just walk over to the next one."

"No. Please. Come. Sit. I sense the disappointment you felt when you found me sitting here. I understand why you would want to sit here. It offers a view that is quite pleasing. I would not want to drive you from it."

Zandy looked doubtful. A clean-cut, black man sitting in the park in the middle of a cool, breezy day wasn't out of the norm. But you never could tell these days. He looked harmless enough, but why should he care where she sat? He didn't know her from Eve.

The man's eyes smiled. "I am as harmless as a dove," he assured her.

Zandy surreptitiously fingered the pocketknife she never left home without. If he laid one finger on her, she'd slice it off with a quickness. Walking toward him, she chuckled and said, "My mother always told me not to talk to strangers."

The man nodded. "I guess I am a stranger to you," he said, smiling. "Tell me, what is it that I can do that will allow you to see me as the friend that I am and not a stranger?"

Zandy sat down on the bench and jokingly said, "Tell me how to get rid of all of my problems, and you'll be my friend for life."

The man chuckled heartily. "I have helped many with their problems. It is my profession. People tell me their most intimate and disturbing problems and I counsel them. I have been told that I am rather good at what I do."

"A counselor," Zandy said, surprised. "That's great. I'm a psychology major. I would've thought you were a college professor or a lawyer of some sort."

"Why?"

"It's the way you talk. You remind me of my English/Lit instructor, except you speak with a slight accent. Are you a foreigner?"

"No."

"Well, you have a great speaking voice, and I can easily see you stuffed in a suit and bow tie standing before a large classroom with a long pointer in your hand or before a courtroom." She laughed, then turned her eyes to the rippling waters in the pond.

The man also looked out over the waters.

Silently, they watched as a family of ducks glided by.

"So what is this problem that you are having?" the man asked.

"Oh, it's a long, ugly story," Zandy answered, her gaze still on the waters. "I don't want to burden you with it."

"If I am to be your friend, you must tell me your problem."

"I was just kidding about that."

His eyes flashed warmth. "Maybe you were. However, I am holding you to your words."

"It's my father."

"What about your father?"

"I despise him."

"Why?"

"He did something terrible to my mother."

"May I ask what it was that he did to her?"

"She loved him very much and he cheated on her and then left her. And me. He broke her heart . . . and mine."

"I see. When did this happen?"

"Almost thirteen years ago. Just before my sister, who's twelve, was born."

"Thirteen years is a long time to hate anyone."

"Not when the person shows no remorse for what he did and when the person continues to flaunt his women in my mother's face."

"Have you ever tried talking to your father? Talking to him might help you to understand the situation better."

"What's to understand? He cheated." Zandy peered at him. "You can't be saying that there's a justifiable reason for him cheating on my mother."

"No. I am not. There is no justifiable reason for it. Communication, though, can provide you with some insight."

"I have nothing to say to him. What I'd like to do is go upside his head with a baseball bat, but that might not be a good idea. He could choke me to death with one hand."

The man smiled. "No, that would not be a good idea."

"Actually," Zandy said, "when I was about eleven years old, I took the chip off my shoulder long enough to ask him why he did it. He told me that he wouldn't talk about the matter with me, that it was between he and my mother. From that day on, I've never had another nice word to say to him."

Zandy waited for the man to say something more. He remained quiet, his eyes once again on the waters. "So what's the solution?" she asked him, smiling. "Should I just go ahead and kill him?"

"No," he said simply, lifting his eyes to the row of golden-leafed trees that served as a backdrop to the pond.

"Then what?" she asked

"Forgive him," he answered.

"Oh, brother!" she groaned. "I thought you were gonna tell me something earth-shakingly profound, and you tell me to forgive him." She shook her head. "I can't do that."

"Have you ever tried to forgive him?"

"Nope."

"Why not?"

"He's so nonchalant, like what happened was out of his control and like it shouldn't matter as much now, since it happened a long time ago. It may have happened a long time ago, but I remember the night he left like it was yesterday."

"You have to let the memory of that night die. It is the only way you can free yourself from the anger you feel toward your father."

"I could never forget that night."

"I am sure that you purposely hold on to and relive that night so that you may continue to feed the hatred and anger you have for your father."

"Maybe."

"So let it go and forgive him. Forgiving your father will not be for him. It will be for you. Untamed hatred destroys the hater more than the hated. Forgiveness, which is born out of love, is the only weapon capable of conquering hatred and freeing the heart, the mind, and the soul."

"I don't disagree with that, but the way I see it, forgiving him may lead to having a relationship with him."

"Would that be so bad?"

"Yes!"

The man chuckled. "No. It would not. There will come a time when you will look back and regret the years that you let your anger rob you of a relationship with your father. Time has a way of bringing many to that point. I have seen it happen often enough to know."

Zandy scoffed. "I have wished for him to die many times, so I can't imagine getting to the point that I regret not talking to him."

"If I had a dime for every time someone has said that to me, I would be the richest man on earth."

Together they laughed.

The man turned his smiling eyes fully on Zandy. "Will you at least try to make peace with your father?"

Zandy opened her mouth to say that she could never do that, but one look in the man's eyes washed the words from her mouth. She found herself smiling and saying, "I'll try."

"Good," he said loudly. "We are now friends. Yes?"

Zandy peered at the man, wondering if he were about to make a move on her. Slipping a hand into the pocket of her jacket that held the knife, she hesitantly replied, "Yes."

The man noted her hesitation and his black eyes flashed warmth. "I was hoping, then, that you might have some candy to share. Friends share."

"Huh?" Zandy asked, confused. "You want some *candy?*"

"Yes, please."

"Oh," she said, sounding dumb in her own ears. She unzipped the front pouch on her windbreaker where she usually kept her candy stash. She rarely went to class — especially her morning classes — without some kind of sweets. The small doses of sugar gave her the spurts of energy she needed to make it until lunchtime. Reaching in the pocket, she pulled out a handful of empty Jolly Rancher wrappers. She'd forgotten to replenish her stash from last week.

"I'm sorry," she said to the man. "I don't have any . . . Yes, I do have some! In my truck. I'll run and get it for you."

"That is not necessary. I—"

"It's no problem," Zandy said, jumping to her feet. "I'll be right back." She sprinted across the lawn to the lot where she'd parked. Within minutes she was back, slightly winded. "Here you are," she said happily and dumped two handfuls of Jolly Ranchers in the man's massive hands.

The man studied the candy like a child in a candy store. Then he carefully placed the candy in the lap portion of his long shirt and picked out one Jolly Rancher. Strawberry-Banana.

Zandy watched him eagerly tear the wrapper off the small piece of candy and plop the candy into his mouth. When he slurped on the candy, her eyebrows rose. *Surely this grown — and obviously intelligent — man did not just slurp,* she thought. She peered at him and there it was again. Slurp. Slurp. Zandy held back a laugh.

The man closed his eyes, savoring the candy. "The Jolly Rancher is now my favorite candy," he said, smiling.

Zandy laughed. "Yes, I can see," she said, thinking that the man sounded very much like a three-year child.

How old is he anyway? she wondered, studying his face. With prominent facial features, the man was attractive but not overly handsome. His skin, a deep bronze, was smooth and taut. Not a wrinkle to be found. *Forty? Forty-five?* she guessed. She couldn't really tell by looking at his face. It was possible that he looked younger than his actual age.

Her eyes dropped to his clothing. He wore a long-sleeved, tan linen shirt that fit loosely over a pair of matching linen pants. The wind lifted and caused the pants to billow around his long, powerful legs.

He definitely doesn't dress like an old man, she thought, her eyes drifting down to his huge feet. She snickered.

"I see you have noticed my new tennis," the man said, opening his eyes. "Do you like them?"

Zandy studied the navy and white tennis shoes with orange bottoms and a neon green Nike swoosh on each side. "Yes, I like them," she said smiling, "but they don't—"

"Yes, I know. They do not coordinate with my clothing. I was not concerned with color when I purchased them, only comfort. And these, my friend, were the most comfortable ones in the store."

"How do you know that?" Zandy asked. "Is that what the salesperson told you? You know, some of them will tell you that so you'll buy the most expensive pair in the store."

"No, not at all. I know because I tested every pair of size thirteen tennis shoes in the store."

Zandy started to shake with laughter. "You're kidding me. You *did not* go in the store and try on that many pair of shoes."

"I kid you not. I tried on exactly twenty-two pair of shoes today. The young man working there was very patient, answering my questions and providing me with great service. The young man even discussed personal issues with me. He told me that he was working two jobs to help his single mother take care of his three younger siblings. I tipped him handsomely before I left the store. I believe I saw tears form in the young man's eyes as I was leaving."

"They were probably tears of laughter, especially if he had to watch you walk out of the store dressed in a tan linen pant suit and neon colored shoes."

The man's booming laughter startled Zandy. With his head held back, he laughed as though he was trying to fill the heavens with the sound of his voice. Hearing the deep resonance of his laughter echo throughout the air, she thought he might have done just that. Smiling, she stood to her feet.

"I guess I should be heading back to campus. I had planned to skip the rest of my classes today, but I feel better now. Thank you."

"You are welcome," the man said, his eyes shimmering brightly from the laughter. "I am very happy to have met you."

Zandy frowned down at the man. "You never told me your name."

"Jabril. My name is Jabril."

Zandy held out her hand to him, and when he placed his hand in hers, she shook it friskily. "It was very nice meeting you, Jabril. Thank you for being a friend," she paused then said laughingly, "and not a stranger. And I'm sorry for giving you a rude look when I found you sitting in my favorite spot. Do you forgive me?" she asked him teasingly.

His eyes twinkled. "Yes, I forgive you. Do you forgive me for sitting in your favorite spot?"

Zandy chuckled lightly. "Yes, I forgive you." She smiled at him then turned to leave. Walking toward the parking lot, she breathed deeply. Laughing and talking with Jabril had lifted the ton of bricks she'd been carrying on her shoulders. She was glad he'd chosen to sit in her favorite spot.

Before pulling out of the park's parking lot, Zandy turned to get one last look at the man she'd met in the park and she laughed out loud. Jabril was eagerly tearing into another Jolly Rancher candy wrapper.

Chapter 13

Z andy pressed the message button on her answering machine as she walked past it to place two bags of grocery on the kitchen counter.

"Zandy, this is *T'Kara*." Zandy smiled when she heard her little sister's saucy voice. "Not T.K., but *T'Kara*. It's forty-two minutes and seven seconds after five o'clock on Wednesday, October the twenty-seventh," T'Kara's message continued. "I know that because Daddy bought me this great, new watch. Call me when you get in so I can tell you about all of the different things it has on it. You should be home soon because you're finished with classes for today and you don't have to work this evening. I'll wait by the phone until you call me. Okay? Okay. Good-bye. Don't keep me waiting because I've got something else to tell you, too. Okay? Love you. Good-bye." The answering machine clicked then fell silent.

Zandy looked at the kitchen clock. It was 6:05. Either she needed to get a life or her little sister knew her daily routines way too well. She'd call her as soon as she finished putting away the groceries.

Before Zandy could put away one bag of grocery, her pager vibrated at the waistline of her pants. Zandy slipped the pager out of its case and read the number. 555-4129. It was T'Kara. Zandy picked up the cordless phone and dialed her mother's number.

The line was answered in the middle of the first ring. "Hi Zandy!" T'Kara said, excited. "You got my page?"

"Hi T'Kara" Zandy replied warmly, remembering to use the proper name. "Yes, I got your page. I thought Mama told you not to page me unless it was an emergency," she teased.

"This is an emergency, but," she added in a whisper, "don't tell Mama I paged you. I might get in trouble."

"I won't tell. So what's the big emergency?"

"Didn't you get my message about my new watch?"

"I got your message," Zandy mumbled peevishly, knowing that T'Kara was about to launch into another long stint about her sweet and wonderful daddy. Zandy wasn't up for it. Not today. "What's the emergency in getting a new watch?"

"Daddy bought it for me. He must have spent a lot of money on it, too, because it has an expensive, leather band, and it has an alarm on it, and a calendar, and—"

"Oh, that sounds nice," Zandy said, feigning excitement. "Where's Mama?"

"In the bathtub," T'Kara answered, but refusing to be thrown off the subject, she said, "You will *really* like this watch, Zandy. It's *tight*."

"I'm sure it is," Zandy said snidely, tossing a package of lunchmeat in the refrigerator.

"And guess what?!"

Zandy really didn't care, but dryly gave the response her sister expected. "What?"

"Daddy bought you one, too! It's your favorite color — hunter green!"

Why would he buy me a watch? she questioned in her mind. He'd stopped buying her things years ago. Zandy knew that he still gave her mother money for her, but he never bought her gifts anymore. She didn't need a watch anyway and even if she did, she wouldn't wear one that he bought.

"Can I bring it over to you?"

"Tonight? Mama's not going to bring you over here. She needs to rest for her early morning shift."

"She'll bring me if you say I can come. If you say 'no', then I'll have to spend the night at Rachel's."

"Why?"

"Because school is out tomorrow for Parent–Teachers Conference. Can I spend the night with you? I know you don't have classes on Thursdays and you don't have to go to work until three. You can drop me off at Rachel's before you go, and Mama can pick me up from there on her way home from the school."

"Shouldn't you be going to the conference with her? You're not trying to dodge a bad grade report, are you?"

"Me make a bad grade?" T'Kara snorted. "That's impossible."

"Well, *ain't* you the one, *Miss Thang!*"

T'Kara laughed into the phone. "I keep trying to tell you that I am, but you don't seem to want to hear me."

"So you still have straight A's, little sister?"

"I don't mean to brag, but yeah, big sister, I've still got straight A's."

"Well, go on with your bad self!"

"I'm going! I'm going!"

Zandy chuckled. "Alright. Tell Mama you can spend the night with me."

"Thanks, Zandy! And I won't forget to bring your new watch."

Yeah, yeah, yeah, Zandy thought as she hung up the phone. If only she could tell her sister exactly what she could do with the watch. She still couldn't understand why her father bought her the watch anyway. She preferred it much better when he seemed to be as indifferent to her as she was to him. It made it much easier to hate him.

Picking up the phone again, Zandy dialed Sasha's number.

"Hello," Sasha answered.

"You sound as bad as I feel," Zandy teased. "Still didn't find the bug in your C program?"

"I finally found it. The program runs fine now."

"Then why do you sound so sad?"

"Tellis," Sasha answered, then asked, "Why are you *feeling* bad?"

"My father, who else? But I don't want to talk about him. What did Tellis do?"

"Nothing. It's just that I haven't talked to him. We're supposed to have dinner with Dr. Avery tomorrow night, and I wanted to make sure he was still going. I've left messages for him, but he still hasn't returned my call. Well, he did leave a message on my machine saying that he would call me soon."

"Did you guys argue or anything?"

"No. We haven't even talked long enough in the past few days to argue about anything."

"He's probably very busy with work or school. Or another girl."

Sasha sighed. "You're being insensitive and cruel. I really don't need that right now."

"I'm sorry. I'm not trying to be mean, just real. At any rate, Tellis not calling is no reason to get depressed. *Ne t'inquiéte pas!* — Don't worry about it! Come and eat some ice cream with me. It'll help wash away our blues, before they consume us."

"It's alright to get fat, as long as we're not depressed," Sasha said laughingly, her spirits rising.

"My sentiments exactly," Zandy responded cheerfully.

"Alright, let me get a pen and paper for the directions, and I'll be right over."

Less than thirty minutes later, Sasha knocked on Zandy's apartment door.

Zandy threw open the door. "Hey, girl. C'mon in."

"Hi," Sasha said, then stepped into the sparsely furnished front room. Her eyes were immediately drawn to the enormous sound system that spanned the full length of one wall, from floor to ceiling. Sasha's eyes bulged at the speakers that stood almost as tall as she did.

Zandy laughed. "I told you I like music."

"*Like* is an understatement. You must have every CD ever made."

Zandy shook her head. "No, just all of the good ones." Pointing to a black futon, she said, "Sit down. You didn't wear a jacket? It's a little windy out tonight."

Sasha walked past a computer monitor resting on a large metallic desk to sit down on the sofa. "I brought a jacket, but it's in the car. I like weather like this." Pausing, she added, "especially at night."

Zandy pointed a finger at Sasha. "*Je te préviens!* — I'm warning you!"

"What?" Sasha asked, surprised.

"I hear that sad, I'm-thinking-of-Tellis tone in your voice. There will be no gloom of any kind in this apartment tonight. Not from you and not from me."

Sasha smiled and nodded. "I like this room. It has the feel of a dorm room, only bigger."

"Yeah, it does. I couldn't bear to share one of those tiny dorm rooms on campus. So I found this apartment, made the front room my castle, and found a roommate to help me pay the rent. I guess I could move into the bedroom, now that she's gone, but I'm so used to being out here."

"This is your bedroom? I would never have known if you hadn't told me. You sleep here on the sofa?

"Yep. It lets out into a bed."

"Where do you keep your clothes."

"I use the linen closet by the bathroom and that file cabinet," Zandy answered, pointing to a six-drawer metallic cabinet near the desk. "There are no papers in that cabinet, only clothes. And I still had a small section in the bedroom closet. It's a pretty big closet."

"You sure are efficient."

"I never have needed a lot to maintain."

"I see. You don't even have a television."

"I have one," Zandy said, heading for the kitchen. "I just never watch it — well, rarely do I watch it. It's a waste of my time. At least I can listen to music and do other things at the same time — like read and study. I put my TV in the bedroom for Kayla when she moved in. It's still back there."

"You didn't tell me your roommate moved out."

"Correction — I *put* her out. She just moved out earlier than she had to. Good riddance."

"Found a replacement yet?"

"Not yet, but I can manage on my own for a few months. I have a few dollars saved up. And my mom will help me out if necessary. You want something to drink with your ice cream? And I hope you like plain old vanilla."

"Water is fine. Thanks," Sasha answered. "And plain old vanilla is my favorite." Turning slightly in her seat to peer at Zandy, she asked, "So what did your father do that put you down in the dumps?"

"Can't talk about it. I'll end up getting upset."

"Tell me. I won't let you get upset."

Zandy groaned deep in her throat. "As if you can stop me. Just the thought of him makes me upset." Walking up to Sasha, she placed a glass of water in one of her hands and a bowl of ice cream in the other. "It's funny, though."

"What is?"

"I didn't get upset last night when I was thinking back to when I was younger and how much fun I used to have with my father. And how . . . crazy I was about him."

Sasha saw the soft gleam in Zandy's eyes and thought of her own father. "That must have been nice, being able to reflect on some of the good times you had with your father, without feeling the animosity you have toward him now."

"I guess," Zandy replied, walking to the kitchen and coming back with her own bowl of ice cream. She sat down beside Sasha. "It's kind of hard to be sad when you're remembering all of the birthday parties and the clothes and other wonderful gifts your

father used to give you when you were a child." She smiled remi-
niscently. "I used to think we were rich. Living in the brick
home that my father built in a neighborhood of ramshackle
homes. To ride through our neighborhood now, you wouldn't
know that the homes were so raggedy back then, but they were.
Too raggedy for my mother to live in, or so my father used to say.
So he built the house, married my mother, and then one year
later, I came along. He spoiled us rotten. But he always pushing
us to do well, too. When he told me that I could be anything I
wanted to be in life, I believed him. I guess my mom did, too.
Because of him, she quit her job as a waitress and went back to
school to get her GED. After that, she became a nurse's aid, and
then finally went to nursing school. Now she's one of the highest
paid RNs in the city. I was so proud of both of them. I couldn't
have picked two better people to be my parents. And for seven
years I had them all to myself."

"Until T'Kara was born,' Sasha interjected.

"Yep, but don't get me wrong. I was looking forward to having a baby sister or brother to play with, but even now, I can't
help but associate T'Kara's birth with the death of my parent's
relationship. And with the death of the close relationship I had
with my father."

Sasha swallowed a scoop of ice cream. "What happened?"

"I don't know where things went wrong, because, as far as I
knew, we were all one big happy family waiting for a new baby to
arrive. But one night, I fell asleep on the couch and I woke up to
hear my parents arguing. Well, actually, it was my mother screaming at my father. I jumped up and ran to stand in their bedroom
door. I remember being so scared. I had never heard them argue
like this before. My father wasn't saying anything. He just walked
around the room getting some of his clothes and stuff and throwing them in a suitcase. My mother was crying one minute and
then screaming hysterically at him the next. She kept yelling,
'Leave! Get out! Don't come back here! I hate you! I hate you! If
another woman wants you, then she can have you! I don't need

you anyway! You hear me! Get out! Get out!' Then she fell across the bed and cried like a baby.

"I ran to my mother and tried to console her, but she wouldn't stop crying. I started crying myself. I looked at my father, trying to understand what he had done to make my mother so upset. The look on his face was cold and hard, like he wanted to rip someone's head off and needed to get away before he did it. That's the look he came home with when one of the guys he hired did something really stupid and dangerous on one of his construction sites. So I knew he was just as angry as my mother was. But when he walked over to me, he smiled and wiped away my tears, and he told me that he loved me. And then he picked up his suitcase and left the room. As soon as my mother saw him walk out of the room, she jumped up from the bed and ran after him. At the front door, she started pulling on him and begging him to stay, but he just shook her off and left anyway.

"I tried to comfort my mother that night, but I couldn't. She cried practically all night long. I kept asking her why my father had left and what happened, but she wouldn't tell me. She never did tell me. I remembered my mother's angry words, though, so it wasn't hard to figure out that the argument had something to do with another woman. Somehow my mother found out that my father was cheating on her. She was hurt and devastated. My mother was about four months pregnant when he left, and if it were not for her best friend, Mae, she would have starved herself and her baby to death.

"When I saw how broken and depressed my mother was after my father left, I started to dislike him, too. But, do you know what really made me start hating him with an intensity?"

"What?"

"He didn't go to the hospital with my mother the night she delivered T.K. Mae called him and told him that my mother was in labor and that she was taking her to the hospital, but he didn't show up at all." Tears sprang into Zandy's eyes. "I was only seven years old, but even I knew that a man had to be really cruel to not go to the hospital when his baby is being born."

"Did he ever explain why he didn't go?"

"What's there to explain? He chose to be with the other woman instead of his wife and newborn daughter. In fact, T.K. was almost two months old before he even laid eyes on her. Even then, he didn't pick her up or play with her or *anything*. I don't know how he could resist her, she was so cute. Everybody used to say how much she looked like him. She really did, and still does, but I never liked to admit it, especially when he treated her like she had the plague. "

"Goodness," Sasha said. "That *is* pretty bad."

Zandy nodded in agreement. "When T.K. could barely walk, she'd stumble over to him and grab on to one of his legs. She would look up at him with those sad-looking eyes she got from him and a silly grin on her face. She would tug at his pants, wanting him to pick her up. If he picked her up, it was only long enough for him to sit her on the couch or somewhere. That seemed to be fine with her, because the moment he picked her up, she went into a fit of giggles. When he put her down, she wouldn't cry, she'd keep on giggling and clapping her hands. She adored him even then. You had to wipe her mouth constantly when he came around because it was like she forgot to swallow or something. She'd laugh and giggle and clap so much that spit bubbles would be running all down her chin. I can't tell you how much I despised him for treating her like that."

"He must have started treating her better, didn't he? You told me that they're really close now."

Zandy rolled her eyes. "Yeah, he did, but it took him long enough. He came to her first birthday party and brought her some toys. Then he started bringing her toys almost every week. My mother had to tell him to stop giving her so much stuff. He didn't listen, though. He started spoiling her rotten, just like he used to do me. And you couldn't have paid him to put her down then. Can you imagine an overgrown, five-year old child being carried around like she was one?"

Sasha laughed.

Zandy shook her head, smiling. "The next thing I knew they were like two peas in a pod. Just like he and I used to be when I was younger."

"Zandy, you and your father can rekindle the relationship you had. It's not too late. You just need to talk to him."

Zandy shook her head, an adamant expression on her face. "I'm glad T.K. has a good relationship with him. It may not always seem like it, but I am. A daughter should have a good, healthy relationship with her father - I think that's very important. But it's too late for us to rebuild the relationship we had."

"Zandy, don't say that. As long as you're both still living, it'll never be too late."

"As far as I'm concerned, he *is* dead. And I have no illusions about reconciling our relationship. My problem is trying not to say anything to T.K. that would infringe upon her relationship with him. She doesn't know the details of what my father did, but she knows that he did something that led to my parent's divorce. Still, she hasn't let it stop her from loving him. She says that everyone needs to be forgiven sometime. I wish I could be like my mother and keep my thoughts about the man to myself and say nothing bad about him at all, especially in front of T.K."

"She doesn't like it when you talk about her father, huh?"

"*Non!* — No! Which means I'll probably get in trouble with her tonight when she comes over because she's going to want to talk about him and that stupid watch he bought me, and I'm not tryin' to hear it."

"Oh, your sister is coming over tonight?

"Yeah, my mother is bringing her over. She's spending the night with me."

"Good! I'll finally get the chance to meet her."

"Just remember to call her T'Kara — not T.K. — and smile when she talks about her father, and she'll love you like a sister."

"T'Kara is such a pretty name, so I won't forget to call her that. And since I love my father just as much as she loves hers, I shouldn't have a problem smiling when she talks about her father."

Zandy exaggerated a groan.

"When she talks about him," Sasha said, coaching Zandy, "just remember the thoughts you had about your father last night. You even smiled when you talked about him a few minutes ago."

"I think I was feeling a little nostalgic last night. Yesterday, I met this man in the park, and he— "

A knock on the door interrupted Zandy.

Zandy stood up. "That must be them. Let me get the door, and then I'll tell you about the man."

Chapter 14

T'Kara strolled through the door as soon as Zandy opened it. "Hey, Zandy!" she said, a wide grin on her face.

"Hey, brat. What took y'all so long to get here?"

"She wanted to stop by the video store first," Zandy's mother answered, stepping into the apartment after T'Kara. Once in the apartment, she hugged Zandy. "How you doing, baby?"

Zandy had always been grateful to have a mother who never stayed mad at her for long, even when she'd done worse things than talking back. She returned her mother's hug. "I'm doing good, Mama. You doing okay?" she asked, still holding her mother firmly in her arms.

"Yes. I'm doing fine."

Mother and daughter looked at each other and knew that their disagreement had been left in the past.

Zandy beckoned for Sasha. "Mama, this is my friend, Sasha. Sasha, this is my mother."

Sasha gazed into the woman's beautiful face. If T'Kara was the spitting image of her father, then Zandy was definitely that of her mother's. They shared the same flawless copper-toned skin, high cheekbones, and dimpled cheeks. Zandy's mother even had the same sandy-brown hair. She wore it swept up in a bun at the back of her head.

Zandy's mother smiled politely. "Hello, Sasha. It's nice to finally meet you."

Sasha noticed the sadness etched around her smile. Smiling back, she said, "Thank you. It's nice to meet you, too."

"And I'm T'Kara," the twelve-year old said, stepping to stand beside Sasha. "I'm Zandy's sister."

Zandy shook her head at T'Kara. "If you could've waited another second, I would've introduced you, too. Sasha, this is my little sister. We call her T.K.," Zandy added, baiting her sister.

T'Kara shot a curt look at Zandy, then turned to Sasha. "I'm her *only* sister, so I see no reason to be distinguished as *little*. And I would *prefer* to be called T'Kara. I'm getting too old to be called by initials." Smiling widely at Sasha, she added. "You must be very nice if you can stand being friends with my sister. She's pretty, too, isn't she Mama?"

"Yes, she is," her mother agreed.

Sasha smiled at the precocious twelve-year old. "Thank you, T'Kara. You're pretty, too."

T'Kara's hair, the same shade as her mother's and sister's, was sectioned down the middle into two thick, long plaits. With a round face and endearing eyes, she favored her big sister, too.

"Please don't tell her she's pretty," Zandy protested, playfully throwing an arm around T'Kara's neck. "Because she's not."

T'Kara threw her arms around Zandy's waist and squeezed her tightly. "If I'm ugly, Zandy, then you're ugly, too, because I look like you!"

"T'Kara," their mother said, "stop playing now and take your bag. I've got to go home and get some rest."

"Zandy won't let me go, Mama."

"Let go off her, Zandy," her mother said patiently.

"I'm not holding her. See?" Zandy raised both hands in the air, and T'Kara's arms were still locked around her waist. Zandy laughed. "She's trying to squeeze the life out of me."

"Stop now, T'Kara. If you don't behave yourself, I'm going to take you back home with me. I mean it."

"Yes ma'am" T'Kara said, releasing her hold on Zandy. She took the overnight bag from her mother's outstretched hand.

"And, Zandy, don't tease her so much. You play as much as she does."

"Yes ma'am," Zandy said, mocking T'Kara.

Both girls hugged and kissed their mother, and with a quick good-bye and wave to Sasha, she was gone.

T'Kara dropped her bag to the floor. "So what are we going to do tonight?" she asked, looking from Zandy to Sasha expectantly. "We could pop popcorn and watch the video I rented."

"First of all," Zandy began, "you're going to take that bag in the bedroom and put it up the right way. And then you're going to take a shower. After that, *you* can watch your video. Sasha and I were talking before you got here."

"Come on, Zandy," T'Kara pleaded. "I want to hang out with you guys. I just got here, and already you're trying to get rid of me."

"I should be heading home anyway," Sasha threw in. "You two probably want to spend some time together."

"No," T'Kara told Sasha, grabbing her by the arm and leading her back to the futon. "You don't have to leave. Sit down. Finish doing what you were doing before I came."

Sasha allowed herself to be pushed down to the futon. "We really weren't doing anything. Just talking."

"Well, then, finish talking. I'll get you some more water . . . and ice cream! Yum yum!"

"Thanks, T'Kara, but I don't want anymore ice cream. Zandy may want some. Hers melted before she could eat it."

"Zandy, you want some more?" T'Kara asked cheerfully from the kitchen.

"Just a little," Zandy replied. Looking at Sasha, she said, "Stop treating her like she's an adult. She's a brat."

"I heard that, Zandy," T'Kara said loudly, "but I'm going to act like I didn't. So what were you two talking about before I came?"

Zandy shook her head, a look of hopelessness on her face. "I guess I should've told you that she's very nosey, too."

"I'm not nosey, Sasha. I just like to ask questions. Isn't that how you learn?"

Sasha laughed and nodded, yes. "Zandy was telling me about this man she met in the park yesterday."

T'Kara was all ears. Anticipation beaming on her face, she shuffled out of the kitchen with two bowls of ice cream in her hands. Giving one of the bowls to Zandy, she inquired, "Did you get his number?"

"Not *that* kind of man," Zandy retorted. "Although he was an attractive man in an intriguing kind of way," she added reflectively.

T'Kara plopped down on the futon between Sasha and Zandy. "Well, then, *what* kind of man?" she asked.

"I mean, he was a man, but he was . . . different."

"What do you mean, *he was different?*" T'Kara asked impatiently. "Did he have four legs or something?"

Zandy fixed a wry smile on her sister. "I'm gonna try to act like you're not here, as hard as that may be." Looking at Sasha, she said, "He was different, but I can't really explain what I mean. You know how you can meet a person and instantly be drawn to them, but not really know why? I mean, deep down inside you know why, but you really can't find the right words to explain it? So you just say, 'it's just something about him' or 'it's just something about her'? Have you ever met someone and felt like that?"

Sasha nodded, yes.

"I know what you mean, too, Zandy," T'Kara piped in.

Zandy looked thoughtful. "I only talked to him for a little while, but I feel like I've known him for years. It's *very* rare that I like a man so much, so soon. But there was just something about him." Vividly recalling Jabril's face, she smiled. "There was something about the way he looked at me and smiled without actually smiling. I know that sounds crazy, but he had this way of smiling with his eyes more than his lips. There was something about the way he seemed to understand me, too. I opened up and talked to him like he was a friend, not a stranger." Looking at T'Kara, she said, "But that doesn't mean *you* should go around talking to strangers."

T'Kara plopped a spoonful of ice cream into her mouth. "*You're* the one who has a problem with talking to strangers, not me. You might want to be more careful."

Sasha snickered. "At first, I thought T'Kara looked a lot like you. Now, I see she acts a lot like you, too."

"I'm going to send her to bed if she keeps interrupting my story."

T'Kara smiled mischievously, eating more of her ice cream.

"Who was he?" Sasha asked Zandy.

"I don't know. I was wondering the same thing last night. I wish I'd found out more about him. I'd like to talk to him again, to get to know him. I asked him if he was a foreigner, but he said that he wasn't."

"He had a foreign accent?" Sasha asked her.

"Not really, but he did speak with a different dialect. His English was sort of crisp and proper. And I noticed that he didn't use contractions when he spoke. That made him sound different, too."

"I speak proper English," T'Kara said, placing the empty bowl on the coffee table. "What's so special about that?"

"Hush or I'm going to send you to bed," Zandy threatened again. "You'd have to hear him talk, Sasha, to know what I mean. I just got the feeling that he's a very important man, or wealthy. I really don't know who he was, but I felt so much better after talking to him. See, I went to the park because I was so upset. I usually like to go to the park when I start to feel a little stressed. The park and the water relaxes me."

"Why were you upset?" Sasha asked.

"My father, who else? I got into an argument with my mother about him, and then he came over just as I was leaving."

T'Kara slumped down in her seat, but said nothing.

Zandy continued. "I talked to the man in the park about my feelings toward my father. He told me that I should forgive him."

"Really?" Sasha and T'Kara asked in unison.

"*Really*," Zandy answered dryly. "He said that hate was self-destructive, that I was only hurting myself by hating my father.'

"That's is true, Zandy," Sasha said.

T'Kara nodded in agreement.

"I know it's true, but like I told him, I just don't have it in me to forgive him. You're talking about letting go of twelve years of hurt and anger. It's not that easy."

"Can't you even try, Zandy," T'Kara implored. "Daddy loves you so much. He's always talking about something cute you did when you were a little girl. Sometimes he looks so sad when he talks about you, too. He misses you. I keep telling him to be patient with you and that one day you'll talk to him. Zandy, if you would just talk to Daddy, you'll see that he's not as bad as you think."

"You just don't understand, T'Kara. If you knew how much he hurt me and Mama, you would understand how I feel."

"Mama told me herself that she doesn't hate Daddy. If she can forgive him, then why can't you?"

"That's because she's still in love with the stupid man."

"He is *not* stupid," T'Kara said angrily, defending her father.

Frowning at Zandy, Sasha placed a comforting hand on T'Kara's shoulder.

"I'm sorry, T'Kara," Zandy apologized. "I shouldn't have said that. I'm glad that you can love him in spite of everything, but I just can't do it. And that's okay, because we're still sisters, and I love *you*."

"No, it's not okay, Zandy," T'Kara countered, tears watering her eyes. "All of my life, I've felt torn between you and Daddy. It's hard to talk to you about him, and it's hard to talk to him about you. Well, I'm really getting tired of it. I want us all to love each other and be friends."

Zandy wrapped her arms around T'Kara's shoulders and pulled her close to her side. "I'm sorry for putting you in that position, T'Kara, but I don't think I can ever be friends with him."

A tear rolled down T'Kara's face. "But you don't even try," she mumbled.

Zandy looked at Sasha, as if expecting her to say something.

Sasha eyed Zandy, as if to say, "If you don't say something to stop her from crying, I'm going to hit you."

"You're right," Zandy admitted to T'Kara. "I don't try, but I'll try to do better in the future."

T'Kara eyes brightened instantly. "You promise?"

"Yes, I promise. I promise to *try*, so don't expect the world from me."

"So you'll speak to Daddy when he comes over next time?"

Zandy rolled her eyes up to the ceiling. "I guess I can at least do that, for you."

"And you won't run from the house when he comes over?"

Zandy looked at Sasha once again for help, but her friend only offered an encouraging smile. Zandy released a deep sigh. "I may have to go to another room, but I'll try not to leave the house."

T'Kara clapped her hands cheerfully. "And you promise to stop calling him '*that man*' and start calling him 'Daddy'."

"Wait, now. Hold up." Zandy stood up, shaking her head. "That's asking for just a little bit too much. I will *not* promise you that."

T'Kara laughed. "Alright. I'll take what I can get," she said, leaping up to envelop Zandy in a bear hug.

Zandy wrapped her arms around her sister.

"You two are going to make me cry," Sasha said.

"Oh, you hush," Zandy told her. "You wouldn't help me out when I needed you to."

T'Kara loosened her hold on Zandy and fell on the futon beside Sasha. Throwing her arms around her, T'Kara said, "I'm so glad you were here, Sasha. If you hadn't been here, Zandy wouldn't have even talked about our father."

"That's not true, T'Kara. I talk about him . . . sometimes."

"Not like this, you don't."

"But she promised to do better," Sasha said, her look reminding Zandy of the promise she'd made.

T'Kara beamed. "Yeah, Zandy, don't forget your promise."

"Hush," Zandy said laughingly. "Both of you just hush."

"Oh!" T'Kara yelled, "I forgot to show you your new watch. It's in my bag. I'll run and get it." Jumping to her feet, she ran toward the bedroom.

Sasha smiled at Zandy. "I always knew I was missing out on something special by being an only child."

Zandy nodded slowly. "I can't imagine my life without her in it."

Chapter 15

Sasha sat staring at the telephone. She couldn't decide whether to call Tellis' home one more time or call Dr. Avery and tell her that she wouldn't be coming to dinner tonight. Of course, Dr. Avery would want to know why.

Telling her that Tellis stood me up is simply out of the question, Sasha reasoned.

She glanced at her watch. 6:50 p.m.

Where is he? The least he could do is call and tell me he's not coming.

Standing to her feet, Sasha walked across the room to the glass patio door. Sliding the door open, she stepped onto the padded patio and sidled up to the patio's rail. The night's cool breeze tantalized her bare arms and flirted with the flap of her knee-length wrap-skirt. The savory aroma of grilled meat wafted through the air, reminding her that she hadn't eaten since breakfast.

I don't want food. I want Tellis.

She wondered if he wanted her as much as she wanted him. Maybe she'd been caught up in a bubble dream, believing that he did. Maybe she'd mistakenly interpreted his attraction to her as blossoming love. He'd never actually told her that he was falling in love with her. Why would she think that he was? Because he called her on the phone? Because he spent time with her? Because he gave her her first real kiss?

Is it possible that he could be dating other girls like Zandy seems to want to believe? If that were the case, then why would he lead me on?

Sasha groaned from within. Tellis hadn't led her on. He hadn't made her any promises. He hadn't promised to be with her, and her alone. He hadn't promised to love and cherish her. He hadn't promised her anything, except to be her friend.

Sasha could feel her heart caving in. Her growing love for Tellis was founded on nothing more than girlish dreams and passionate illusions. Even worse, she'd fallen in love with a guy who hadn't fallen in love with her. Tears slowly crept into her eyes. She gripped the rails with both hands and shook her head in disbelief, the tears flowing down her face.

How could I have been so naïve and stupid? Am I so desperate to be with a man that I would fantasize a relationship with him?

Sasha wiped the tears from her face. *Pull yourself together,* she silently commanded. *Don't be a baby. Be strong.* Closing her eyes, she willed herself to be strong and not cry. And then she heard that familiar, devilish voice in her head that she was beginning to hear more and more, reassuring her and exalting her. *You've made it through much worse than this,* the voice said. *You're the one who survived the worse hand that God could ever deal a living soul. Yes, you're the one who survived the slaying hand of death. Your mother's death. Like the mortician who embalms a corpse with preservatives and perfumes, you embalmed your grief-stricken heart with the strength of your character and your will to overcome. Like the magician who mysteriously hides the rabbit in the hat, you mysteriously hid your bitterness toward God in the deep chasm of your soul. No one knew it was there, so well did you hide it. Your friends didn't know. The church didn't know. Not even your father really knew. Your bright smile and holy façade fooled them all. You fooled them because you're wise and because you're strong, not because you're naïve and stupid. Naïve people aren't smart like you, and stupid people aren't overcomers like you. If Tellis doesn't love you and chooses to be with someone else, you will overcome that, too. He's only one man in the sea of many. He can easily be replaced with another. Find yourself another man . . . a willing man.*

Sasha opened her eyes. "If what Zandy says about guys is true, then Tellis would've left me sooner or later anyway," she mumbled, walking back into the apartment.

The phone began ringing just as she drew the blinds closed over the patio door.

Tellis, she thought and sprinted to the phone.

"Hello."

"Hi, Sasha. This is Tellis. I was just calling to let you know that I wouldn't be able to make it to dinner tonight at Dr. Avery's. I apologize for calling so late. I thought I'd be able to make it, but I've been tied up. You're not too upset with me, are you?"

"Well, I was really hoping that you would go with me, and of course, Dr. Avery is expecting to see you."

"I know. Tell her that I'm sorry I can't make it."

"Is everything alright? You haven't called me. I've even left messages for you."

"Everything's fine. Just got a lot of things going on right now. I got your messages, but I haven't had a whole lot of time to talk. Listen, I have to run, but I'll call you soon. Okay?"

Sasha didn't believe him, but said, "Okay," and hung up the phone.

She had to face the fact that Tellis was involved with something that was more important to him than she was, and her gut feeling told her that that something was another girl.

Dr. Avery strolled down the walkway from her home dressed in a three-piece duster, tank, and pant set. The sophisticated ensemble was tie dyed in subtle shades of green and gently flowed with her every step.

"Hello, Sasha," she said, greeting Sasha warmly with a hug. "Where's Tellis?"

"He wasn't able to make it. I didn't know he wasn't coming until the last minute."

"I'm sorry that he won't be dining with us. I was looking forward to seeing him." Smiling, she added, "But I'm glad you could come."

Sasha had seriously thought about not coming. But staying home and drifting into a state of melancholy would only prove that she had given Tellis the power to break her. She refused to wallow in misery like a helpless little girl lost in the ways of the world. No, she'd learn to play "the game" as well as he. If he chooses to be with someone else, then so would she.

"I'm glad I could come, too," she told Dr. Avery.

"Let's hurry inside. It's getting chilly out here." Dr. Avery ushered Sasha into the house. "Hang your coat up in the closet," she instructed, "then come on back to the kitchen. I need to check on the pot roast."

Sasha looked around, admiring Dr. Avery's living room as she always did when she visited. Harmoniously designed with off-white European furniture, nineteenth-century inspired motifs, age-old art, and handpainted collectibles, the room was classically stunning. Sasha glided an appreciative hand over the polished stone surface of an expansive handwrought iron console as she walked to the closet just off the living room.

"You need any help?" she asked Dr. Avery as she entered the kitchen.

"Yes, thank you." Dr. Avery pointed to a replicated antique cabinet graced by a wide cornice top and glass-fronted doors. "Why don't you grab the plates and glasses. Since Tellis is not here, we can have a cozy little dinner here in the kitchen. Is that alright with you?"

"Sure," Sasha answered, moving toward the cabinet.

"I'm glad to see you looking more like yourself tonight," Dr. Avery said, casting Sasha a wry look.

Sasha smiled. "Thank you."

"Does that mean you're feeling better, too?"

Sasha shrugged. "I'm alright."

Dr. Avery spooned large helpings of succulent pot roast and mixed vegetables into a casserole dish. She covered the dish and placed it in the center of her kitchen's round, handcrafted table. She then returned to the stove for the mashed potatoes. They were irrefutably the most scrumptious mashed potatoes in the world. Everyone who'd eaten them had told her so.

"Did Tellis say why he couldn't make it?" she asked Sasha.

Sasha stiffened. She'd been hoping that Tellis' name wouldn't be mentioned anymore. "No," she replied flatly, placing two glasses on the table.

Dr. Avery raised an eyebrow. "Is something wrong?" she asked.

"No."

"Are you sure?"

"Yes."

Dr. Avery placed the bowl of steaming hot potatoes on the table, then approached Sasha. Her eyes searching Sasha's face, she said, "I sense that something is wrong, and I'm positive that it has something to do with Tellis. What is it, sweetheart?"

Sasha could feel her lips starting to tremble. She crimped them tight and shook her head. "Nothing," she replied, walking to stand near the kitchen window. She crossed her arms and stared out into the blackness of the night. "It's nothing."

"Don't tell me that when I can clearly see that it is *something*. Now, as far as I know, Tellis is a nice, intelligent young man, but people talk and . . . is he trying to force you to do something you don't want to do?"

Sasha chuckled sarcastically, shaking her head. She turned from the window to look at Dr. Avery. "You've got it all wrong. In fact, you've got it backwards."

"Wha-at?" the instructor asked, obviously shocked. "What are you saying, Sasha?"

"Does that surprise you, Dr. Avery?" Sasha asked, a diabolical smile fixed on her face. "Does it surprise you to know that the girl you thought to be so sweet and innocent wants to have wild sex with her so-called boyfriend? Does it surprise you," she continued, her voice rising sharply, "to know that the only reason this girl, the daughter of a sanctified, hell-fire and damnation preaching man, hasn't lost her virginity to that boyfriend is because he's too busy with something else?" Sasha swiped away the single tears that fell from her eye. "Or *someone* else, for all I know. I really don't care which is true."

Dr. Avery recovered from her state of shock and walked toward Sasha, her arms outstretched. "Oh, baby," she said, enveloping Sasha. "I didn't know you were holding so much inside. Shhhhhh," she cooed, patting Sasha as she sobbed quietly. "It's going to be alright. All this means is that you're normal." Dr. Avery chuckled lightly. "You're supposed to be experiencing these type of feelings."

Sasha pulled out of Dr. Avery's embrace to look at her. "You don't understand. I'm not supposed to be having these kinds of feelings. I've been taught better."

"Do you think that good teaching exempts you from human nature? Sexual desires are a natural part of the human experience, Sasha. Don't allow yourself to think otherwise. But neither can you allow yourself to think that sex is an experience that should be callously pursued as though it is nothing more than a kiss or an embrace. It is far more than that. Your body — your virginity, your virtue — is one of God's most precious gifts to you. Do you know how special you are, to be such a beautiful young lady with your gift still intact? Not many can boast the same." Dr. Avery pulled Sasha back into her arms and squeezed her tightly. "I'm so proud of you. It takes a person of great strength and character to do what you've done. I know your father is very proud of you, too."

Sasha stepped out of Dr. Avery's arms. The instructor had unknowingly pushed her hot button. "See, that's exactly what I'm talking about!" she fired at Dr. Avery. "Everybody wants me to live out my father's expectations. What about me?! What about what I want to do?!" Her voice dropped two notches lower.

"I'm so sick and tired of living up to everyone else's standards. I'm old enough to make my own *cotton-picking* decisions."

Dr. Avery smiled patiently. "You're right, Sasha. You *are* old enough to make your own decisions, and I should *not* have used your father as a reason why you should be proud of your virginal state. But, baby, you've got to acknowledge the fact that your parents have a lot to do with who and what you are. They taught you that sex outside of marriage is wrong because they wanted to shield you from the shame and humiliation that is often associated with promiscuous sex. It took me a long time to understand that God knew what He was doing when He condemned fornication and adultery. He knew that a sexual union between un-covenanted partners would ultimately lead to the overwhelming displacement and disintegration of men, women, children, and ultimately, society. You don't have to look long and hard at the world around you to know that this is what has happened and is still happening.

"So just because you're old enough to make your own decisions doesn't mean you should make *irrational* decisions. Sex is a beautiful thing, Sasha, but you'd be doing yourself a great injustice if you engage in it before you're married. Always remember: if a man doesn't view your chastity as the most inimitable gift you can give to your husband, then he's not worthy of you. Alright?"

Sasha crossed her arms and looked at the floor.

"Just tell me that you will at least consider what I've said."

"I'll think about it," Sasha mumbled.

"Look at me, Sasha." When Sasha lifted her head and looked at her, Dr. Avery smiled and asked, "Is that a promise?"

"Yes," Sasha said, unable to resist smiling back.

"Well, come on and help me finish setting the table. We need to eat before the food gets too cold."

"These potatoes are delicious, Dr. Avery," Sasha said. "Mashed potatoes are my favorite and these are the *best* I've ever tasted."

Dr. Avery beamed. "Thank you. Help yourself to some more, if you'd like. But save room for my banana pudding. It's very good, too."

Sasha smiled openly at the instructor. "Then I'd better not eat any more potatoes."

The doorbell rang, grabbing their attention.

Dr. Avery looked puzzled. "Who could that be?" As she stood to her feet, she said, "Oh, how could I have forgotten? That's the gentleman coming to pick up the book. Excuse me, Sasha." She placed her cloth napkin on the table and hurried to answer the door.

Within minutes, she was back. A tall, bronze-skinned man dressed in a two-piece, brown linen garment trailed her.

"Sasha," Dr. Avery said. "This is . . . I'm sorry," she said, turning to the man, "but can you tell me your name again?"

"Jabril," the man answered kindly.

"Jabril," Dr. Avery repeated. "Jabril, this is Sasha, one of my students and a very dear friend."

Sasha stood to her feet, "Hello," she said, extending a hand toward the man.

Jabril approached the table and shook Sasha's hand. "It is an honor to meet you, Sasha," he said, holding her hand a little longer than was necessary.

An honor? Sasha thought, a puzzled look on her face.

"Sasha," Dr. Avery said. "Could you please entertain Jabril for a moment? I need to run to my library and locate that book. Jabril, I apologize for not having the book ready for you. When Professor Thompson called me and said that you'd like to borrow the book, my intentions were to pull it out as soon as I ended my conversation with him. But, somehow it slipped my mind. I'll go and get it now. It should only take a moment."

"I am in no hurry," Jabril said to Dr. Avery as she hustled out of the kitchen. Turning to look at Sasha, his eyes smiled. "How are you this evening, Sasha?" he asked.

"Fine. Thank you," Sasha responded. "Would you like to sit down?" she asked him.

"Yes. Thank you." Pulling out a chair adjacent to Sasha, Jabril sat down.

Sasha sat in her chair, feeling nervous under the man's steady gaze. "Would you like me to fix you something to eat?" she asked for lack of anything else to say.

This time the man smiled with his lips. "No, thank you. I am not hungry. I apologize for interrupting your meal."

"Oh, that's alright," Sasha said, giggling nervously. "I was just sitting here stuffing myself with Dr. Avery's delicious food. Actually, you're late. You should've interrupted my meal five minutes ago. Now, I may have gained four or five pounds."

Jabril's laughter rumbled deep in his throat. "Well, then, let me apologize for not coming sooner. Arriving late is not something I have ever been accused of. I will try not to be late in the future."

Sasha looked curiously at the man, as if she knew him but couldn't place his face. She opened her mouth to ask his last name, but Dr. Avery breezed into the kitchen, carrying a large leather bound volume.

"Here it is," she said to Jabril. "I hadn't looked at in so long, I had to remember where I'd placed it on the shelf."

Jabril stood to his feet, his eyes still on Sasha. "I will be speaking at The Garden of Prayer church on Saturday night. I would like it very much if you would attend the service."

"Oh, really?!" Sasha said, standing up. "That's the church I attend. Elder Earl is my pastor. I knew about the Saturday night service, but I didn't know we were having a special guest as the speaker."

"So you will be there?" he asked her, his eyes intent.

"Yes," Sasha replied.

"Then I shall not be late," he said, smiling at her.

Sasha smiled and shook his outstretched hand. "It was nice meeting you, Jabril," she said. "I look forward to seeing you on Saturday night."

Jabril nodded to Sasha, then turned to Dr. Avery. "I would like to invite you to the service as well, Professor Avery."

"Thank you. I'd like to come. I've been planning to visit Sasha's church for some time now."

"Thank you kindly for allowing me to borrow your book," Jabril said. "I will return it to you on Saturday night."

"Keep it as long as you need it. I have no immediate use for it."

"Thank you, Professor Avery," he said, shaking the instructor's hand. "It was a pleasure to meet you."

"It was a pleasure to meet you as well, Jabril."

Both Dr. Avery and Sasha saw Jabril to the door. They waved good-bye to him as he walked down the walkway and then off down the sidewalk.

Dr. Avery closed the door. "Where is his coat, I wonder?" she asked. "It's getting cold out there."

"Probably in his car," Sasha answered. "But, then, where is his car?"

"I suppose he parked on the main street and walked over. He wasn't sure which campus house I lived in."

Sasha looked curious. "What kind of book was that?"

"A book on the Hebrew language. It details the meanings and forms of Ancient Hebrew, the language of the Bible, and it analyzes the dialectal differences between Mishnaic Hebrew and Modern Hebrew as well."

"Interesting," Sasha said thoughtfully.

"Which? The book or the man?"

Sasha smiled. "Both, actually."

"He's *definitely* an interesting man. When he told me that his name is Jabril, I wondered if it was his first name or his last. The manner in which he spoke his name, though, stopped me from asking. He said his name as if it was both his first *and* last name, as if the one name represented the total man. Now, *that* I find interesting. Don't you?"

"Yes. I do."

"And he's *handsome*, too."

Sasha cocked a questioning eye at the pensive look on her instructor's face.

Chapter 16

The mouth-watering aroma of cooking burgers and frying fish filled the campus Snack Bar and escaped into the halls of Warren Hall, luring students in to partake of its fast food delights. Day students, who lived off campus and had no access to the cafeteria, eagerly made their way into the campus diner. And board-paying students, who had daily access to the cafeteria, but preferred to have their taste buds tantalized by savory foods like huge, juicy burgers and tasty French fries, followed close behind. Unaffected by the growing line at the food counter, the two capable cooks filled orders and moved the line along quickly.

Sasha and Zandy had beaten the Friday lunch crowd. Seated at a table near the entryway, they were already devouring their meals.

"Sasha, do you know that today marks two months of friendship for us?" Zandy asked, her voice raised high enough to be heard over the chatty students in the room.

Sasha thought a second. "You're right. It *will* be two months."

Zandy raised her cup filled with Coke in mid air. "Here's to two months of friendship," she sang out. *"Santé!"*

Sasha tapped her cup to Zandy's. *"Santé!"* she said, Sprite spilling from the cup. Wiping her hands, she said, "I assume *'santé'* means 'cheers'."

Zandy nodded. "That's right." She pointed the long fry in her hand at Sasha. "All in all, you've been a pretty good friend."

Mock indignation suffused Sasha's face. "Excuse me, but are you saying that you've been a better friend to me than I've been to you?"

Zandy popped the fry in her mouth. Smacking her lips, she raised one brow and peered at Sasha. "First, you hold out on me about your relationship with Tellis. *Then* you snap on me because you thought I talked to Dr. Avery about your relationship with him."

"What about all the times you teased me unmercifully? And all the times I've poured my heart out to you and you, with your crazy self, always made a joke about something I said."

"You're right," Zandy admitted, chewing on another fry, "but there's nothing like being falsely accused." A pathetic look crossed her face. "Nothing like it."

Sasha kicked Zandy's foot under the table.

"Ouch!" Zandy yelled, a smile breaking out on her face. "You can't be kickin' me like that."

"Well, stop looking like that! I did apologize. Remember?"

"I remember. And I apologized for teasing you so much."

"So we're even."

Zandy grinned. "We're even." Taking a quick slurp from her cup, she raised it in the air. "Here's to two more months of friendship."

Sasha didn't raise her cup. "Only *two* more months?"

"Girl, with your past record, I gotta take this thing two months at a time."

Sasha kicked Zandy's foot again.

Zandy laughed. "I'm just kidding. I can tell that we're going to be friends for a very long time. Probably forever."

"How can you tell?"

"I just can. It's a feeling I have." Spinning around in her chair, Zandy looked toward the food counter. "That cheeseburger was good. I should've ordered two."

"Two! You're going to get as fat as a pig."

"Not hardly," Zandy said, turning back around. Eyeing Sasha's plate, she asked, "Are you finished with that fish sandwich?"

Sasha pushed her plate toward Zandy. "Yes."

Zandy took a huge bite of the half-eaten sandwich. She washed it down with a gulp of soda. "So how are things with you and Tellis? Did he ever get around to calling you?"

"Yes, but we didn't really talk."

"Why not?"

"He just called to tell me that he wouldn't be able to go to dinner with me at Dr. Avery's. Then he said that he would call me later."

"Did he say *why* he hadn't called?"

"He said he'd been busy."

"You don't believe him?"

"Would you have believed him?"

"Probably not."

"I don't believe him, either. I think he's seeing someone else."

"Why do you think that?"

"Because he seems so distant lately . . . and because of the things you said about him."

"I didn't say anything negative about *him*. I told you about how guys are in general . . . and Tellis is a guy."

"I just have this feeling that something is not right."

"So you're planning to break up with him?"

"I'm not sure if we were really going together. I may have just assumed we were."

"Are you okay? You don't feel heartbroken or anything, do you?"

"A little, but I'm okay. I just need to learn how to guard my heart more and how to play the game better. Like everyone else does."

"Hold up, now. What do you mean by that?"

"There're more fish in the sea. Isn't that how you would look at it?"

"What do I have to do with this? He's not cheating on *me*."
Sasha pulled her plate back across the table. "Give me my food back. You can be so insensitive."

Zandy grabbed the last bite of the fish sandwich from the plate and plopped it in her mouth. After swallowing the food, she said, "I'm sorry for coming off as insensitive, but you should make your decisions based on how *you* feel, not on what I would do. Next thing you know, you'll be blaming me for everything."

"Fine," Sasha snorted. "I *will* make my own decision. If Tellis doesn't call me and actually *talk* to me before the day is out, I'm going to start seeing someone else. Now, that's *my* decision."

Zandy's eyebrows rose like mountain peaks. "What? Are you telling me that you've hooked you another man already?"

A tall, dark-skinned girl with black, blonde-streaked hair spoke to Zandy as she passed by.

"Hey, what's going on?" Zandy responded, barely looking up at the girl. "C'mon, Sasha, give me the scoop. Have you found someone else?"

"Maybe," Sasha answered coyly.

Zandy threw an open hand up in the air. "That's my girl! Give me a high-five!"

Sasha slapped her hand into Zandy's, awkwardly landing her first high-five. Proudly, she said, "I thought you would approve."

Zandy sat back in her chair, admiring Sasha. "I feel like you're my protégé and that I've taught you well. Just remember, though, that *you* made this decision, not me." Leaning across the table she asked, "Who is it?"

"Who is who?"

"Don't play dumb with me, Sasha. You know who."

"Dexter Williams."

Zandy stiffened. "The Dexter Williams that plays basketball for Tougaloo?"

"Yes."

Zandy threw her hands up in dismay "Sasha, you can't date Dexter. He preys on the fresh and innocent. Don't you know what kind of reputation he has?"

"No, and I don't care."

Zandy rolled her eyes, shaking her head at Sasha. "I thought I'd taught you better than this."

"He seems like a nice guy to me."

"Yeah, as nice as a wolf in sheep clothing. Have you talked to him?"

"Not a whole lot. He's been trying to talk to me for a while, even before I met Tellis. I just ignored him. He slipped me his number one day, but I never called him." Sasha paused, then said, "but I will."

"No, you're not. I'm not going to let you."

Sasha shrugged her shoulders. "That's what I'm going to do if Tellis continues to be aloof with me."

"Just call Tellis one more time. He probably *has* been too busy to call. Besides, it's not like it's been weeks. It's only been a few days."

Sasha shook her head defiantly. "I've made up my mind, and I'm sticking – "

"Speaking of the devil," Zandy interjected dryly, her eyes focused beyond Sasha's head.

Sasha turned in her seat in time to see Dexter coming through the door. He spotted her and smiled. Zandy watched him as he approached the table, rolling her eyes from his round, bald head down to his long, bowed legs. She twisted her lips into a frown when he squatted beside Sasha's chair.

"Hey, Sasha," he said in a low voice. "What's going on?"

"Nothing," Sasha answered, her smile strained. "Just having lunch with my friend, Zandy."

"What'z up, Aleczandria," he said.

Not bothering to return the greeting, Zandy crossed her arms and stared at him through narrowed lids.

Dexter shrugged and turned back to Sasha. "I've been waiting for you to call me. How much longer do I have to wait?"

Sasha swallowed. "Not much longer," she said.

"I'll be waiting," he said, briefly touching the area below her chin with his forefinger.

Zandy grunted in disgust as he walked away. "I don't care what you say, I'm not going to let you go out with him."

Sasha smiled like she had a secret. "If Tellis doesn't call me by tonight, I'm calling Dexter tomorrow and inviting him out on a date."

"You can't go out with him tomorrow night. You have to go to church."

"Oh, I forgot about the Saturday night service! I do have to go to that. I promised Jabril that I would come."

"Jabril?! You *know* Jabril?!"

"What Jabril do you know?" Sasha asked, wondering why Zandy had become so excited.

"The man I met in the park the other day! His name is Jabril!"

"But you never told me his name. Now that I think about it, I think he *is* the same man."

"He fits the description I gave you of the man in the park?"

"Yes. He did."

"Did he have this way of smiling at you with his eyes? And is he a handsome man in an intriguing kind of way?"

Sasha's head bopped rhythmically. "Yes," she replied.

"That's Jabril!" Zandy exclaimed. "Where did you meet him?!"

"He came by Dr. Avery's last night to borrow a book."

"And he told you that he was going to be at church on Saturday night?"

Sasha nodded, yes.

"Good. I'll get the chance to see him again."

"So you're going to church Saturday night?"

"Yep. One of the missionaries from the church called me. She thanked me for filling out the visitor's card and she told me how happy they were that I attended the Sunday service. She asked me if I would like to be a part of the program for Saturday night. It's supposed to be a service for young people. I told her no, but to put T'Kara on the program for a poetry reading. She likes doing stuff like that. At first I was going because T'Kara would kill me if I didn't. Now I'm going because I want to see Jabril."

Sasha looked doubtful. "Do you really think it's the same man? Don't you think that's too much of a coincidence?"

Zandy smiled knowingly. "Oh, it's the same man. You just don't confuse men like Jabril."

Twenty pairs of eyes watched Dr. Avery as she stood in front of the Holmes Hall classroom and assigned the final paper of the semester. She stressed that the paper must be in accordance with the guidelines outlined in her course syllabus and that it must be submitted on the day of the final. No excuses will be accepted. No extensions will be given.

The students listened, but only with half an ear. They didn't feel Dr. Avery needed their undivided attention at this point: they had her course syllabus, they'd been in her class long enough to know that she didn't play when it came to her no-extension policy, and, most of all, they were ready to go. It was Friday afternoon, and they were looking forward to starting their weekend, soon.

Sasha impatiently tapped the rubber end of her pencil on the desk. She wondered if she should call Dexter tonight, instead of waiting until tomorrow. *He looked so handsome when he came in the Snack Bar today,* she thought, smiling. *And where did he get those beautiful, bowed legs?*

Zandy sat across from Sasha. She was looking forward to her weekend, too — she had a date tonight and it promised to be a sizzling one — but the thought of another paper weighed heavy in her mind. Her hand shot up in the air, beckoning Dr. Avery's attention.

"You have a question, Aleczandria?"

Zandy nodded. "Dr. Avery, isn't there a way we can get around writing this paper? Like, if we have an 'A' average by the end of the semester?" The few 'A' students in the class looked hopefully at Dr. Avery. None of them were looking forward to writing the ten-page paper.

Dr. Avery wasn't having it. "Aleczandria, you know the rules of my class. They're in the syllabus, like always. An 'A' average only exempts you from your final exam, not your final paper."

Zandy shrugged. "I think you should be exempted from both if you have an 'A' average. You don't want to grade all of those papers anyway, do you?"

"I'm perfectly fine with grading *all of those papers*, but thank you for asking. This semester is almost over when you consider the upcoming Thanksgiving and Christmas holidays, and this paper is your last major assignment. Use the remainder of your time in this class to complete the paper and to study for the final exam."

Zandy smiled, fiercely shaking her head. "Oh, I won't have to take the final."

"Is that so?" Dr. Avery asked, smiling back.

"C'mon now, Dr. Avery," Zandy whined. You *know* I have an 'A' in this class."

Dr. Avery looked wide-eyed at Zandy. "*Really?*" she asked, her smile widening. "I didn't know that. I guess I'll have to look again."

Zandy groaned and congenial laughter spread over the room.

Dr. Avery's eyes scanned the class. "If there are no more questions about the paper — legitimate questions, that is," she said, cutting an eye Zandy's way. "Then you all may go."

The students quickly filed out of the room. All of them except Zandy and Sasha.

Zandy leaned across the aisle to Sasha. "She's just trying to scare me. She knows I have an 'A' average." Standing, she flung her book bag over her shoulder and walked to stand near Sasha. "And if I *don't* have one, I'm only one or two points off. She can give me that. Or maybe I can make up those points on one of her pop quizzes. C'mon, so we can go and talk to her."

Sasha chuckled as she stood, throwing her book and pencil into her book bag. "*We?*" she asked with raised brows. "*We* don't need to talk to her. I *know* I have an 'A' in this class."

Zandy rolled her eyes and sighed. "What-*ever*, Miss Einstein." She pulled Sasha by the arm. "Just go with me for support, then."

They made their way to the front of the class just as Dr. Avery was closing her briefcase. She smiled as they approached. "Hello, ladies. What can I do for you?"

Sasha returned the greeting, but Zandy skipped the preliminaries. "Dr. Avery, what's my average in this class?"

"I don't know, Aleczandria," Dr. Avery answered, hunching her shoulders and looking decidedly innocent. "I haven't computed class averages yet. You have all of your work, don't you? You can compute your grade average up to this point."

Zandy's eyes pleaded. "I've gotten an 'A' or a high 'B' on almost everything."

Dr. Avery smiled at Zandy like she was a three-year old. "I guess you forgot about the homework assignment you didn't turn in."

"See, Dr. Avery, that's what I'm saying — without that homework assignment I should be only a point or two away from an 'A' average. You can *give* me two measly points."

"Aleczandria, you should know me better than that. Besides, you may need more than two points. Did you also forget about the 'C' you made on that pop quiz?"

Sasha glared at Zandy. "You made a 'C' on a quiz? They are so *ea-sy*."

"Oh, hush," Zandy said. "You're supposed to be supporting me here. Besides," she said, turning to Dr. Avery. "I wasn't feeling well that day, but I got out of bed to come to your class. Your class was the *only* class I went to that day, Dr. Avery, because I like it so much. And as far as that assignment, I told you that I just completely forgot about it. You *know* I usually turn in my work."

Dr. Avery chuckled heartily. "You're just too much, Aleczandria," she said, then lifted her briefcase from the desk and walked off toward the door. "Make sure you study for your final exam, Aleczandria," she said over her shoulder. "Sasha, I'll see you tomorrow night at church."

Zandy called out, "I'm going to church, too, Dr. Avery. Can I get a couple of points for that?"

Dr. Avery didn't answer, just gave them a good-bye wave as she passed through the door.

Sasha shook with laughter. "Points for going to church? Now I've heard it all."

Zandy stomped her foot. "Man!" she pouted, "I don't want to have to take that exam. I know she's just pulling my leg, trying to stress me out. C'mon. Let's go. I've gotta go home and figure out my average."

"I'm sure the next time Dr. Avery sees you, she'll tell you what your average is," Sasha told her as they walked down the hall of the building.

"Maybe, but I'm not going to wait for her to tell me. I need to know as soon as possible." Zandy thrust open the heavy door that led to the outside. "This is serious."

On the sidewalk, Sasha asked, "Did you really forget to turn in that homework assignment?"

"Girl, *please*. I never forget any work I have to do. I kept procrastinating with writing that paper. I finally said that I'd write it the day before it was due, but I messed around and went to a party. I partied so hard, I didn't have enough strength to even *lift* a pencil."

"But *now* everything is *serious*," Sasha said, teasing Zandy.

Zandy made a face at Sasha. "No, it's always been serious. At least from the time I realized that if I didn't work hard, I'd have to rely on some *man* to take care of me. And you *know* that I'd rather *die* than to let that happen." Leaning to hug Sasha, she said, "I'll see you later, girl. I need to get home."

"What are you doing this evening? I may give you a call."

"Oh, I forgot to tell you: I have a date with this guy tonight."

"A date? Have you been holding out on me, Zandy?"

"No. There's really nothing to tell."

Sasha's eyes twinkled with interest. "Is this one of the dates where you love'em then leave'em?"

Zandy winked. "I don't know yet," she said, a sly smile on her face. "I'll have to wait and see." Waving good-bye, she turned and walked off down the sidewalk.

"Hey, Zandy," Sasha called out to her. "Let me know if you need help studying for Dr. Avery's final exam."

Zandy stopped long enough to stick her tongue out at Sasha.

Sasha watched her friend hurry off down the sidewalk. When a throng of approaching students finally swallowed Zandy up, Sasha turned with a smile on her face and walked off in the opposite direction.

Chapter 17

F riday night, Tellis stood in front of his bedroom mirror and lightly sprayed his bare chest with Jean Paul Guatierre cologne. Tonight, he would be with his baby, and he planned to be smelling nice and looking good when she saw him. She'd bought the cologne for him and whenever he wore it, she was like putty in his hands. He smiled. She was always like putty in his hands. Still, it was now his favorite cologne.

He stared at his reflection. The low, square-cut fade. The golden-brown skin tone. The thick, silky eyebrows. The sensual, hooded eyes. The perfectly formed nose. The thin mustache that connected to a well-groomed beard on his chin. The small tuft of hair that accentuated the lower rim of his beautifully shaped lips. The powerful arms that swelled with generous muscles. The robust chest that narrowed to a flat, rippled midriff.

In his opinion, the face in the mirror was attractive enough, but the body was more than attractive — it was fit for the calendar of the world's finest men. He'd never idolized his model good looks — like so many others did — but the condition of his body had always been important. He worked hard to keep it in tip-top shape. Tonight, his girl would see his naked body for the very first time. He was sure that she'd be pleased. Studying his reflection, he nodded his head, as if he could already see her hands roaming his hard body.

From the closet he pulled out a deep red, short-sleeved shirt and slipped it over his head. Tucking the shirt in his black slacks and buckling his belt, he walked to the mirror once more. The shirt hugged his torso, emphasizing his muscled physique. He'd seen the Latin singer, Ricky Martin, on television dressed in a shirt of a similar style and thought he'd look good in the shirt as well. He'd been right. The fit was perfect.

Satisfied with his appearance, Tellis walked out of his room and down the stairs, into a spacious and elegantly decorated foyer. The house was quiet. His parents had gone out for the evening to a dinner party. Walking through the 3,000 square feet custom built house, he made sure that all the doors were closed and secured. Returning to the foyer, he set the alarm and left the house.

With cougar-like grace, Tellis slid his tall frame into the seat of his 1987 Toyota Celica. A hoopty, his friends called it. They all drove the latest model cars and ragging on his car was one of their favorite pastimes. After years of teasing him, they finally concluded that either he had a serious screw loose in his head or he had very bad credit.

Tellis laughed as he backed out of the driveway. His friends were wrong, on both accounts. Every screw in his head was bolted tight, and his savings account held more than twenty thousand dollars, thanks to his money-conscious father who started teaching him financial responsibility at the tender age of five.

Still, his friends didn't let up on him. They couldn't understand why he wouldn't buy a new car. Didn't he realize that he was missing out on loads of honeys by driving that banged up jalopy?

"Loads of honeys" was a stretch, but they were right — he *had* scared off a few girls with his dented, fading blue car. They'd been disgusted and highly offended at having to ride in the car, especially when they had to enter through the driver's side to get to the passenger's side.

Tellis hadn't cared. He'd chalked them all up to being selfish and materialistic and definitely not worth his time. Because of them, he began using his car as a way of weeding out the females in his life. And there had been quite a few to weed out. He'd had more breasts and rear-ends thrown his way than he could handle. And he had tried to handle them all at one point in his life. It just got to be too much. Before he could get to know one girl, another one — more enticing than the last — came along, and he could never resist the temptation to seduce and conquer.

And the way they started grilling him got to be too much, too: Where did you go? Who were you with? Why haven't you called? And they were always falling in love, too. One night in his arms, and they were ready to spend the rest of their lives with him. Handling the questions they bombarded him with had been easy: he just told them what they wanted to hear. But he didn't know how to handle that love-at-first-sight thing. Besides, heartbreaker was not a role he enjoyed playing. So, as a graduating high school senior, he vowed to change his womanizing ways.

But sistas made it hard for a brotha, he thought as he drove along the dark streets.

As soon he'd set foot on Tougaloo's campus, the madness had begun all over again. The ladies swarmed him like flies do honey. Still, he'd remained focused and resisted the urge to play. That's not to say that he stopped dating altogether. He did date, but he dated with a purpose. He was tired of empty relationships, relationships with sex as the only foundation. He wanted the real thing.

Now, as a junior and one year from graduating, he'd accomplished his goal — he'd disciplined himself enough to stop the flow of women in and out of his life. But a few still hung around. He was in the process of getting rid of them, though, because he'd finally set his heart on the one woman he was going to spend the rest of his life with. Just yesterday, he had been at work when it hit him like a ton of bricks: she was the one.

He was falling in love with her and he knew that she was falling in love with him. He could tell by the way she looked at him. He had every reason to believe that she was worth all the others he'd been casually dating put together. The way he felt about her was enough to make him think about marriage. It was enough to make him think about having babies with her. It was even enough to make him want to buy a new car, and no other woman had affected him in that way before. In fact, she'd passed his car test with flying colors.

"Your car says a lot of positive things about your character, Tellis. I like it," she'd said the first time she'd ridden in his car.

"You like *it*?" he'd asked. "Are you referring to my car or my character?"

Smiling, she'd answered, "Both. I like them both."

Tellis had smiled back. *Good answer*, he'd thought, and his feelings for her had soared.

Now, he wondered what kind of car he should buy. What kind of car would she like? Would she like a flashy, red sports car like the Corvette his playboy of a brother, Trent, drove recklessly around town? Or would she like a sports utility vehicle like the Lincoln Navigator his oldest brother, Thomas, an orthodontist, had recently bought for his wife and three children?

Tellis smiled. His girl was simple. She would like anything he bought. That's why he was going to marry her. She didn't know it yet, but as soon as it was appropriate, he would put a ring on her finger. Until that time came, he'd shower her with all the love and affection she could stand. And gifts. He'd shower her with those, too.

Parked outside her place, he reached over to the passenger seat and picked up a beautifully wrapped single red rose and a large box of chocolates. She loved chocolate candy with nuts in it. There were enough in the box for her to eat to her heart's delight.

He stood at her door a moment before knocking. He needed a little time to compose himself. He wondered if she was as excited about tonight as he was. He knew that she was. When he'd spoken to her on the phone a few hours ago, and they'd both agreed that tonight was the night for them to consummate their relationship, she'd become breathlessly excited. Her excitement had made him nervous. He'd been celibate for more than six months now, and he wondered if he should be trying to remain that way. Celibacy had been good for him — it helped him to feel more grounded, like he was in control and not his genitalia. And more than anything, he wanted a relationship that wasn't dictated by sex, like all the others he'd been in. He wanted a relationship that was based on love and commitment and one that was wholesome and good.

He'd alluded to the very same thing just yesterday when Minister Makil, the youth minister from the church, had called him and invited him out to a special Saturday night program. They'd hit it off instantly and for almost an hour, they talked about the Lord and sports and school. And women. Tellis had been surprised at how candidly the young minister had spoken about relationships and sex. He'd said that God — a God of order and covenant — ordained sex between man and woman, but only when the covenant of marriage had been made between the two first.

With the subject of sex never too far from the focal point of his mind, Tellis had welcomed the discussion. He'd shared with Minister Makil his current state of celibacy, but said that it was more for personal reasons than for spiritual. He'd explained to the minister how one day — out of the blue — he came to the realization that, because of his uninhibited sexual liaisons, he was misusing and debilitating his own body and those of the females, too. Minister Makil had immediately told him that that was not a thought that came out of the blue, but that it was of the Spirit of God, seeking to instruct him in the way of life and truth.

Tellis hadn't disagreed with the minister, but told him that he'd been denying himself sexual pleasures only until he had totally committed himself to one special lady. And now that he had done that, he didn't think he had the strength to remain celibate. Minister Makil told Tellis that the Lord had given him the grace to be celibate and that he could do the same for Tellis. He then led Tellis into prayer, in which Tellis accepted the Lord as his Saviour and asked God to give him the strength he needed to live upright before Him. Tellis had hung up the phone pleased with the kindred spirit he'd found in Minister Makil and with the fact that he'd given his life to the Lord. And he'd had every intention of doing all that was good and right in the eyes of God.

But that was before he'd spoken with her. The minute she'd invited him over for their special evening together, his resolve began to weaken. And nothing in him – not even the words Minister Makil had spoken or the prayer he prayed – was enough to kill the urge to be with her.

His feelings ran deep for this girl, and he wanted to be with her, in every possible way. She wanted the same thing. What else mattered?

Taking a deep breath, Tellis raised a fist to knock on the door. *It's not good for a man to touch a woman*, a quiet voice said in his head. His hand froze in position, just before making contact with the door. That's the same thing Minister Makil had said to him. The minister had laughingly told Tellis that that was one of the first things he'd learned after he got saved — one touch led to another, then another, then another . . . . Tellis' hand fell to his side. For a split second he thought about turning around and going home, but when he looked down at the flowers and candy he held, he began to envision the salacious pleasures that waited for him behind the closed door. His hand sprang up and he knocked hard on the door.

Within seconds, the door opened slowly, and in the opening stood one of the most beautiful women he'd ever seen. Her attractive face, enhanced with dark, seductive shades of makeup, literally took his breath away. His eyes lulled with desire as he slowly drank all of her in.

Her hair, parted in the center, laid sleek and straight along the sides of her face. Her shirt – black and sleeveless with a zipped front — exposed a fair amount of her taut midriff. Her skirt — black, tight and very short — revealed shapely thighs and beautiful legs. Her feet, with carefully manicured and painted toenails, were nicely encased in a pair of black, high-heeled sandals.

She'd said she'd be ready for me, but my, my, my, Tellis thought, looking in her eyes.

She smiled. The smoldering flames in his eyes told her that she'd achieved the glamorously alluring look she'd been shooting for. Taking him by the arm, she pulled him into a dark room and closed the door. Sniffing the rose he mutely handed to her, she thanked him. When he handed her the candy, she leaned into him and gave him a soft kiss on the lips. He held her to deepen the kiss, but she pulled out of his arms, smiling. Laying her gifts on a table, she turned back to him with the smile still on her face and took him by the hand. He followed her as she led him to her bed.

Tellis hadn't expected things to move so fast, but if it was okay with her, then it was okay with him. He'd been dreaming about this moment for some time, and now his dream was about to become a reality.

At her bedside, where a candle burned with a soft glow, he wrapped her in his arms and kissed her. Snaking her arms up his chest and around his neck, she gripped the back of his head and pulled it toward her, deepening their kiss.

The kiss went on for minutes, and Tellis could feel his passion rising. If the look in her eyes meant anything, her passion was rising, too. Slowly, he pushed her down to the bed, and then bent to one knee and kissed the soft flesh of her inner thigh. He heard her moan. Sliding his hands down her smooth, bare legs to her feet, he slipped off her sandals. He then wrapped his large hands around her small ankles and stood to his feet, placing the length of her legs onto the bed as he did so. She leaned back until she was lying prostrate on the bed, smiling as he leaned over to kiss her again. She hungrily returned his kiss, slipping her arms around his waist to pull him down beside her, but he resisted.

Stepping back from the bed, Tellis slipped off his soft, leather shoes. Without taking his eyes off of her, he unbuckled his belt and pulled the hem of his shirt out of his pants.

Silently, she watched him.

In one swift move, Tellis pulled the shirt over his head and let it fall to the floor.

She smiled at him, her eyes registering appreciation for his muscle-ripped body.

Joining her on the bed, he lay along side her, taking her hand in his. He kissed it. "I love you," he said to her.

"I love you, too, Tellis," she replied softly.

He ran a finger along the edges of her lips and then kissed them. He kissed her cheeks, and then her chin. Burying his mouth in the curve of her neck, he trailed deep kisses along the delicate curve of her collarbone. She moaned again, pressing her nails into the hardness of his back.

It's not good for a man to touch a woman, the voice said again.

Tellis heard the voice, but his body didn't. His adept hands began to roam over the upper part of her body. He heard the sharp intake of her breath when his hand briefly touched the tip of her breast through the soft fabric of her shirt. He felt her body quiver beneath him. And the way she arched her chest toward him, he knew that she liked what he was doing and wanted more of it.

Aiming to please, he reached to the front zipper of her shirt and pulled it down until the shirt was completely unzipped, exposing her full breasts, veiled by a black, satin bra. He slid his finger along the crevice of her breast, down to the bra's clasp.

A bra that opens in the front, he thought, a devilish smile on his face. *She's making this so easy for me.*

He placed his thumb and middle finger on the clasp, and pressed the ends together to unhook the bra. The clasp wouldn't give. He pressed again. The clasp remained intact. Shifting his body in the bed, he put both hands on the clasp and began to jiggle it. One end of the clasp shifted up as if to open, but stopped short. In the little light offered by the candle, he strained his eyes to see why the clasp wouldn't part. As far as he could tell, nothing appeared to be blocking the clasp from opening. Frustrated, he jerked at the clasp. Still, it didn't budge. Agitation began to eat away at his passion. His hands began to tremble.

"Let me do it," she said softly in his ears. Pushing his hand aside, she reached for the clasp.

"No," he said, a tinge of harshness in his voice.

"It's okay. I can do it."

"No," he said again, moving away from her and sitting up on the edge of the bed.

Her brows knitted, she asked, "What do you mean *no?* I can undo the clasp, Tellis. *It's no problem.*"

"It *is* a problem. I can't do this."

"You can't do this?" she asked, an incredulous look on her face. "Just because you couldn't unfasten my bra, *you can't do this?*"

Tellis didn't answer.

"That doesn't make any sense, Tellis. Tell me what's wrong," she pleaded.

"I don't know," he said, perplexed by his own reaction. "I don't know."

"You have to know *something*, Tellis. What's wrong?"

Tellis shook his head, as if confused. "I've been thinking . . ."

"Thinking?" she said, her voice rising. "You're not supposed to be thinking. You're supposed to be . . . making love to me."

"I know, but —"

"But what? Don't you want to?"

"Yes."

"No, you don't," she said, contradicting him in an adamant voice. "Because if you did, that's what you would be doing. Do you know how long I've waited for this? Do you know how frustrated I'm feeling right now?"

Tellis bowed his head and said nothing.

Zipping her top and scrambling out of the bed, she stood before his bowed head. "Tellis, look at me. I want to ask you something, and I want you to answer me truthfully." When Tellis raised his eyes to hers, she asked, "You said you were thinking. I don't need to hear the person's name, but are you thinking about someone else?"

Tellis hesitated before answering, "No."

"Why the hesitation, Tellis? Either you are or you aren't."

Tellis bent over and picked his shirt up from the floor. Standing, he slipped it over his head. "I may not have the best track record when it comes to women, but I've been really trying to make it right. So when I say that I love you, I mean it. I *know* that I love you. And I'm not in love with anyone else. There's no one else I want to be with more than I want to be with you."

"Then what's the problem?"

"I don't know," Tellis answered, shaking his head and looking off. "I don't know if I'm doing the right thing."

She frowned. "What do you mean? Didn't you tell me that sex is always right between two people who really love each other?"

Tellis sighed. "That's how I used to feel," he mumbled, as if talking to himself.

"What do you mean by that?" she asked, her frown deepening.

"Look," he said, "I've got to go."

Her brows rose high. "You're just going to leave?" she asked, her voice rising to an angry screech. "Without explaining anything to me? Tellis, we talked about this and we decided that tonight was our time to be together, and now you're just going to walk out? Just like that?"

Tellis avoided the troubled look in her eyes. Buckling his belt and stepping into his shoes, he said, "It doesn't matter what I say, you're not going to understand. You're going to be angry. And I really don't want to argue with you right now."

The sincerity in his voice warmed her heart, and she moved to stand near him, wrapping her arms around his waist. Softly, she said, "I don't want to argue, either. Tell me what's on your mind. I'll try my best to be understanding."

Tellis looked down into her eyes. She was right — he did owe her an explanation. But how could he explain what was wrong with him when he himself didn't fully understand it. Simply telling her that his untimely reluctance to be with her may have had something to do with him giving his life to God yesterday would probably get his eyes scratched out. What woman would want to hear that from the man she was desperate to make love to? "I know that I owe you an explanation," he said pleadingly, "but I can't really give you one right now. Just give me a little time to get myself together, and then we'll talk. Okay?" Without waiting for a response, Tellis laid a quick kiss on her lips and practically ran from the room.

"Tellis!" she called out after him. "Tellis!"

But Tellis was gone.

"I can't believe he just walked out on me like that," she muttered angrily.

Chapter 18

"Knock, knock, knock," Zandy yelled, stepping through the front door of her mother's house. "Where are you guys?" she called out in the empty den as she headed for the kitchen. The smell of fried chicken filled the house, and Zandy's stomach responded with a growl. Going straight to the stove, she grabbed a chicken leg from a plate piled with meat.

T'Kara bounded into the kitchen. "Hey, Zandy," she said, slightly winded. "I heard you, but I was putting on my shoes. How was your date last night?"

Zandy rolled her eyes and pursed her lips. "It was alright."

"What's his name?" T'Kara asked.

"Can't tell you," Zandy replied with an I've-got-a-secret smile, then bit off a piece of the crispy chicken.

T'Kara grimaced, then said, "Well, do you like my hair?"

Zandy's mouth was too full of chicken to answer. She twirled the chicken leg around in the air, motioning for T'Kara to turn so she could see all of her head.

T'Kara was only too willing to obliged. She strutted in a circle, pumping her head full of sandy-brown ringlets with both hands.

"It's pretty, T.K. Who did it?"

"Mama took me to Rob-Robin. And I'm gonna let you slide with calling me T.K. this time because I'm so excited."

Zandy laughed out. "Rob-Robin? I know you didn't call him that to his face. Some gay guys like to go off on people, you know."

"He likes it when I call him that."

"Well, *Rob-Robin* did a good job on your head," Zandy said, munching on the chicken. Pointing the chicken at T'Kara's blue checkered jacket and short matching skirt, she asked, "When did you get that outfit? It's cute. Except for the color, it looks like mine."

T'Kara looked at the hunter green suit Zandy wore and twisted her lips into a mock-sneer. "Mine looks better, though." She giggled when Zandy threatened to bop her with the chicken leg. "Daddy bought it for me when we went shopping last weekend. I wore it so that he could see me in it tonight. He's coming to church to hear me say my poem."

Zandy stopped chewing. "What'd you say?"

T'Kara was too busy picking out her own piece of chicken to notice the frown on Zandy's face. "I said, Daddy is coming to church with me, you, and Mama tonight. He's in the bedroom talking to Mama right now."

Zandy's eyes narrowed to knife-like slits. "Where's his truck? I didn't see it outside."

"Sherrell dropped him off. I think something is wrong with her car, so she's been using Daddy's truck. I didn't even have to beg him to come. He said, 'yes' as soon as I asked him, even though he knew Mama was going, too."

Zandy felt mad enough to chew nails. She threw her chicken leg in the garbage can. Her appetite was shot. "Bump that! If he's going, then I'm not."

T'Kara's face became a mass of frowns. "Why not?" she asked sharply.

"I'm just not, and I'm going to tell him, too." Zandy's angry strides carried her to the kitchen doorway.

T'Kara ran behind her and grabbed her by the arm. "Don't do that, Zandy. I want both of you there. P-leeease, Zandy. You promised to do better. You promised!"

"I never promised to go anywhere with him!" Zandy retorted, shaking her arms from T'Kara's grip. Seeing the pained expression on T'Kara's face, she said in a soft voice, "Look, T.K., I know you're thinking that maybe they're going to get back together, but it's not going to happen. If they were going to get back together, it would've happened a long time ago. So stop wishing, okay? Do you remember the man I met in the park the other day? Well, I was thinking that he would be perfect for Mama. He's going to be at church tonight, and I want to introduce him to both of you. If he sees her with Walter, then he might be scared off. You're gonna really like him, T.K. I can't wait for you and Mama to meet him." She reassured her sister with a warm smile, then with determination in her steps, she headed toward her mother's bedroom "I just need to get rid of this piece of scum first."

Tears popped into T'Kara's eyes as she watched Zandy walk through the den and into the hallway. *Zandy is about to destroy everything*, she thought sadly.

Zandy barged down the hall and stopped abruptly at her mother's bedroom door. The door stood wide open, and no one was in the room. Zandy frowned. *Maybe they're in the backyard*, she thought. Just as she turned to head on down the hall, she heard soft voices. Stepping gingerly into the room, she peeped around the wall toward the bathroom. The bathroom door was slightly ajar and she could hear soft whimpering. It was mother. *Why is she crying?* Zandy wondered. She tip-toed closer to the bathroom door. Her father was consoling her mother.

"Shhhhh, Dot," he said, using his pet name for her mother. "Stop crying." His tone was soothing. "I found the tissue. Come here. Let me wipe your face."

"Walter," her mother sobbed softly. "I'm so sorry it has taken me this long to . . . to talk to you. I could've saved us both a lot of heartache." Her voice sprang into a squeak. "I've missed you so much."

Zandy wanted to hit the wall, or at least slap some sense into her mother. *It wouldn't do any good. She's so weak. How can she even be talking to him after what he did to her? What in the world is she thinking?*

Zandy could hear her father still cooing her mother, telling her not to cry. Whenever she'd hurt herself as a small child, he would comfort her in the same way and he'd always made her feel better. But hearing him now made Zandy want to choke the very life out of him. *Mama, he's playing you like a slot machine, and you can't even see it. I oughta ring his thick neck.* Her fingers clenched at her sides as she heard him speak to her mother in a husky, calming voice. "It's all in the past now," he said. *That's fine for him to say! The no-good dog!* "I'm glad we had this talk, too. I'm glad for the talks we've been having for the past couple of weeks . . ."

Zandy wanted to hit the roof. "Talks? What talks?" she mouthed angrily. *Since when? . . . I wonder if T.K knew,* she thought, darting angry eyes toward the front of the house. *Probably not. She definitely would have told me.*

"We both understand what went wrong, and now we can move on, together," her father continued softly. "I've even talked to Sherrell. She wasn't too happy about me leaving, but she's always known that I'd never stopped loving you — they all knew that. So, we just need to go on from here. There's no need to keep talking about the whole thing, is there?"

Zandy strained to hear what her mother had to say, knowing that it would be something stupid. "Walter, I can't let it go that easily. I'm trying to, but I can't." *Finally, some sense. Tell him to get his cheatin' behind the steppin', Mama. The jerk.* "I was wrong," her mother said. *Wrong for what? For not accepting his mess? What-ev-er!* "I was so wrong to do what I did," her mother croaked.

Zandy threw up her hands in disgust. *She's apologizing to him.* Angry beyond measure, she paced in a small circle. The urge to burst into the bathroom and do her mother's job for her — throw her father out of the house, for good — was just too great. She clenched her teeth, fighting to calm herself.

"Dot, I told you. It's in the past, and there's no need to keep talking about it," her father said sternly.

Zandy could always tell when her father was starting to get annoyed. He'd suck in a deep breath and he'd speak in a tight, harsh tone, like he was doing now. *He's got his nerve.*

Her mother was annoyed, too. *But she has every right to be.* "There *is* a reason to keep talking about it," her mother said. "Do you honestly think I can just forget what happened? For the past thirteen years, I've thought about nothing else, every day of my life. When you left me, my life was turned upside down. If it hadn't been for the love I have for my girls and the love they have for me, I never would've made it. So I can't just forget it, Walter. I have to talk about it. I *need* to talk about it. I know that we've been talking lately, and it's helped me more than I knew it could. But, still, talking is only the first step. How do we just pick up the pieces and move on as if the past never happened? I don't know if we can do that. I just don't know if I can do that, Walter."

Zandy silently egged her mother on. *Tell him, Mama! Set him straight!*

The harshness left her father's voice. "Baby, what do you want me to do?" he asked patiently. "Just tell me what I can do to make this easier for you?"

Zandy had the answer to that. *You can get your useless behind out of here and never come back! That's what you can do!*

"You can listen," her mother pleaded softly. "I need you to listen to me. Whenever I need to talk about it, just listen to me, Walter. Because when I cheated on you, it was the worst thing I could have ever done. And I'm so sorry, Walter."

Zandy's chin drew back into her neck, her face a mask of frowns. Surely she hadn't heard her mother right.

"I never meant to hurt you. I was lonely . . ."

"I understand, baby, and I'm sorry I wasn't there for you."

"No, Walter, you were a good husband. A good father. You always wanted the best for us. You were always pushing me to do better, to be better. Sometimes I felt like you didn't think I was good enough for you, but now I know that you pushed me because you loved me . . ."

Zandy couldn't believe her ears. This couldn't be true. There was no way in the world that this could be true. *My mother? My mother cheated on my father? No way,* she thought, shaking her head slowly. *There's no way* . . . Her entire body began to tremble, but she stood rigid and listened for her mother to say something that proved she'd heard her wrong. But her mother only repeated over and over again how sorry she was for hurting her father. Then she heard soft groans and loud kisses coming from the bathroom.

Zandy's body began to shake violently. She raised trembling hands to cover her face as tears burst into her eyes and ran down her cheeks. A gulf of pain hit her in her stomach and she doubled over from the blow, falling to her knees. *Oh, God. Oh, God. Please, no. This can't be true. It can't be.* Squeezing her eyes shut, she struggled to hold back the tears and the nausea overtaking her. Feeling the nausea traveling up her throat, she clamped her hands over her mouth and struggled to her feet. Her weak and trembling legs carried her to the doorway where she fell once again to her knees. With all the strength she could muster, she latched on to the doorjamb and pulled herself to her feet. Disbelief and shame engulfed her as she flung herself from the doorway and down the hall.

"What did Daddy say, Zandy?" T'Kara asked, leaping from the sofa. "Is he still going?"

Zandy rushed past T'Kara like death and hell were behind her and dashed out the front door.

T'Kara rushed to the door and called after her sister. "Zandy!" she yelled. "What's the matter?! Where are you going?!" She watched as Zandy fell to her knees in the grass and vomited loudly. T'Kara rushed out of the house and down the steps "What's wrong, Zandy?" she asked, seeing the tears flowing down her sister's face. T'Kara reached out to touch her, but Zandy brushed her hand away and stumbled to her feet. T'Kara watched as she jumped in her SUV and sped off down the street. T'Kara slowly walked back to the house.

"T'Kara," her mother called out sternly, walking into the den. "Why were you yelling like that? I could hear you from my bedroom." Dorothy Davis, dressed in a green suit with a flared skirt, walked up to her daughter, a disapproving expression on her face. But the frown on T'Kara's face prompted her to ask, "What's wrong, baby?"

"I was trying to catch Zandy."

"Zandy was here?"

"Yes ma'am," T'Kara answered. Noticing her mother's wet eyes, she asked her, "Are you crying, too. Did you and Zandy have an argument or something?"

"No-o-o-o, baby," her mother said, hugging her. "I haven't even seen Zandy. She must've gotten upset and left when she realized your father was here. Like she always does." She wondered how Zandy would take the news of she and Walter reuniting, but she already knew the answer to that — *Zandy will be furious, especially when she learns that I was the unfaithful one and not her father.* To T'Kara she said, "Zandy'll be okay."

T'Kara pulled out of her mother's arms and looked up at her. "Well, then, what's wrong? Why are you crying?"

"Nothing's wrong, T.K.," her father said, coming up behind her mother and wrapping his arms around her. He kissed her mother on the cheek. "She's just happy."

T'Kara's eyes widened and her mouth opened to the shape of an 'O'.

Her parents chuckled at her expression. "Surprise," her father said, smiling down at her.

T'Kara somehow managed to get her mother out of the way and she slammed her body into her father's, gripping him with tight hug. She snuggled her face into his chest. "Oh, Daddy! I'm so happy!"

"Baby, you're messing up your father's suit," her mother chided softly. "And your hair."

T'Kara pulled out of her father's embrace, giving him her brightest smile. "I'm so happy, I can burst."

"I'm happy, too, T.K.," her father said, smiling back at her.

T'Kara was too excited to correct him on the use of her name. "When are you coming home?"

Her father turned his smile on her mother, "Well, your mother and I have a few things to work out first."

"Like what?" T'Kara asked.

"Well, like we're going to get married . . . again."

T'Kara let out a loud hoot and began to jump up and down. She clapped her hands wildly, grinning from ear to ear.

"When are you getting married? When?! When?!"

Her father grinned at her excitement. "Calm down, T.K.," he said, trying to steady her. "We're going to get married soon." He pulled her mother into his arms and lightly kissed her forehead. "Very soon."

T'Kara shook her head as if the sight before her was too good to be true. "God does answer prayer," she said and enveloped them both in a hug. "I've been praying for years that you would get back together. And, boy, did I have to pray hard — you hardly even *talked* to each other," she said, giving them both a disapproving look. Then she smiled. "But I never gave up. I never stopped hoping. Never. I love you both so much and I'm so happy you're back together."

"We love you, too, baby," her parents said as one.

T'Kara smiled into her mother's eyes. "Real smiles look good on you, Mama,"

Fresh tears sprang into her mother's eyes. "Thank you, baby," her mother croaked. "We'll be leaving for church soon. Are you ready to go?"

"Yes ma'am," T'Kara answered, "but first I need to call Janay and Marcus and tell them my good news." T'Kara turned to sprint off down the hall.

"Hold it a minute, now," her father said in a questioning voice. "I thought we agreed that you're not old enough to be talking to boys on the phone yet."

"Daddy," T'Kara said, looking at him like he didn't have a clue, "Marcus is not a *real* boy — he's my friend, just like Janay is my friend."

Her father looked skeptical. "I don't know," he said, shaking his head.

"Daddy, I like Marcus because he's very smart and because he's a good friend. But he's as skinny as spaghetti and he wears bifocals. Tell him, Mama. Tell Daddy what Marcus looks like."

Her mother nodded, a smile on her face. "He is a pretty skinny young fellow," she said.

"Trust me," T'Kara said. "When I start calling boys on the phone, it definitely won't be Marcus. He's *way* too goofy for me." With that, she turned and sprinted toward her bedroom.

Angela D. Shearry

Chapter 19

"I understand that we have a poem recital tonight by a young lady who's visiting with us for the first time," the young emcee for the program said. "Where is T'Kara?" she asked, scanning the crowd. When T'Kara stood to her feet, the emcee smiled and waved her forward. "Let's give her a warm welcome as she comes."

T'Kara had been enjoying the comfort of her father's arm tossed loosely over her shoulder and her mother's hand clasped tightly in hers. She'd wanted to pinch herself, to make sure she wasn't dreaming. Both of her parents were there, together, with her. Tonight, because of the youth program, almost all of the young people sat on one side of the church, and the adults on the other. But T'Kara had chosen to stay with her parents. She'd been enjoying the program, but ever so often she'd look up at her parents and thank God for bringing them back together again. God had answered her prayer, and she hadn't even seen it coming. She should've known, though, that something had changed because her father had started to call the house more often lately. Of course, he'd always speak to her first, but then he'd asked to talk briefly with her mother. She wondered which one of them had made the first move, not that it really mattered. She was just glad that her mother had forgiven her father and taken him back. T'Kara was convinced that her mother had always loved him anyway, which is probably why her relationships with other men never lasted. And T'Kara was happy they hadn't lasted. The men had been nice enough and she had even liked some of them a lot. But T'Kara chose to believe that only one man could make her mother happy — her father. And only one woman could make her father happy — her mother. And she had been right. After all these years, they still loved each other.

When T'Kara heard her name, she rose from her seat and walked to the front of the church. When the applause subsided, she cleared her throat and spoke loud and clear into the microphone. "I'm happy to be here tonight, and I want to thank you all for letting me be a part of your program." She looked over the congregation to where her parents sat snuggled together and she smiled brightly. "And I want to thank God for my mother and father being here tonight, too." Breaking her eyes away from her parents, she looked over the crowd for Zandy. Not seeing her, T'Kara continued. "I'm going to recite a poem that I wrote, and I want to dedicate it to all the young people here tonight. The name of the poem is, "I Choose." I hope you like it." Clearing her throat again, she recited:

> *I don't care who's unhappy,*
> *I choose to have joy.*
> *I don't care who's sad,*
> *I choose to laugh like a child with a new toy.*
>
> *I don't care who's falling,*
> *I choose to rise to the top.*
> *I don't care who gives up on their dreams,*
> *I choose to fight for mine, and never stop.*
>
> *I don't care who follows the crowd.*
> *I choose to do my own thing.*
> *I don't care who fears to stand alone,*
> *I choose to fear nothing.*

I don't care who does dumb things,
I choose to be smart.
I don't care who drinks and smokes,
I choose to never start.

I don't care who doesn't believe in God,
I choose to always believe.
I don't care who listens to the devil,
I choose not to be deceived.

I, T'Kara Davis, choose to be the best I can be,
Because being less than the best is not good enough for me.

Thunderous applause followed T'Kara back to her seat. Some of the people even stood to their feet as they clapped for her. Sasha was one of them. She hoped she wouldn't forget to tell T'Kara just how much she liked her poem. Sasha's eyes scanned the crowd for Zandy, knowing that she must have been very pleased with her little sister's poem. Standing on the raised platform reserved for the musicians, Sasha could clearly see the faces of every one in the church. Zandy wasn't out there. *Where is she?* Sasha wondered as she sat down.

"Praise the Lord!" the emcee said. "Wasn't that a beautiful poem? It's such an encouragement to my soul when I see young people like T'Kara choosing God because He *is* the best. And we know that only in Him can we be our best." Shifting her glasses on her nose, she said, "I want to thank all of the young people who participated on the program tonight and for the young people who served as ushers. As you all know, we have a guest speaker with us tonight, but before Minister Makil comes to introduce him, Elder Earl has requested that I sing a solo. Pray for me as I attempt to sing, "I'm Still Holding On."

Sasha turned up the volume on the organ and played an introduction for the emcee. She'd played for Laurien before on a number of occasions. In fact, Laurien was the only reason Sasha sat at the organ now. Before the program started, Laurien had asked Sasha if she would play for the participants who would be singing on the program. Sasha had politely refused. Then Laurien told Sasha that the church organist had not yet arrived and asked if she would play until he came. Sasha agreed and reluctantly made her way to the platform.

Now, Laurien stood before the congregation with her eyes closed. She leaned her head full of thick braids back and began to sing with a voice that was airy and incredibly enchanting. Sasha followed her with little effort. She'd played the same song for Laurien, a sophomore at Jackson State, when she'd entered a voice competition for college students last year. Laurien had won first place. She'd said that Sasha's masterful playing had tipped the judges in her favor. But Sasha knew that Laurien would've won — hands down — even if she'd sang a cappella.

Laurien had wanted them to be close friends. When Sasha had started attending the church, Laurien would call her occasionally, sometimes to invite her out and sometimes just to talk. It didn't take Laurien long to figure out that Sasha wasn't interested in a close friendship with her. Sasha had always liked Laurien, but she preferred not to be buddy-buddy with someone as involved in the church and in the Lord as Laurien was. Sasha had enough church friends to last her a lifetime and at this point in her life, she preferred friends who were less rigid and more exciting to hang around. Like Zandy. The thought of Zandy made her search the crowd again. There was still no sign of her.

Sasha's fingers paused for dramatic effect as Laurien's voice began to crescendo dramatically. Then Sasha's fingers pounced on the keys, and she played the final notes as Laurien brought the song to an arresting end.

Sasha clapped along with the congregation as Laurien praised God to her seat. Minister Makil stood up in the pulpit and made his way to the rostrum. Sasha knew that he was getting ready to introduce the guest speaker and she wanted to get off the platform before Jabril got up to speak. She felt naked for all to see when she sat up there. As she leaned over to get her purse from the floor, the church door opened and she sat back up, expecting Zandy to walk through the door. It wasn't Zandy who walked in, but Tellis, dressed in a chestnut-colored suit. Sasha smiled in spite of herself, but then her lips froze and her body stiffened. A girl followed closely behind Tellis, and even from where she sat, Sasha could see that the girl was very pretty. Sasha's stomach turned over with jealousy. Her eyes followed the two as the young usher led them to vacant seats just off the middle aisle. As soon as Tellis was seated, his eyes began to roam the congregation, as if searching for someone. Sasha looked away just before he spotted her, still seated at the organ. Sasha wondered who the girl was, but was shaken out of her thoughts when a loud voice boomed over the church. Startled, she jumped in her seat.

"Praise God!" Jabril shouted in a fulminating voice. Walking out of the pulpit, he beckoned the congregation to its feet. "Praise God!" he repeated loudly. "Isn't He worthy of your praise? Hasn't He done great and marvelous things?"

Sasha watched as the Saints — including Elder Earl and Minister Makil — sprang to their feet and began to break forth in praise. Cries of "Thank You, Lord" and "I love You, Lord" could be heard all over the building. Even the young people began to praise God. Sasha could feel the Spirit of God moving in the church, and her eyes pricked with tears. *I should be praising God, too,* she thought. *In spite of everything, I have a lot to be thankful for.* Clenching her teeth, she thought, *No. I won't do it. I've made up my mind to pursue another life, and I've come too far to go back now.*

Not wanting to appear as unwilling to praise God as she was, Sasha lifted her hands and began to stroke the organ's keys, causing loud, rapturous music to float within the walls of the church. Back home, whenever she didn't want to pray during the worship service, she'd get on the organ and play, and no one was ever the wiser. The music she played just seemed to boost the Saints into more praise.

"We do not need the music of instruments tonight!" Jabril proclaimed loudly. "Let your praise and your worship be music unto the ears of the Lord!"

Sasha's hands froze. *Surely he's not talking about me. Is he?* Her eyes darted anxiously over the church, trying to locate him in the midst of the people. The church was scattered with people. They were in the aisles. They were in the front of the church, and they were in the back. They were in the choir stand. They were everywhere. Shouting and praising God. *And way too many of them have on white*, she thought as she searched for Jabril's white linen.

Finally, she spotted him. He was standing in the middle aisle praying for Dr. Avery. Sasha hadn't known that Dr. Avery was there.

She must have made it to church before me, Sasha thought. *Otherwise, I would've seen her come in.*

When Jabril turned from Dr. Avery, he turned his eyes on Sasha. *Why is he looking at me?* she wondered. *I'm not the only musician here.* Embarrassment rushed through her. *What about Zaynia . . . and Delandré?* Sasha's eyes slid from Jabril's to the section where the drums sat, just a stone's throw along the wall from the organ. Her eyes widened in dismay. Zaynia, the thirteen-year old drummer danced and shouted around the drum set with her eyes closed. Two missionaries jumped clumsily around Zaynia, desperately trying to snatch the pair of drumsticks she flailed in her hands without getting their eyes poked out.

Sasha jerked her head around to the corner spot of the platform where Delandré usually stood when he played the bass guitar. Delandré hands were stretched high in surrender to God and tears poured down his face.

Sasha's stomach did a huge flip-flop. *I guess he was talking about me*, she thought. Slowly she turned her eyes back to Jabril. His gaze, direct and fierce, was still locked on her. Sasha was mortified. Jabril had evidently seen through her tactic. She lowered her head, her eyes falling to her hands, clasped in her lap. *I know that I'm wrong, but does he have to look at me like that? Like I'm the devil incarnate or something. What happened to the nice man who came to Dr. Avery's home? This can't be the same man.*

Had Sasha known the truth of the matter, she would've known that Jabril *had* been looking at the devil. His spiritual eyes had penetrated the outer casing of her flesh and traversed the very depths of her mind and soul. And within those secret places, Jabril saw the slithering spirit of the Enemy, lurking, scheming, and anticipating the crowning moment when he would strike and destroy.

Jabril had come to make sure that that moment would never arrive.

Pointing his right hand toward Sasha's bowed head, Jabril began to rebuke, in a loud voice, the spirit of the Enemy, commanding him to loosen his hold on Sasha, to take his hands off of God's beloved vessel of purpose. He rebuked the unholy passions that stirred in Sasha's flesh and the anger and bitterness that threatened to be her spiritual downfall.

"I guess I *am* acting like the devil," Sasha mumbled thoughtfully.

Jabril kept praying.

Sasha shook her bowed head slowly from side to side. *I don't mean to. I just . . . can't . . . seem to help it.*

Jabril kept praying.

Sasha's shoulders slumped and her eyes closed. *I want to live my own life. I want to make my own choices.*

Jabril kept praying.

Tears welled up in Sasha's eyes, and she raised her hands to cover her face. "But I'm so tired . . . so tired of fighting," she mumbled into the palms of her hands. Whimpering, she said, "God, help me. Please help me."

In a voice that erupted with the power and anointing of God, Jabril declared, "In the name of Christ Jesus, I command you, thou spirit of the Enemy, to *go!*"

A piercing scream rang out over the church, pulsating in Sasha's ears, and she was on the floor, rocking back and forth on her knees and squeezing her folded arms around her stomach before she realized that it was she who had uttered the gut-wrenching scream. Tears poured from her eyes in heavy streams. "God, help me!" she wailed. "Oh, God, help me!"

Sasha tried to stop her body from jerking and swaying, but the Spirit of God was stirring in the pit of her stomach and spreading through her body like fire.

She tried to stop the tears from flowing, but when she thought of the lustful desires that had overtaken her heart, she cried even more.

She tried to stop calling out to God, but He was the only One who could save her from the path of the destruction she'd been tumbling down, fast and out of control.

Leaning over from her knees, she buried her face in the carpeted floor and begged God's forgiveness. Her muffled cries and anguished sobs were heard over the church as the Saint's praises began to subside and they made their way back to their seats. Sporadic cries unto the Lord could still be heard, but Sasha's disconsolate sobs caused many eyes to be riveted on her.

"Mama, is Sasha alright?" T'Kara asked, concern shadowing her face.

Looking down at T'Kara through teary eyes, she whispered, "She's alright, baby. Sometimes, when you pray, you cry because you realize that you've done some things that God doesn't like and you want Him to forgive you." She looked down at T'Kara's father, sitting on the pew with his head bowed in prayer. "And then," she added, smiling, "sometimes you cry because you're so thankful that He *has* forgiven you and given you a second chance."

When T'Kara opened her mouth to ask another question, her mother motioned for her to keep quiet.

Tellis also wondered if Sasha was alright. He stood at his seat and watched her, his face strickened with worry. He wanted to go to her and comfort her, but he wasn't sure if he'd be stepping out of the protocols of the church. And he wasn't sure she'd want to be comforted by him. He was probably the last person she wanted to help her. *That's not important right now*, he thought. *She's obviously in agony, and somebody should be trying to see if she's okay. Why is everyone just standing around looking at her? Shouldn't someone be helping her?* His hands gripped the back of the seat as every moan and groan from Sasha tore at his heart. He'd seen other people cry in church when they were being "delivered" but he couldn't bear Sasha's cries. Ignoring the questioning gaze his accompanying guest locked on him, he moved to go to Sasha.

Just as Tellis turned to step from between the pews, two missionaries moved toward Sasha. Tellis stood still and watched as the missionaries leaned over her.

"Let her alone," Jabril said in a voice that was like gentle thunder. Making his way from the back of the church to the front, he said in a loud voice, "Contrary to what some of you may think, this daughter *is* being comforted." His eyes softened as he looked over at Sasha crouched on the floor of the platform, weeping softly. "It is the arms of our God that cradle her. For He is the Father of mercies, and the God of all comfort." Jabril's piercing eyes swept the entire congregation. "If there are any among you who are troubled and afflicted, you must do as this daughter has done. Cry unto God, and He will comfort you with a peace and a love that is everlasting!"

At that moment, the door of the church flew open and crashed into the wall. Heads swung around to the back of the church, startled by the loud thud that resounded throughout the sanctuary. Those who had a clear view of the door, drew back in shock. Those who didn't, strained their necks to see what was happening. And Jabril, standing in direct view of the door, stood calmly and watched Zandy as she stood trembling in the doorway.

With eyes brick red from crying, face smeared with mascara, hair wildly tousled, and clothes in disarray, Zandy stumbled through the door of the church looking like a woman gone mad. She'd spent the last few hours in her parked SUV wailing in sorrow. Not even the breathtaking view of the park's pond, glimmering with the yellow and orange reflections of the setting sun, could bring comfort to her grieving heart. Now, her tear-blurred eyes searched the faces of the people. *She's supposed to be here*, she thought. *Where is she?!* Her eyes pleaded with the people as she staggered down the aisle on weak legs. *Just tell me where she is!*

Finally, one of the sisters of the church stepped into the aisle and wrapped a steadying arm around Zandy's trembling body. "What's wrong, sweetheart? Are you looking for someone?"

"My friend," Zandy said, whimpering. "I need to find my friend."

"What's your friend's name?" the lady asked patiently.

"Her name is . . . uh . . . Sasha."

"Oh, you mean Sister Lindsey. Let me take you to . . ." The woman paused, remembering where Sasha was. "Is there someone else here who can help you? I can—"

"No" Zandy said, pulling out of the lady's arm. Continuing down the aisle, Zandy resumed her search for Sasha. She saw Tellis reach out to her, but she kept walking. She saw Dr. Avery trying to get past a few people in the pews to get to her, but she kept walking. Finally, she looked up and saw Jabril. Tears popped into her eyes. "Jabril," she said softly, then rushed up the aisle to the front of the church.

As Zandy approached Jabril, he raised a hand and silently motioned for the two missionaries to bring Sasha to him.

"Oh, Jabril!" Zandy cried, stopping just short of crashing into him. The tears fell from her eyes and her words came out rushed and garbled. "I messed up, Jabril. Real bad. It was me, not him. I was so wrong. So wrong. My father, he . . . I can't believe it. The things I said to him. Mean and ugly things. I treated him so . . . so . . . I just can't believe it." Sighing heavily, she raised her hands and covered her face in shame.

Jabril saw Zandy's family quickly walking up the right aisle of the church with worried looks on their faces, but he raised a hand to halt them just as they stepped beyond the first pew. They all stopped in their tracks, but Dot, intent on getting to her daughter, rushed ahead. Moving quickly, Walter reached out strong arms and pulled her back. Wrapping one arm around Dot and the other around T'Kara, he held them securely against him. "Zandy's alright," he told them assuredly. "Don't worry. She's alright."

Placing a gentle hand on Zandy's bowed head, Jabril said, "Daughter, I speak peace into your spirit. Even now, the peace of God is comforting you."

Zandy inhaled a deep breath and released it. Wiping her face with her hands, she looked up into Jabril's smiling face. She opened her mouth to speak, but was distracted when she saw Sasha approaching. "Sasha!" she said, turning to her with outstretched arms. Sasha fell into her arms and hugged her tightly.

Everyone watched silently as the two held on to each other, each one drawing strength from the other.

Jabril beckoned the two girls to him when they finally loosened their hold on each other. Together they walked, hand in hand, to stand before him. He looked them both in the eyes before speaking. "Tonight, God has heard your cries and your sins have been forgiven. So, by the power and authority given unto me, I release you, in the name of Jesus Christ, into your purpose and your destiny. From this day forth, your lives will never be the same, for God has called you with a special calling. He has anointed you to do great and mighty things for His name's sake. Through your lives and ministry, rooted and grounded in the perfect love of your Lord and Saviour Jesus Christ, many souls shall be saved and many lives shall be made whole. Satan and all of his angels cannot prevail against you, for the hand of the Lord is upon you. In faith shall you go, believing all things are possible through Jesus Christ." Laying one hand on Sasha's head and the other on Zandy's, Jabril said in a strong voice, "God has great things for you! God has great things for you! God has great things for you!" Then stretching forth his hands high in the air, he raised his face heavenward and said, "Father, tonight, Your will has been done! For these, thy prodigal daughters, have come home! Let the angels in heaven make merry!" and looking over the congregation, he added, "Let the Saints of God rejoice! Come now, and receive your sisters with open arms."

Enthusiastic applause reverberated around the sanctuary as many of the Saints moved out from behind the pews and hastened to the front of the church to greet Sasha and Zandy. Before Sasha realized it, a tall, heavyset sister of the church eagerly enveloped her in a bear hug and planted a big, wet kiss on her cheeks.

But none of the Saints reached Zandy before her family did. Her mother and little sister rushed her at the same time, throwing their arms around her and squeezing tightly. Her mother repeatedly asked her if she was okay, and Zandy smilingly told her that she was. When Zandy looked up and saw her father, her smile faded and tears threatened to spill from her eyes. He approached her slowly, a wary look in his eyes, but his eyes filled with surprise when Zandy fell against him and threw her arms around him.

"Daddy, I'm so sorry," she sobbed. "I'm so sorry."

Tears of joy fell from Walter's eyes as he crushed his daughter to him. "I'm sorry, too, baby," he told her. When Zandy continued to tremble and cry in his arms, he soothed her like he did when she was a little girl. "It's alright, baby," he said, "It's alright."

T'Kara watched in awe as her father and sister clung to each other. Two of her prayers answered in one day was almost too much to bear. She could've watched them hug each other forever, but her mother, seeing many of the Saints waiting to greet Zandy, finally separated the two.

Zandy reluctantly stepped out of her father's arms and wiped her face with a tissue someone had pressed in her hands. Then smiling warmly, she accepted countless handshakes and hugs from the Saints of the church. When Dr. Avery approached her, Zandy's smile spread to a grin.

"I checked your grades," Dr. Avery began, feigning a stern gaze, "and you do have an 'A' average, *but*" she stressed, "it's a borderline 'A', so you can't afford any slip-ups."

Zandy beamed. "Thank you, Dr. Avery," she said, hugging the instructor.

With a smile on her face, Dr. Avery gave Zandy a tight squeeze, then turned and headed toward Sasha.

Sasha stood a few paces from Zandy and accepted her share of hugs and words of encouragement. When she saw Dr. Avery approaching, Sasha moved to meet her and took her by the hands. "I want to thank you for being so patient with me the other night at your home, Dr. Avery. Now I can appreciate the things you told me, and I'm sorry for behaving so badly. Do you forgive me?"

Kissing Sasha on the cheek, Dr. Avery replied, "Yes, I forgive you." Then, giving Sasha a hug, she moved out of the way to allow others to greet her, too.

Finally, when the crowd of people started to dwindle, Tellis walked up to Sasha. She looked at him with a blank stare and he felt unsure of himself. "Hi," he said.

"Hi," Sasha responded kindly.

"Um . . . this is Quinteria," he said, pulling the girl that was with him forward. "Quin, this is Sasha."

"Hi, Sasha," the girl said, her wide smile making her look younger than she first appeared.

Sasha looked into the girl's beautiful face and wondered why she didn't feel that same spurt of jealously she'd felt when she'd first laid eyes on the girl. Shaking the girl's hand, she smiled back. "Hi, Quinteria. It's nice to meet you."

"Quin's my niece — my oldest brother's daughter," Tellis said. "She came over to spend some time with my mother, but she's been with me all day." He chuckled. "I got some mean, envious looks from guys in the mall today. I think they thought she was my girlfriend."

Sasha smiled, not daring to admit that she'd had a similar thought.

"Your girlfriend?!" Quinteria exclaimed, playfully shoving him. "How could they think that, Uncle T, when I'm only sixteen?"

"Maybe it's those long legs you have," Tellis told her, chuckling.

"And your pretty face," Sasha said, complementing her.

Not bothering to respond to her uncle's comment, Quinteria looked at Sasha and said, "Thank you."

Tellis' smile faded as he looked pointedly at Sasha. He wondered if she was angry with him. She didn't appear to be, but he wanted to be sure. Turning her away from the people milling about, he spoke in a low voice. "I know that we can't really talk right now, but I just want to tell you that I'm sorry . . . about the other night. I didn't know how to tell you that I'd given my life to the Lord. I was so confused that night. I know that I should've expl—"

"Tellis, there's no reason for you to apologize to me. I should be apologizing to you."

"For what?"

"For throwing myself at you."

"You didn't throw yourself at me, Sasha."

"Yes, I did. I was wrong, and I apologize."

"So, you're not mad at me for running out on you when we were supposed to make . . . have our special evening together?"

Sasha smiled at him. "No, I'm not mad . . . anymore. I'm glad you ran out. You saved me from doing something I would've regretted."

"So," Tellis whispered, "do you still love me?"

Sasha looked bashfully around her before replying, "Yes, I still love you."

A charming smile split Tellis' handsome face. "I love you, too," he said, then pulled her in for a hug.

Sasha returned the hug, then stepped away from him. A concerned look in her eyes, she asked, "Tellis, do you think you can still love me without us . . . you know? Because if you can't, then I can't stay in this relationship."

Tellis shrugged. "I don't know," he began, shaking his head. "I don't know how long I can last, but I can promise you that whenever we get together, we'll be married." Smiling, he added, "Is that alright with you?"

A tender smile came to Sasha's face, and her eyes brightened with unshed tears. "That's perfect. Thank you, Tellis," she said, wrapping her arms around him again. "Thank you so much."

Epilogue

To My Father:

I know how surprised you must be to receive a letter from me – and not the usual phone call – but I felt the need to write to you instead of calling. I wanted you to know just how much I love you and just how fortunate I am to have you as my father. You're probably thinking that I've told you this a thousand times before, but this time is a bit different. More than any other time in my life, I feel such a magnitude of love and appreciation for you. It would take forever for me to explain exactly how I got to this point, but I can sum it up by saying that God has touched me in a profound way.

Last night, I went to church and it was an incredibly glorious night for me. A man was there by the name of Jabril. God used him in a mighty way during the service, and so many souls were blessed, including mine. He told me and my friend, Zandy, that God had anointed us to do great works in His name. When service ended and the people had left, Jabril sat in the sanctuary with Zandy and me alone, and he ministered to us. We were so excited about the things he told us and we asked him many questions. Many he answered, but some he said we'd have to seek God for answers to. Sitting there, alone with Jabril, Zandy and I felt like the disciples must have felt in the presence of Jesus when He taught them. Jabril is a man of great wisdom. I wish I knew more about him – his full name, where he lives, whether or not he has children, etc. – but I don't. Whenever I thought to ask him a personal question last night, somehow it always slipped my mind. It must have been the excitement of the night. I guess I know the most important thing about him, though, and that is, he is an anointed man of God. Zandy is convinced that Jabril is an angel from heaven. The thought popped into her head on our way to church this morning, and she wouldn't let it go. I laughed at the idea of Jabril being an angel, but maybe she's right. At any rate, he is definitely an angel in our eyes. Because of him, I renewed my vows to the Lord and Zandy has given her life to the Lord.

Daddy, I can hardly wait 'til the Thanksgiving Holiday rolls around. I'm really looking forward to seeing you. There's so much I want to talk to you about as well. I can't get into it all right now, but I feel like the pitfall I fell into after Mom passed could've been avoided if I'd had a better understanding of who God is. I ask myself now if I really loved the Lord all the times I said I did, and as much as I hate to admit it, I think the answer is a resounding "No." I say that because deep down inside of me, I see now that I loved the laws of the church more than I loved God. My relationship with God was a superficial one. I didn't know Him. I sought Him, but I didn't know Him. If I had known Him, I would never have known the hatred and bitterness that flourished in my heart against Him after Mom passed. The source of that hatred and bitterness was not my love for God. The source was self-righteousness — my own form of godliness — and self-pity. I understand that now, and I'm going to change. I will no longer be just a church member going through the motions of the church. I will boldly throw myself at the feet of God, not because I'm right, but because I'm wrong; not because I'm fixed, but because I'm broken. I want to move into a deeper relationship with Him. I want to know Him. I want to love Him.

There's so much more I want to talk to you about when I get home, and I know that you will be open and receptive to my thoughts and opinions — you always are. That's one of the reasons I love you.

And I do love you very much.

Your daughter,
Sasha

To My Father In Heaven:

Zandy and I agreed that it might be a good idea to start keeping a daily journal. Jabril said that we should expect You to do great things in our lives, and we want to keep an accurate account of everything. I wanted the first entry in my journal to be a "thank you" to You.

There's just so much to thank You for. I cannot even find the words to express the gratitude I feel for the grace and mercy You've extended toward me. More than anything, though, I thank You for forgiving me of my sins and for casting them into the sea of forgetfulness, never to be remembered again. You replaced the bitterness I had in my heart against You with love, and You cast out the rebellious spirit that was in me and gave me a mind to please You. I'm so thankful to You. Though I still don't understand the reason my mother had to die so young, I do understand that she didn't die because You didn't love me. I allowed my hurt and disappointment to lead me to believe that You didn't answer my prayer to heal her because You didn't love me, because I hadn't pleased You enough. Today, I know that You love me, and today, I have found something to be thankful for in my mother's death. I'm thankful that she was a holy woman when she died and that she lived a full life before she died — not in age, but definitely in happiness. Many mothers — even some who are still living — have not been as fortunate as my mother was before her death.

I thank You, too, for allowing Jabril to cross my path. I realize that I was on my way to destruction, but he helped me to turn my life around. He spoke words of life and purpose into me, and now I feel like the dead coming alive. I pray that You will reward him greatly . . . wherever he is.

I also want to thank You for bringing Zandy and Tellis into my life. I can remember a time when I would never have befriended them because they didn't fit the church's "image" of true holiness. But in my opinion, they are two of the most kind and loving people I have ever met, and I know for a fact that they have a sincere mind to do Your will. Bless and keep them, I pray.

Your daughter,
Sasha

P.S. *I've spent the last few years of my life running from You. Thank You for not letting me get away. Oh, the joy that fills my soul to know that with all of the running I did, I never made it out of the palm of Your hand!*

To My Father:

What do I say? Where do I start? How do I ask you to forgive me for all of the horrible things I said and did to you for so many years? You've told me that you've forgiven me and that you've put it behind you, but how can you forgive me so easily? Can you really and truly forget? You say that you can, that you already have. And when I see the love in your eyes when you look at me, I can't help but to believe you. I guess it is me who can't forgive myself.

Nevertheless, I will spend the rest of my days trying to make it up to you, Daddy. I love you so much. I realize now that I have always loved you. The volatile anger I carried inside just made it easier for me to suppress the love I felt. Last night, when God delivered me from all of that anger, the first thing I felt as I stood at the alter was His peace, then I felt a rush of love overtake me. Love for you. It hurts me to know that I allowed years of hate — rooted in my erroneous childhood perception — to be compounded in my heart. And to know that you suffered my mean-spirited and cruel ways for so many years without ever saying anything to put the blame where it should've been, makes me love you even more. You could've told me that you hadn't been unfaithful to Mama — and that she, in fact, had been unfaithful to you – but you never did. Even now, tears fill my eyes when I think of the love you must have for her — a love that moved you to protect her even when she'd been disloyal to you. Now I can understand why she never stopped loving you and why she was always deeply hurt when I disrespected you. I don't exactly know what led Mama to do what she did, but I know that she's spent the last thirteen years regretting it — like I now regret the things I did.

I'm so glad that you've found it in your heart to forgive us both. I'm so glad that you and Mama have reunited. I'm especially glad that you want me to move back home so that we can make up for some of the time we lost. I'm so excited, I was willing to break my apartment lease to move back. But the apartment manager released me from my lease. Isn't God good?! I can move out any time I want and not have to pay an extra cent. I've decided to move out this coming Saturday, so tell Mama and T'Kara to get my room ready because I'm coming back home!

Daddy, I know that we can't recapture the years we lost as father and daughter, but my prayer is that we will at least try.

Your daughter,
Zandy

To My Father In Heaven:

As my first journal entry, I want to thank You, God, for all the wonderful things you've done in my life:

1. *I thank You for loving me enough to save me from my sins.*

2. *I thank You for giving my father the heart to forgive me. I left home because I never wanted to see him, but now I want to spend every free minute I have with him. It feels good to finally be able to say that I love my father.*

3. *I thank You for my special friend, Sasha, and for entwining our destinies.*

4. *I thank You for my mother. In spite of everything, I still love her very much. With the same love my father drew from to forgive me, I draw from to forgive her. Besides, I can't waste any more time hating anybody for anything.*

5. *I thank You for my sister, T'Kara. If it had not been for her unshakable belief that "God can fix anything," who knows where our family would be right now.*

6. *I thank You for Jabril, whom I will forever believe is in heaven with You right now. He touched my heart in so many ways, and I will never forget him. Since I'll probably never see him again down here, I can't wait to see him again when I get there.*

7. *And more than anything, I thank You for Jesus! Like no one else I've ever heard before, Jabril explained how Jesus became my sin on the cross and died that I might live. As Jabril spoke, I thought about many of the sins I'd committed during my short lifetime — some too shameful to even think about — and I cried and cried. I cried because, for so many years, I let the devil use me — my heart, my mind, my body, my mouth, every part of me — as*

a weapon against the love of Christ. I know that no weapon the devil uses can stand up against the love of Christ, but, still, I couldn't help but wonder how often did the devil yell to God that Christ's death on the cross was in vain and used my life as his proof? The thought saddened me so much that I vowed to never let the devil have reign in my body ever again. I will not be a pawn for his glory! I have been redeemed by the love of Jesus and only Him will I serve! So I thank You again for the love of Jesus!

Sasha and I are so excited about our new lives in You. Jabril said that we are chosen vessels and that You have called us to do a special work for the kingdom of God. On one hand, Sasha and I couldn't help but feel special when Jabril ministered to us, but on the other hand, we are persuaded that You have called every living person to do a special work — it's just a matter of them bringing their lives under submission to You. Sasha and I asked Jabril what is the work You've called us to do. He told us that we would need to seek You for direction. He said that You would reveal to us the direction we should take. So we have decided to seek You in fasting and prayer until You give us a vision for our lives.

Whatever the work is You've called us to do, we want to be able to impact the lives of people in the same way that Jabril did ours. We want to draw souls to You.

Be with us, Father, I pray, as we strive to do Your will. And whatever trials and tribulations come our way, help us to recall the words that Jabril spoke into our hearts so that we may remain faithful to You in all things.

Your daughter,
Aleczandria

P.S. Hi God! It's me T'Kara. I also want to give thanks to You. I thank You for bringing my family back together again. I can't wait until Zandy comes home. We're going to have so much fun! I'm so happy that she and my father have made up and that my mother and father are getting married again. I know that there are a lot of kids in the world who are praying that You will bring their families back together again, too. I don't know exactly what it was that caused You to answer the prayers I prayed for my family, but I'm going to be praying that You answer those kids prayers, too. There's no feeling like the one you get when your family realizes that they really do love each other. Thank You for helping my family to feel the love that they have for each other. And, God, I ask that You let our love for each other grow stronger and stronger each and every day.

And there's one other thing I need to ask You, God: Can You give me the strength to run very, very, very fast? Zandy is going to come after me when she finds out that I've written in her journal, and I need to be able to get away from her very fast. ☺

Thanks God,
T'Kara

QUICK ORDER FORM

Fax orders: Toll-free: 1-877-542-4078. Fax this form.
Telephone orders: Toll-free: 1-877-542-4078.
Email orders: sales@fromheaven2earthbooks.com
Postal Orders: **From Heaven To Earth Publications**
  P.O. Box 166138, Irving, TX 75016-6138. USA.

<u>TITLE</u>	<u>PRICE</u>	<u>QTY.</u>	<u>TOTAL</u>
The Prodigal Daughters	$13.95	_____	_____

Sales Tax: If you live in the state of Texas, add 8.25% for each copy.
U. S. Shipping: Add $2.00 for the first book and $1.00 for each additional book.
Total Amount Enclosed: $ _____

Credit payments: ❏ Visa ❏ MasterCard
Card number:_____ Expires: ____/____
Name on card: _____

❏ Please ship an autographed copy of *The Prodigal Daughters* to me.
❏ Please ship an autographed copy of *The Prodigal Daughters* to a relative/friend as a gift from me.

Ship to: (Please Print)
Name:_____
Address:_____
City:_____ State:_____ Zip:_____ -_____
Telephone:_____

If you are purchasing a book as a gift for another, please print your name and a contact number should questions arise concerning your order:
Name:_____
Contact Number:_____
Comments: _____

Every copy autographed.

Angela D. Shearry